HER FAMILY SECRETS

ALISON LYLE

Her Family Secrets

ISBN: 978-1-0684850-0-8

First edition

For Jeff

The clock starts... now.

1
Colin

After thirty long hours in Labor and Delivery, Dr. Colin Clarke finally kicked off his shoes and let out a long, slow breath—home at last.

Then came the sound.

Ping.

An urgent message pulling him back into the chaos he had just escaped.

Twenty minutes later, the elevator doors opened, and Colin stepped onto the ward, hiding his exhaustion behind a mask of calm.

"Hey, Selena," he said, hanging his coat and looking up at the nurse's board. "Are the Hansons here?"

"On their way. But that's not why I called," Selena said, pulling her hair into a messy bun. "We're completely slammed. I have three in the hall, waiting for rooms. Two more are on their way up. Dr. Park has a breech in 808W. Please, Doc..."

He took the chart and flipped through. "You know it's gonna cost you."

"Chicken tamales for lunch tomorrow?" Selena smiled.

"Nah... You can wait for Dr. Park."

"Please?"

"Red chili pork."

"Oh, come on." Selena rolled her eyes. "I'll have to slow-cook the pork shoulder for—"

He handed the chart back.

"Oh, all right. Pork," she said. "Liz is on her way up."

Outside the room, Colin listened as screams faded to moans. When the room fell quiet, he gave a rapid-fire double knock and pushed the door open.

He would have introduced himself, but the patient was on all fours, her head buried in the hospital pillows. She rolled over to face him as he washed up and pulled on gloves to examine her.

"My nurse tells me you only just realized you were pregnant?"

"Yeah." The patient's hands twitched, and her eyes darted around the room. Stringy hair coated in grease and sweat fell over her face, but it couldn't hide the meth sores on her cheeks. Marks on her arms told more of her story. Her enormous pupils, when she finally turned to face Colin, left barely a sliver of ice blue.

He closed his eyes for a moment and remembered the baby in the dumpster. The paper towels wet with blood and amniotic fluid. The little boy desperately suckling the plastic bag, clinging to life.

"I'm glad you came here today," he said. "We'll take good care of you."

The woman squirmed her legs and scratched her arms.

A few minutes later, Colin pulled back, having finished the exam. "Well, it looks like we're about to have this baby." He pulled off the gloves, dropping them in the trash.

Liz entered with the instrument tray. He gave her the nod that meant, *Move quick.* She nodded back, grabbing additional supplies. They could read each other perfectly. Watching the patient's nails pierce into her own skin as if to claw away imaginary bugs, Colin looked back at Liz. They'd been in this situation before. She nodded. The restraints were ready if needed.

After the baby was born and moved to the NICU for withdrawal, Colin signed off on the chart and handed it to Selena.

"Pork. Don't forget," he said with a wink.

In the staff lounge, he found Liz.

"Marie Hanson's on her way up," he said, checking his phone. "Her contractions are four minutes apart."

"Thirty-eight weeks? With her first?" Liz laughed. "Not happening tonight, buddy."

"I'll be holding that baby before dinner."

"Speaking of dinner," Liz said, grabbing her purse, "I need onions."

He walked her to the elevator, stole a quick kiss goodbye, and watched the doors close between them.

Hours later, Colin dropped his keys in the ceramic bowl and found Liz in the kitchen. The smell of basil, garlic, and fennel simmered with a rich Cabernet as she browned some ground pork. Her secret Italian sausage recipe.

"How'd it go with Marie?" Liz asked.

"Not even close." He picked at a crispy bit on the edge of the pan as he kissed Liz on the neck. "You were right."

She swatted his hand with a wooden spoon. "Knock it off, it's for the lasagna."

"You're killing me," he said, wrapping his arms around her waist as she crumbled the meat. "Can't you just make a Bolognese? Lasagna takes too long."

"Whining is so unattractive." Liz pulled a saucer from the cabinet to cradle the spoon, poured Colin a glass of wine, and kissed his lips. Her eyes met his.

He swirled the glass, inhaled the bouquet, and frowned. "Again?"

She nodded, tucking brown curls behind her ear. "Next time," she said, winking and forcing a smile as she poured more wine into her own glass. "Now go take a shower. Trent's bringing his new girlfriend, and I'm dying to meet her."

"You better be nice." Colin curled his fingers and pawed the air with a shrill yowl. The same old dance. The bad news swept under the rug.

"What does that mean? I'm not catty." She laughed, then

tilted her head to the side. "Okay, maybe a little catty."

Colin sipped his wine. "I know you were on Nancy's side in their divorce."

"Yeah, well, he did cheat with every—"

"Not every."

"Okay, not *every* woman. But close."

"That's true. Moron. He had a great life with Nancy. Now he has to split their money and their kids. Did he show you pictures of his new apartment?"

"That dirty hole in the ground? Yeah... Sad."

Colin swirled his glass, watching burgundy lighten at the rim. "I don't see why anyone would bother building a life together and then throw it all away. It's a huge waste. And for what?"

Liz turned off the stove and skimmed the grease into a coffee mug. "All I know is you better be nice tonight."

"Have I ever done anything less than perfect?"

"Go take a shower."

"You're sure you're all right?" Colin knew she wouldn't want to talk. He'd read it on her face at the hospital, and he'd known it the minute he saw her upon arriving home. He could always read her.

She shook her head. "I already called central scheduling. They can fit me in tomorrow afternoon for a D&C."

"Trent has three C-sections, and he's overbooked for appointments. I don't think he—"

"Good thing I'm his favorite patient."

"Only because you butter him up with his favorite food." He opened the box of noodles.

Liz winked. "Don't worry. Tomorrow I'll be as good as new, and we'll try again next month." She layered the ingredients in her favorite casserole dish, then glanced at Colin. "Don't look like that. It could be worse."

He knew that was true. Things could always be worse. Knowing that didn't take away the sting of another miscarriage.

2
Colin

"There he is, late to his own party," Trent said, shaking Colin's hand and lowering his voice as he pulled him in close. "Liz told me. Sorry, man. I'll get her in right away."

Colin shrugged it off with a smile of appreciation and turned to Trent's girlfriend of the month. "You must be Cami," he said, taking her hand. "It's nice to meet you. Trent's a lucky man..." Blah, blah, blah. He said the right things to make her feel welcome, showing interest in her work and laughing at her jokes, all the while praying that Trent would reconcile with his ex-wife and return to being the power couple everyone admired.

"She's my soulmate," Trent said, clinking his glass with hers.

Colin wondered if she was old enough to drink as she blushed and batted her eyelashes—fake eyelashes, plastic and spiderlike. Colin caught Liz smiling and batting hers as she turned away. He smiled, but a lump caught in his throat. The image of their dead baby floating in his wife's uterus flashed abruptly in his head.

They carried on through the dinner party like it was just another night.

"What?" Colin asked, having lost the thread of the conversation.

"Cami hired a decorator for my apartment," Trent said. "The

painters start tomorrow. Which reminds me, I'm jam-packed all day. Can you swing by and let them in?" He reached into his pocket to find his keys.

"Sure, no problem." Colin took the keyring, twirling it on his finger.

"Oh, no way," Liz said, carrying out the salad. "You're trusting Colin with your keys? The man who hadn't locked his door in months when we first met because he couldn't find his keys?"

"On second thought..." Trent laughed and held out his hand, beckoning them back.

"Don't be ridiculous." Colin ran through the house to the entry hall and fished around in the bowl. Back on the patio, he smiled, holding up his keys. "I've matured," he said, puffing up his chest. "I have this handy tracking device on my keyring."

"You're welcome," Liz said, slicing bread.

"Don't listen to her—she's just as bad at losing things as I am." Colin twisted Trent's keys alongside his own. "Don't you worry. Your keys are safe with me."

Colin refilled everyone's glass.

"Thanks, man," Trent said, turning to the spread of food. "My favorite. Looks amazing, Liz."

Liz smiled. "Dig in, everyone." With patients going into labor at any moment, and seeing as lasagna wasn't the best eat-on-the-go food, there was no time to waste in getting to it.

As they ate, the conversation turned, as usual, to work at the hospital and the new patient portal computer system. Liz joined in with the nursing team's complaints. Then, she gently shifted the chat to general topics, making sure to include Cami as she shared slices of chocolate marble cake.

Colin switched to sparkling water just in case any patients called in the middle of the night, looking for a sober doctor to deliver their baby.

Trent switched to water too. Checking his phone, he nodded to Colin. "Sorry, man, duty calls." He stood to say goodbye. Cami crossed her arms, turning away. Trent leaned over to whisper in her ear. She hesitated, then seemed to think twice and stood up like a spoiled child, stomping away from the table and looking for her purse so she could leave.

As Liz dressed for bed, Colin checked his phone, worried it must be broken, unable to remember the last time they'd had a dinner party he wasn't called away from. To have bonus time alone with his wife bordered on miraculous. He stopped thinking about his good fortune for fear fate would notice and call him away.

"So?" Liz called from the bathroom.

Colin could hear the smile in her voice, and he knew she wanted to talk about Trent's new girlfriend instead of the difficult discussion of their fourth miscarriage and what, if anything, they could do differently in the future.

"You already know what I think," he said.

Liz gave a sigh and passed by him to the closet. "Is it selfish of us to want him to get back together with Nancy?"

Colin hesitated. He hadn't thought it selfish to question how Trent and Nancy's divorce would affect the two couples' dynamic: Trent and Nancy, Colin and Liz. When Nancy left Trent, Colin had hoped she'd return. Then she'd left their OB/GYN practice and started her own. In just a few months, everything had changed. Still, Liz was pregnant again, and they'd be able to pour all their attention into the baby.

But then the baby. Gone. His gaze settled on Liz's belly. "Yeah, maybe we're being selfish. In our defense, Trent is being an idiot."

"Right? I just miss how things were, and now with Nancy gone, I'm stuck babysitting Trent's flavor of the month."

Colin couldn't help but laugh. "Cami's his soulmate, Liz."

"Stop it." Liz feigned anger, then laughed, pulling Colin onto the bed.

"No," Colin said, standing up. "We have to talk for a minute about the baby."

"The pregnancy."

"What?"

Liz sighed again and walked into her changing room to sit at her makeup table. "I no longer think of *baby* when I get pregnant. My brain can't see that far ahead. I just think pregnancy and hope to get through one. If the pregnancy results in an actual baby, then we can use the word."

"We're doing everything right," Colin said, leaning on the doorframe.

"I guess. Trent had an idea..."

"Trent and his experimental ideas. No, Liz, we don't want to risk our baby's future with one of his ideas."

Colin sat down on the bed next to her. She rested her head on his shoulder. "So, what? We just keep doing what we've been doing and hoping for a different result?" She rolled her eyes.

"It's not quite like that. There have been plenty of women, patients we've delivered, who've had the exact same issue. Low progesterone—"

"I know, I know..." she said, holding Colin's hands. "Then their bodies just kicked in and did what they needed to do."

"It happens all the time, and I was thinking we could try—"

"But how many times..." Her voice trailed off as she leaned over and turned out her lamp. "Let's not waste this time alone, having the same old conversation about my hormones. It's so boring."

Colin turned out his own lamp and tossed the extra pillows on the armchair, then jumped in beside Liz.

"And what, my darling, would you not find so dreadfully boring?"

"Eww, stop talking like that." She laughed and covered her face. "There is something..."

"What is it?" Colin folded his pillow and bent his elbow, facing her in the dark.

"Nothing, really."

"Don't do that."

"Do what?"

"Whenever you're excited about something, you start to say

it, and then you hold back."

"It's just—" She adjusted her pillow and let out a sharp exhale through her teeth. "You're right. I do begin to tell you things and then hold back. It's just, well, silly, I guess. I've been working on something for a while now, and I was thinking... I meant to tell you, but you know how it is when you wait to say something and then you lose the opportunity? Not telling grows, and it becomes this huge—"

"I'm here to listen. I promise I'll share my thoughts only if you ask." He rubbed his fingers across his lips, zipping them shut, but then remembered she couldn't see him in the dark.

"Okay, okay," she said.

Colin's phone lit up the room before he heard the ping. He groaned and rolled over to check it.

"Marie Hanson's water just broke," he said, kissing Liz. "Sorry, I really do want to hear about whatever huge plan you're cooking up."

"You don't have to say sorry." She turned on the lamp and stood up. "I think I'll have another slice of cake."

"Wrap me one to go?" he asked as he dressed.

3
Colin

On the drive to the hospital, he wondered what Liz had been working on. He could tell from her voice, even in the dark, that her expression was grave. It wasn't like her. Since their first delivery together, he'd known she was different from any woman he'd ever met. Now, wondering about her secret worried him. His mouth watered, craving his own secret. He didn't have time. He hated that he didn't have time. Then again, he hated his secret. He hated himself for needing it more and more.

At a red light, he looked at himself in the rearview mirror and promised he'd stop once and for all. He'd stop for Liz—and for the babies who died because of his own secrets.

Then a voice in his head made him wonder if Liz knew the truth he'd been hiding. Was that what she wanted to discuss? As he pulled into the hospital's parking garage, he did his best to clear his mind.

"Looks like someone's moving in," Selena whispered. Marie and Donald Hanson arrived, carrying three fluffy pillows and a bulging suitcase.

Colin hugged Marie and patted Donald on the shoulder.

"We're finally here," Colin said, leading them into their

birthing suite.

"I can't even believe it." Marie sat on the edge of the bed. "Is Liz not here tonight?"

"Sorry," Colin said, "she's taking a few days off."

"Good for her, but I was hoping..."

She made those pleading eyes all his patients made. The ones they made when they arrived at their first prenatal appointment to ask, plead, beg, and bribe Colin and Liz to be the team to deliver their baby. He always made a big show of scheduling his life around that one special patient. In truth, Colin had never missed a patient's delivery. In fact, he'd delivered in the parking lot once when a patient's husband called from the car to say she refused to move. Another time, he'd sprinted six blocks in the rain when a woman pulled off the road and felt the baby's head.

The same care was true of his nurses. Selena had been with Colin for over twenty years. He trusted her with his life. Then, of course, there was Liz. They'd met when she came on board as a temporary traveling nurse to shore up a staff shortfall during a four-month baby boom. Colin made sure they found it in the budget to keep her on permanently.

Marie's next contraction brought Colin back to the present, and he backed out of the room to leave the couple to settle in.

When morning came and Marie's labor stalled, Colin sent her out to walk the halls while he ducked into the staff lounge for a nap. Twenty-three minutes in, his phone pinged. He cringed as he saw the message from Gerrard Coffey—the hospital's new chief community and social impact officer—announcing he was on the L&D floor to meet with Colin.

He'd managed to avoid Coffey for the past week after reading the email with the subject line announcing *An Exciting Opportunity for the Hospital*. Colin knew "exciting opportunity" was code for more work on an already overworked team. He hoped that by avoiding Coffey, the eager new administrator would find an exciting opportunity for the Telemetry floor instead.

"Dr. Clarke, you're a hard man to hunt down," he said, following Colin down the hall and into the stairwell.

"Just busy." Colin smiled to see one of the bosses at work so early in the morning. He'd seen Coffey out smoking on the roof one day, and it had occurred to Colin that not many people smoked anymore. He hopped down the stairs, enjoying Coffey's panting and wheezing as he tried to keep up. Not very professional, but fun.

"We've secured a contract with the city."

Colin stopped on the fourth-floor landing and turned around. Coffey caught up to him, still struggling to catch his breath.

"Contract for what?"

"We'll be handling all pregnant migrants."

Colin worked out the numbers based on statistics. "That's got to be four hundred new patients."

"Three hundred eighty-seven. So far."

"Three hundred eighty-seven patients who've probably received zero prenatal care. Have you considered the potential for lawsuits?" Colin knew it was a difficult situation, but he'd probably end up adding the majority of the patients to his own already bursting practice.

"It's no secret we've been hurt by Platford Hospital building their luxury maternity wing. We don't have any more room to expand, so we can't compete. This is the only way forward for us."

Coffey was right. They tried to grow, but as a small hospital just outside Chicago, Southwest General couldn't compete. Without the money and Coffey's "exciting opportunities," the hospital might close.

"I'll make it work," Colin said and shook Coffey's hand. Then he raced down the stairs, through the staff hall, behind the emergency room, and into Outpatient Surgery.

"Hey, man." Trent was typing on the computer outside the recovery rooms.

"What time is she scheduled for?" Colin asked, looking at the screen.

"We're already done."

"You're done?"

Trent stopped typing and looked up. "Sorry, there was a last-minute opening. Liz didn't want you to worry."

"It's okay," Colin said. "How'd it go?"

"She did great."

Colin walked into Liz's recovery room and smoothed her brown curls through his fingers. One bounced back and shimmered in the light. He kissed her forehead, watching her sleep, and whispered, "I'll be back soon."

He walked back into the hall. "Hey," he said to Trent. "Did anything new show up from the sample I sent to the lab?"

"I don't think so." Trent tapped away at the computer. "No, your boys are as healthy as a twenty-year-old's. Great motility..."

"Maybe a more detailed genetic workup? We don't really know—"

Trent sighed. "There's nothing wrong on your end. It's Liz's hormones."

"I know, I just thought..." Colin checked his watch. "Anyway, how many new patients do you think you can take on?"

"I don't know." Trent skimmed Liz's chart on the computer screen, shaking his head. "Maybe five, but I just started dating Cami, and the last thing I need is another woman complaining I'm too busy for her. Why?"

Colin's phone pinged. "I gotta get back upstairs."

4
Colin

Colin stood outside Marie's room, listening for the contraction to pass before he entered. As it reached its crescendo, Donald wouldn't shut up. How Colin wanted to throw the door open and smack those husbands who made any noise during a contraction.

"I don't know what you're trying to prove. My sisters and cousins all had C-sections," Donald said. "You just schedule it and arrive at a decent hour. By lunch, you're relaxing with the baby in one hand and a turkey sandwich in the other. Now—would you mind looking at me when I talk?—now this nurse is saying this could go on all day, and we've already been here all night. Why? So you can gloat that you're a better woman than my sisters?"

Colin heard Marie's breathing subside with a steady exhale. He stepped into the room.

"How are we doing, Marie?" Colin asked.

"They're getting stronger," she said.

"Can we get her an epidural or something?" Donald said, sidling up to the bed and giving Marie's shoulder a brisk rub.

"I don't want one." Marie's eyes were focused on Colin.

He watched Donald's hand as the man rubbed his wife. His nails were stained yellow.

"Donald," Colin smiled, "might I talk to you in the hall?"

Donald followed him out of the room.

"This is exhausting, am I right?" Colin said in a hushed voice. "And to think of the days when the fathers would hang out in the waiting room, eating and relaxing with a nice cigar or a pack of cigarettes." He raised his eyebrows.

"Yes. I'm all for being more involved, but really, what can I do here? She's not listening to a word I say."

"I sympathize with you, for sure. I have a few free minutes—why don't you go up to the roof? There's a coffee shop with amazing muffins and—one of my favorite spots—a smoking section. Take some time and come back refreshed. We'll take care of Marie."

The relief on Donald's face was all the thanks Colin needed.

In the room, after examining her, Colin helped Marie out of bed to lean forward and sway as another contraction began.

"Does that help?" he asked.

"Yes, but my lower back..." She winced and began to moan.

Colin's hands curled into tight fists. He stood behind Marie, massaging her back with small, steady circles as the contraction peaked and she swayed and hummed in a steady rhythm.

Selena peeked her head into the room and nodded. When the contraction ended, Colin went out and found her at her station.

"Liz is asking for you, and Michelle Sullivan's water just broke at work. She'll be here in thirty minutes."

"This is her sixth," Colin said with a frown.

"Let's hope she makes it." Selena raised her eyebrows.

"I'll grab my keys in case she doesn't."

Colin raced down the stairs, through the staff hallway, behind the Emergency Room, and into Outpatient Recovery, to Liz's bedside.

"Hey."

"Hey," she said. She was eating a shortbread cookie.

"Marie Hanson's asking for you."

"Oh." She set down the packet of cookies and pulled her blanket off. "How far?"

"Just three." Three centimeters dilated. Not even halfway.

She pulled the blanket back on and picked up her cookies. "There's time."

"Don't even think you're coming up for the delivery," Colin said, peeling the foil cover off an apple juice cup.

"I might as well—I'm no use here."

"I already told her you're taking a few days off."

"Fine, make me sound lazy." She smirked and drank her juice. "Colin..."

"Yeah?"

"We need to talk."

"I know."

They had been trying for a baby since their wedding six years earlier. They'd accepted the first miscarriage by focusing on the silver lining that they actually could get pregnant. The second was tougher. It showed low progesterone levels. Colin and Trent, Liz's obstetrician, agreed that artificial hormones could help until her body started functioning properly. Everyone said, "Third time's the charm."

Not quite. And then with the fourth, it seemed to become a familiar part of their life together. *We'll try again. Next time will stick.* Their new mantra.

Colin's phone rang, and he answered.

"Marie's ready," Selena said.

"What can I say? I've got the magic touch."

"Yeah, well," Selena said, "why don't you get that magic touch back up here lickety-split before I have to catch this baby myself?"

"On my way, boss." Colin hung up and kissed Liz on the forehead.

"Marie?" Liz asked, smiling as she opened another packet of cookies.

Colin hesitated at the door. "It'll happen for us too. Talk later?"

"Go on, I'm fine."

Colin knew she really was fine. There were no double meanings when it came to his wife. What she said was the truth.

He not only loved and appreciated that about her, but he also respected her more than any other woman he'd ever met. Even Selena could be polite to patients, then pull a face as she left the room. Not Liz. She wasn't affected by other people's words or actions. He'd seen that in their first delivery together.

By the time Colin arrived at Marie's room, Donald seemed revived from his hit of nicotine. He was standing beside his wife with his mouth shut. Good man.

"Here we go, Marie." Colin moved quietly around the room, getting ready for the delivery. He watched as the baby's hair appeared with each contraction.

And then, the miraculous moment. The moment Colin had witnessed so many times before. The euphoria that came to wash away any negative emotions. The rude comments from Donald about Marie competing with her sisters, the fears, the unknown. Gone. That moment when even the word "miracle" fell short.

He'd always been happy to be the doctor, the bystander to other couples having that moment. Until he married Liz and opened himself up to wanting it for himself. Now, as he thought of their fourth baby's remains being dissected in the lab, he wasn't so sure he'd ever experience it himself.

After finishing with Marie and taking a photo for his office, he left Selena to prepare the new family of three for their move upstairs to recover.

The staff lounge was empty.

Anxiety gripped his chest, and he tried to control his breathing, leaning on the table for support. His hands shook with adrenaline. He felt foolish and looked at the door. Now that he was alone, tears filled his eyes, and he wiped them away.

His phone pinged with a text from Spence, his assistant at his office. *A bus of pregnant women just arrived.*

Colin wiped his eyes and took a breath. Twenty-three minutes of sleep in three days was not enough. He needed sleep. Wanted a release. He knew his secret vice would get him straight, but he didn't have time. He took another breath and responded, *Be right down*, then called Liz. It didn't seem quite right to ask her to take an Uber home after what she'd just endured. Still, he knew she'd understand.

5
Owen

Owen Ryan was born and raised in an Irish Catholic neighborhood on the South Side of Chicago. His wife arrived from Ireland as a teen to the North Side. When they met and married, they decided to raise their family on the South Side, closer to Owen's work. Times weren't always easy for the couple, but they held tight to each other through the roughest times. Unfortunately, the rough times kept right on coming.

While Owen had been to Ireland just a handful of times over the years for weddings and funerals with Sarah, his wife had never forgotten her home. As the tough times continued, she imagined fleeing to the safety and peace of her idyllic childhood. She dreamed of the lambs in spring. Her home, Westport, tugged at her heart.

When the doctor said the words, "Early onset dementia," Sarah knew it was time to go home. She'd known too many friends and family who'd planned to return one day only for life to take hold and keep them firmly planted in America. Then that inevitable day would come when their bodies broke free and made the final journey in a casket or urn to be buried in their homeland.

Sarah refused that fate. When the doctor said those words, she and Owen decided to make the final journey a joyful homecoming instead of a sorrowful parting.

Over the years, as Sarah's dementia stole her away, Owen tried his best to carry on and keep his spirits up. When the economy changed and their retirement savings weren't doing as much as before, Owen found himself looking for work. It wasn't so bad, and if he were to be honest, finding a job was a nice respite from being Sarah's sole caregiver.

Tonight, at five minutes to eleven, Owen started the bus in the parking lot of Knock Airport. It wasn't a busy airport for most of the year. Lately, he'd found a few lively newcomers—refugees from war—to chat with along the way back into Westport. There, he'd take a break before switching over to the 450 route to Achill Island.

"Good morning," he said to a young woman lifting a stroller loaded down with bags as she carried her baby onto the bus.

"Castlebar?" she asked.

"Yes, of course," Owen entered the destination and took the money as the ticket printed, pointing for her to take it with her. He watched as she struggled to collapse the stroller and settle into a seat.

A family stepped up to buy tickets to Westport.

"On holiday?" Owen asked, looking over the mom's shoulder.

"Yes," the woman said, smiling. "Málaga."

"Great, great," he said, pointing to the tickets as they printed.

Then, there she stood.

Lika had been living at a hotel with other refugees on Achill Island until a few weeks ago. She had left for London, looking for work. Owen watched her pink-painted fingernails pick through her Euros as her lips moved and counted the money. She knew the routine. She knew the price of a one-way ticket to Westport. She knew to take her ticket from the machine. Owen had explained it would be cheaper to buy a Leap Card from the post office. She'd always waved off the idea, claiming she wouldn't be around much longer. But here she was, back from London. Defeated.

"No luck?" Owen asked, checking over her shoulder for more passengers and closing the door when no one else appeared.

"Two days of work at a hotel and then a week of waiting... for nothing." She shrugged.

"Sorry to hear that. I'm sure something'll turn up."

"I hope so. They just reduced our benefits."

"I saw that in the paper. People are getting desperate."

"Yeah." She tucked her ticket in her wallet and found a seat.

The mother from Málaga approached Owen as he drove. She held tight to the bars and stumbled a bit, showing him a brochure for a hotel.

"Is this a good place to stay for a family?"

Owen knew all the hotels and restaurants, the best ones and the worst ones. Plus, of course, the ones that gave him a little bump in his wallet if his bus happened to stop off out front.

He made his recommendations with his eyes on the road most of the time. The rest of the time, they were in the rearview mirror, on Lika.

The rest of his shift passed without incident. Afterward, Owen stopped off at the SuperValu for a bouquet of pink and yellow flowers to replace the limp roses on Sarah's nightstand.

His body ached as he pulled into the driveway. A nice hot bath would do the trick.

"Will you please get a cleaner in here?" Marni, Sarah's caregiver, asked before even saying hello. "My cousin has been cleaning for ages and will give you a discount. I won't be able to carry on in these conditions."

"I'm sorry, I know the smell is—"

"Disgusting. Maybe you're used to it. I don't see how Sarah can rest peacefully in her own home all day long with such a stench."

Owen closed his wife's bedroom door and followed Marni to the front. She pulled on her coat in a huff and slung her purse over her shoulder.

"If it isn't clean by tomorrow, you'll need to make other arrangements."

"I understand."

Owen watched her drive off and looked at the fuchsia bush

in the yard. It had grown quite a bit since they arrived. Sarah had planted it from a cutting, a housewarming gift from her nephew's wife. Owen wondered if she would even remember it now. He pinched off a branch to add to her bouquet. When he placed it down beside her, she didn't seem to notice the flowers. Or Owen.

At the end of the hall, Owen fished out the key hanging on a chain tucked under his shirt, opening the room Marni was so adamant that he clean up. Walking in, he locked the door behind himself. The pungent stench filled the space. He reached onto the shelf for the Vicks VapoRub and smeared a glob under his nostrils. It helped a little.

6
Colin

Colin's eyes opened to Liz's curls dangling in his face. She smelled of coconut and Chanel No. 5.

"Monica Sedgwick just showed up on the floor," she said. Colin looked at the clock. *Three full hours*, he thought. He felt groggy from so much sleep.

"She's scheduled for noon," he said, stretching and pulling the covers over his head with a groan.

"I made coffee." Liz pulled the blanket from him. "I'd be happy to dump a bucket of ice water on you."

"Would you?"

"Gladly." Liz's laugh told him everything was back to normal. Their beautiful life was just as it had always been. The desire to complete the perfect picture remained, but in those little moments, everything felt right. He pulled her in close.

His phone pinged with that annoying sound. He groaned as he picked it up, then smiled as he read the text.

"What is it?" Liz climbed over Colin to read. He pulled away.

"Can't I have any secrets from you?"

"No," she said, getting up and pulling on her navy-blue scrubs.

"Where do you think you're going? You need to take it easy."

"Don't change the subject. Besides, I already read it. I don't know what you're hoping to find."

Liz couldn't understand this side of Colin—the desire to know the truth of his past. To find the mother who'd given him up. Okay, not just to find her. To show off the amazing life she'd missed out on. Wasn't that what people said? The best revenge was living well. If only he could have a couple of clever children to round out the picture, but even without them, his life had turned out enviable. He needed her to see that.

"I can't explain it," he said. "It's just something I need to do. Closure or something, right?"

"I just hate to see you get your hopes up every month when you go to that silly meetup and think she'll walk through the door. It seems like every time she doesn't show, you come home more and more let down."

"Do I?" he asked, reading the automatic notification again. *A new DNA match has RSVP'd to tonight's meetup!*

His phone pinged again. Results from one of the new migrants he'd seen late into the evening last night. Colin frowned.

"Damn. Just as I suspected. Come on, I'll let you work half a shift, but no more."

"Oh, thank you, sir. So kind of you to let me, sir." She winked and ran downstairs while Colin headed off to shower.

The day started with his scheduled C-section turning into an emergency C-section. Then his first migrant patient, a twenty-year-old woman from Venezuela, returned for the results of her ultrasound.

Selena arrived with Colin's pork tamales and tucked the container into the staff fridge.

"Come on," Colin said, "I need your help."

Selena followed him to translate the difficult reality to the young mother.

"She swears she still feels the baby moving," Selena said, rubbing the woman's back and handing her a box of tissues.

"Please explain that when she moves, the weight of the baby

shifting within the fluid can sometimes feel like the baby is moving. There is no heartbeat. There's nothing we can do." He wondered how long she'd been dreaming of her baby's future life in America; all the while, it was dead.

Selena explained.

The woman sniffled and whispered, "Are you sure?"

"Sí. Lo siento," Colin said. "Please explain the procedure and have her call any friends or family. She needs all the support she can get."

Selena nodded, and Colin left the room to prepare. He bumped into Liz in the hall.

"Are you all right?" she asked.

"Of course. Just a tough one."

"I heard. I'm ready when you are."

Things could go horribly wrong with childbirth and babies. Most people coped by imagining those things only happened to other people. Colin had seen many deformed babies. He saw premature babies, those with holes in their hearts, and babies with sixth fingers and toes. Others with Down syndrome. He tried his best to manage any anomaly with compassion and professionalism. Nothing affected him more than a stillbirth. It wasn't just the dead baby—which was bad enough. It was the process of preparing a woman to endure the pain and emotion of delivery, knowing in the end there would be no perfect euphoria. She would have to dig deep and push with no reward for all her effort.

The best Colin could do was hope his patient's body responded well to the Pitocin as he brought on her labor.

Soon, the room grew somber as she wailed in pain, exhaustion, and grief. Colin kept his head down while Liz moved calmly, assisting and encouraging. Selena supported the distraught husband as he fell to his knees in shock.

After Colin closed the door to the grieving room, he paused and took a few deep breaths before stepping into the joyful room of a couple expecting their third healthy daughter.

Once the baby was born and pictures were taken, Colin

looped around the ward, finding Liz in the lounge.

"I'm heading home," she said.

"You feel okay?"

"Yeah, just tired."

"Get some rest. I have patients waiting in the office. If I get a minute to get away... Valparaiso?"

"Oh, yes. Please."

Valparaiso was their favorite spot for tacos. The owners had closed down a few years ago due to family infighting. Colin and Liz were so devastated by the loss that they'd paid the brothers to reconcile and reopen.

"Flour tortillas." Liz always reminded him.

In his office downstairs in the Physician Pavilion, Colin moved from room to room. He took a breath before each visit and checked each patient's reason for coming to match his mood as he entered.

"Excuse me, Doctor." Spence knocked at the door and poked his head in the room. "We have another bus here."

Peeking out into the chaotic waiting room, Colin saw a line of women in all stages of pregnancy filing in, filling every seat. More arrived, squeezing into any open space. Spence handed out clipboards and tried his best to answer questions in his limited high school Spanish, then ran back to his desk in search of more pens.

Colin called Spence over.

"Do me a favor. Run upstairs to the staff fridge and grab the big red container for me."

Spence glanced back at the room bursting with eager patients. "Gladly."

"It'll just be a few minutes," Colin said to the crowd, ducking down the opposite wing of exam rooms. He listened for Trent's voice and waited for the door to open.

"See Spence at the front. Have him schedule you for next Monday," Trent said as a very pregnant woman swayed out of the room.

"Hey, man. How's Liz?" Trent asked, dropping the patient's folder on the out-tray and walking to the next room.

"She's great. Already back at work."

"She promised to take a few days. She's worse than a doctor."

"Speaking of doctors..." Colin smiled.

"What's with that look?"

"You know how I had all those new patients yesterday?"

"The migrants who haven't had any care, and now we're expected to work some sort of magic? Didn't you already have one stillborn?"

"Well, yes, but most are routine exams. And since I took care of things yesterday, I figured you'd—"

"Is that all the noise I hear?" He flipped through his next patient's chart.

"Come on, I have three C-sections coming in soon, and Liz needs me to swing home. And"—Colin waved Spence over—"I have Selena's homemade pork tamales."

"Oh, you're killing me."

"Can I get a few?" Spence asked.

"They're Trent's," Colin said. "You'll have to ask him if he's willing to be a team player and share."

"Oh, all right. I guess we can't have Liz leaving you. Go ahead. Go play good husband for the afternoon, and I'll manage the entire practice. I am the better doctor, after all."

"Thanks, man." Colin opened the container and grabbed two tamales before Trent snatched it away.

As he drove to Valparaiso, his stomach growled. When he arrived, he looked for an empty spot. The parking situation was always a problem on the busy road. Customers complained about not being able to run in and out to pick up their orders. Most people just double-parked and risked a ticket. Colin waited for a pickup truck to pull out, then parked. Prying open the molding of his car door, he fished around, grabbing a cheap phone in a little leather case with a single key attached. He dropped his real phone and keys with their tracker keychain inside the molding and pressed the seam shut, then hailed a cab.

A few blocks over, the taxi let him out in front of his apartment. He'd had it since leaving college and kept it for rental income after paying off his student loans and finally being able to afford a house. When he met Liz, he sold that house as soon as their new one was built, but he kept the apartment all the while.

The mailbox was stuffed with manila envelopes, wedged so tightly that he had to yank one free. Pills rattled inside—too many. This wasn't just out of hand; it was spiraling. He needed to stop.

Climbing the stairs to the third floor built his anticipation. He counted the stairs every time, and always around thirty, his mouth would begin to water. He usually waited until he was inside the apartment to call her, using the second phone hidden in his car's door. It had just one number saved. But this time, after thirty-five steps, he couldn't wait.

In the apartment, he undressed, hanging his pants carefully on the antique mahogany valet his father had given him. He draped his shirt over a hanger to keep away the wrinkles. His watch, wallet, second phone, and single apartment key he arranged on the velvet pad.

Colin pulled on a pair of jeans and a T-shirt. Cool and casual, he thought as he looked in the bathroom mirror. That was when the ticker tape of thoughts started playing and replaying through Colin's head. The devil and angel duking it out. The anticipation, the excitement, the desire followed by the release. Then the guilt, frustration, regret.

"This is not something a real man does," he said to himself, washing his hands as if preparing for surgery and looking into his reflection. "Just one more time and then, really, that's it." He'd made the same promise to himself every time. All part of the ritual.

He'd think of the news reports. The sympathy for the young girls affected. Young girls. Children really. Yes, older too, sure, but not so much. Young girls. Yes. Young. Sweet, innocent, young girls. Tortured souls.

“What kind of man are you?” Colin clenched his teeth as he asked his reflection.

“You’re disgusting and filthy,” he responded to himself.

He’d thought having the perfect life with Liz would fix this problem. Perhaps when they finally had children, that was when he would stop.

“I will,” he promised. “I will have to stop then. God, if you give us two healthy children. I will stop.”

Colin knew God wouldn’t believe his pathetic bargaining. He didn’t even believe himself.

“It’s shameful. You’re a disgrace, you pathetic, disgusting shell of a man. If people only knew the real you—”

The doorbell rang. “She’s here,” he said with a smile.

He exhaled and his mouth watered. Looking at himself one last time in the mirror, he hated who he’d become. He knew he wasn’t ready to stop. He opened a manila envelope, swallowed several pills, then headed to the door.

7
Owen

The room's stench filled the entry when Marni arrived the next day. Owen made no attempt to stop her from running out, screaming that she'd never return.

Locking Sarah into their bedroom—for her own safety, of course—he set out for a lovely day driving the bus from the airport to Westport, followed by a nice little break. After, he'd drive all the way out to the edge of Europe on Achill Island, all the while hoping to see Lika along the way. The poor thing.

The day's drive was uneventful. At the final stop, Owen got out to walk around, stretching and massaging his lower back before getting back on board to head home.

Just as he was losing hope, there she stood. Waiting on the return loop, heading from the hotel to the shops in the Sound.

"Any luck?" he asked as he entered her destination into the ticket machine and took her money.

"Still nothing." She shrugged and tore the ticket away.

"Do you have any experience as a carer?"

"Not really," she said, and turned to walk away. Then she hesitated and added, "I did take care of my grandfather when he had his hip replaced two years ago."

Owen looked in the mirror to see if anyone seemed to be listening to their conversation. As usual, that leg from Dooagh to Keel was pretty light.

"If you'd like to give it a try, my wife's carer just quit." He handed her a slip of paper with his phone number.

"Thank you so much," she said, blinking away tears. "I can start right away."

"Call me tonight, and we'll work out the details."

It's good to help young girls, Owen thought as he drove, feeling proud of himself, stealing glances and smiling at her in the mirror. The poor thing had lost her family; she had nothing until Owen offered her a lifeline. His excitement rose as he thought of those tears of relief filling her eyes after trying so hard for months to find decent work. And now Owen had done something that would change her life forever. He was her hero. It felt good. He couldn't save his wife from the awful dementia that stole her away, coating her mind in tar. But he could help a kind young lady try for a better life.

At the next stop, an elderly man carrying a broken umbrella climbed aboard.

"Hiya, Pat," Owen said.

"Hey, Owen." He nodded. "Did you hear? Found a body in the bog."

"Another?" Owen asked.

"Bet you thought you left that big-city crime behind you when you moved out here."

Owen agreed. "Just awful."

The man nodded and found a seat.

At home, Owen had to clean up Sarah first. She'd sat in her own filth all day while he was on shift.

"Sorry, love," he said, dabbing cream on her chafed skin as he told her about his day.

"I found you a new caregiver. I'm sure she'll be better than that old bat."

Helping her from the bed to her chair, Owen turned on the television with the built-in VCR that they'd brought from home.

"Total body burn?" he asked, popping in a tape.

As soon as the familiar music started, Sarah's foot began tapping along to the beat. Owen dragged the step aerobics platform to the open space. He eyed the pink, purple, and yellow dumbbells lined against the wall.

"It's been a long day... five pounders today?"

Grabbing the purple set, Owen climbed up and down, curling his biceps to the beat. Sarah stared. She used to smile. Before that, she'd been the one climbing, kicking, and marching. At first, Owen had felt silly. But those long hours driving the bus left him stiff and hunched over, so he gave her videos a try. And he loved it.

In the evening, Owen went to the locked room down the hall. He pulled the key from around his neck and opened the door. The cages were caked with excrement, urine, and snot.

Owen scrubbed the walls and floor. The yellow stains and stench were embedded in every surface. He dragged the cages out, one at a time, to the courtyard and unwrapped the hose. The hose was not like their hose in America, just a short length of narrow tubing with a jagged-cut end. The pressure was too low to aid in the cleaning. He pressed his thumb into the opening to force the water to spray as best he could, splashing his pants in the process.

Finding a brush in the bathroom, Owen scraped and scrubbed the cold metal bars well into the night. Then he dried everything down with a towel from the rag bin and opened the windows to air the room. Stepping outside, he began to dig a hole.

The area around the fuchsia plant was already too full. Owen dropped the shovel into the base of the palm tree. A funny thought ran through his mind. The first time they'd viewed the house, Sarah had said the palm reminded her of Ireland. For Owen, it felt out of place seeing the tropical plant thriving in the cold, rainy west of Ireland. A storm two years back had given the palm a thorough thrashing. It still hadn't recovered. *Hopefully, the fresh compost will help the poor thing*, he thought as he dug around the base, dropping in the remaining pile from the cages.

By morning, everything was fresh, clean, and ready for Lika.

"Right on time," Owen said as he saw her walking up the sidewalk. She looked eager and bright-eyed to start the day. "Good girl."

"Thank you again," she said.

He showed her around the house, starting in the living room and dining room. Then he introduced her to Sarah.

Lika seemed to hesitate, not knowing what to expect of Sarah's condition, but Owen knew she'd get the hang of things in no time. *She's a bright girl—and ambitious*, he thought to himself as he watched her.

In the kitchen, he offered her a cup of tea or coffee.

"Coffee would be great."

"Lovely. I have a pot ready."

He poured them each a cup and took his pills.

"There is one last room, just down the hall here." Owen led the way, fishing the key from around his neck. "I've cleaned it up. As you see, it's still a bit messy." Opening the door and allowing Lika to pass by him into the room, he watched her stop in place before he pulled the door closed.

"Oh," Lika said, shaking her head as Owen turned the key in the lock.

"You'll get used to the smell."

"Oh, it's—" She swallowed. "It's not that bad, really... I don't mind."

Good girl.

8
Colin

Colin opened his apartment door. His smile slackened as he looked at the girl standing in the hallway. She had a pencil twisted up in her hair and smudges on her glasses.

"You having a party here, or what?" she asked.

Colin grabbed the bags from her hands and closed the door on her.

Turning off the TV and pulling the coffee table close, Colin thought of the young girls. People would have sympathy for them but not for Colin. *You dirty old man,* he thought. He hated what he was about to do, yet even though he hated it, every moment of it, he loved, craved, and needed every one of those moments. Every bit. The good, the bad, the glimpse of euphoria that his patients got to experience but he and Liz never would.

No. Not Liz. She couldn't enter that space.

He opened the packages and laid out the contents in just the right order.

The three orders of beef and mushrooms first, then two shrimp pad Thai, followed by eight egg rolls. The timing was off somehow. The pills were clouding things, and his hands felt heavy. The egg foo young might have to be thrown away. Not enough time.

Unzipping and wriggling out of his jeans, he grabbed the first beef and mushroom container.

The anticipation of it touching his tongue sobered him just enough to enjoy that first bite. Letting out a little moan of delight, Colin dropped the fork and began scooping the food with his hand, stuffing it into his mouth. The beef was tender. The mushrooms were sautéed and squiggly. The brown sauce rushed down his throat, swallowing it all without chewing. Then the second container, and on and on.

The shrimp in the pad Thai were bigger than usual and would require chewing. He didn't have time to chew. One caught in his throat, and he coughed. He tried to breathe. *Take it easy, slow down,* he thought. There was nothing worse than peaking too soon. He picked around and tossed the biggest shrimp on the floor. The ritual had not been followed perfectly.

A moment of worry popped into Colin's head. *What if I can't get a release because I didn't eat those shrimp? It must be done in the correct order.* He picked up the shrimp from the floor and ate them, then forced the remainder of the pad Thai into his mouth. If he slowed down to think about what he looked like in that moment, he'd hate himself even more. He kept going.

And then, the pain. His stomach rebelled with belches of air. Sweat poured from his forehead. He wiped it away, smearing brown sauce and bits of crushed peanuts and cilantro on his face. He wiped his hands onto his T-shirt and sprawled out on the couch, which was stained with every past binge.

Taking a breath, Colin sat up and grabbed the first egg roll. Dipping it into the homemade sweet and sour sauce, he took a bite, chewed twice, and swallowed. Again. Dip, bite, two chews, swallow. He hated the process. He hated himself. It had to be the last time.

Every documentary he'd seen sympathized with the poor young girls afflicted with this horrible disorder. "Not the sort of thing real men do, is it?" Colin would always ask the reporter from his side of the TV screen. He'd seen only one interview of a man with the same problem, but that man couldn't function in life. *At least I'm not that bad,* he thought. That made him think of his perfect life with Liz. No. She must not enter into this space. That line could not be crossed.

Dip, bite, two chews, swallow. Time to finish. There wouldn't be time for the egg foo young.

He raced to the bathroom, and the release felt glorious. Beads of sweat mixed with tears in his eyes. His eyelids pressed tight as he heaved and strained over the toilet. He reached for the handle and felt a flush before opening his eyes. Then he stood up, enjoying the last moments of bliss. But soon, the weight of regret hit him again.

In the shower, he scrubbed away the grease oozing from his pores. The scalding water completed the ritual.

After dressing, he looked in the mirror. He straightened his tie and fastened his watch. "You clean up nicely, Doctor," he said to his reflection, an attempt to replace the guilt with confidence.

Colin had joined the ancestry group after he and Liz married. As head of obstetrics and gynecology, he felt ready to prove a point. He was happily married to an incredible woman. Now, he wanted to show the woman who had given him life—and gave him away—that she had made a huge mistake. After a few years of searching, he'd started to give up. Then an auto-RSVP would ping, dragging him back.

The meetups began online. Then, a keen relative with ties to the Blackstone Hotel set up monthly gatherings in the English Room. Attendees signed in on a dry-erase family tree to see the connections. Many of the names were so far apart it looked more like an archipelago scattered through an ocean than a tree with connected branches. Colin's name was always written far away from the others. Listening to people refer to their findings from many generations ago was tedious. But now and then, someone would make a more recent connection. Colin could hope.

That night, a new name was closer to his island. The DNA match. Not a parent or sibling, yet closer than any other. He read the name, Fiona Cavanaugh, and made the rounds, saying hello, checking name tags.

"Hello, Fiona." He held out his hand, introducing himself to the frail woman in a wheelchair. As they chatted and compared notes, it became clear they weren't related in any meaningful way.

"Hey, cuz." A hand squeezed Colin's shoulder. He turned to see Felix Everett. Although the next closest DNA match, he was still nautical miles out to sea, yet Felix insisted on them referring to each other as cousins.

"Nice to see you, Felix."

"I see you've met our beautiful young cousin, Ms. Fiona."

Fiona blushed and smiled at Felix.

"Come on, let's go get a drink. Fiona? Shot of tequila? Red Bull?"

"Just water," Fiona said. "Thank you."

At the bar, Colin squeezed a lime into his water while Felix delivered a glass to Fiona.

"Still no Liz?" Felix asked when he returned, ordering a whiskey and pulling a can of Red Bull from his pocket to pour into it.

"Liz? No." He'd asked the same thing every month since Colin joined the group.

Felix looked around the room at the motley crew of relations. "Yeah, she's probably right to avoid associating with us. I'm starting to think she doesn't exist."

Colin laughed and sipped his drink.

"Check it out, Cousin Beth's here with the T-shirts. Come on."

Colin trailed Felix, who was almost skipping. He wanted to grab the shirt with the image of their ancestor, Colonel Hodge Port Washington VIII.

He stared at the advertisement on the shirt. Everything Liz had said about the meetup was true. It was a waste of time—and a joke. He knew it wouldn't fix whatever was wrong inside him. Yet there Colin stood, trying on the family T-shirt. "Colonel Hodge Port Washington VIII's Miracle Gout Elixir—made from the rarest rattlesnake venom," stretched across Colin's chest. An absolute joke. He glanced around the room at his distant relatives, all descended from an actual snake oil salesman. Liz had been right to laugh.

"Hey, cuz." Felix pulled another Red Bull and a folder from his coat pocket. "I have some incredible businesses we're still funding for. I thought of you for a few. Trust me, you'll want to get in on these."

Colin browsed through a few "world of medicine game changers" and other sketchy tech firms.

"TSS?"

"The Squatter Squad. You've seen reports in the news of squatters, right?"

"Yeah."

"Well, it can take forever to get rid of them. Even if you do, your house is trashed," he said, tapping the logo. "TSS. It's a squatter remediation service."

Colin skimmed the brochure. Two options: Taken or Exterminated.

"What do they mean by taken? Taken where?"

"They took the troubled teen boot camp model and tweaked it a bit. The important thing is the squatter's gone just as quick as they arrived."

Colin half-listened as he read about the anonymous app used to engage the service.

"If it's anonymous, what's to keep me from using it for someone other than a squatter?"

Felix leaned in closer, lowering his voice. "They're working out the kinks. Feel free to take that with you and hit me up with any questions." He showed him another. "Look at this one—we'll be the sole facial-recognition provider for Homeland Security. Some serious CIA-level tech." He flipped the pages in Colin's hands. "Tech gadgets, if you like that sort of thing. Wait, I remember you do not." He flipped again to yet another business. "This one will be of interest to you. At-home dry-cleaning machine. Convenient, practical, money-saving... money-making, am I right?"

Colin nodded.

Another thing Liz seemed to understand that Colin tried to ignore was the ulterior motives of all his newfound relations.

Colin pulled out his checkbook before leaving to swing by Valparaiso for Liz. He could hear her voice: "Flour tortillas, *don't forget.*"

9
Colin

After making the rounds the next morning, Colin slipped away to the staff lounge for a few moments of sleep. Sweet, beautiful sleep.

His phone pinged forty minutes in, and the door to the staff lounge opened.

"Gina Smith's on her way up with her mother," Liz said, poking her head in.

"What are you doing here?" Colin asked, checking his watch.

"I was bored at home."

"I missed you too," he said, getting up.

"You're an idiot."

"Strange, right?" Colin said, rubbing his eyes with his fist, building to a yawn.

"That I agreed to marry you? Yeah, it is strange."

"No, Gina Smith having a baby."

"Not for me—I'm much younger than you."

They stopped at the nurse station. Colin elbowed Liz. "Move over."

She sat down and rolled her chair away from the computer. Colin checked his notes. Gina Smith was one of the first babies he'd delivered. Now she was about to deliver her own. Full circle.

Starting out as a doctor, Colin had wanted to have everything just right before having a family of his own. He hadn't planned to wait until fifty to start trying for his first baby. That just sort of happened. He easily piled up one success after another and postponed having kids. He figured that someday, life would calm down. Then he could turn his attention to starting a family.

As the hours ticked by, the L&D unit was quiet, except for two of Trent's patients walking the halls. Colin went to check on Gina, hoping he'd be able to sneak in a few more minutes of sleep afterward. Finding Liz in the room, he stood off to the side as she sat on the edge of the bed and lifted Gina's blanket.

"Let's go ahead and see where we're at," Liz said. "Sorry. Exhale. Nice and slow. There you go, Gina. Good work." She turned to Colin and nodded. The baby would arrive in time for dinner. That news was better than being able to go back to sleep.

The delivery went to plan, and for the first time in months, Colin and Liz left the hospital together at the end of her shift.

"What are your plans for tomorrow?" He untied his shoes and placed them on the shelf in their changing room. Liz wiped her eye makeup off in the mirror.

"Fertility support group in the morning, then lunch with my mom and baby basics class downtown."

He stopped unbuttoning his shirt. "I thought Selena had this month."

Liz looked at him through the mirror. "I'm okay, Colin. Our miscarriages have nothing to do with teaching a bunch of pregnant women how to care for their babies."

He walked over to her and rubbed her arms. "I know."

"Really." She turned and kissed him. "You don't need to worry."

He knew she was right.

"Hey, what did you want to talk about the other night?" Colin asked.

"It's nothing really, and I'm exhausted after today..." She

stood and pulled the clip out of her hair, making her curls bounce around her face and shoulders. "I'd love to just veg out with some stupid show."

He followed her into the hall. "Do you have a gambling problem?"

"What?" She stopped on the stairs and laughed.

"Drugs? Starting a knitting business? Tell me the truth, have you..." He switched to his most serious doctor voice. "Have you decided to buy a new car?"

"Obviously, you've lost your mind." She laughed again and continued down to the kitchen.

Colin followed. He'd thought his silly guesses would hide his need to know without coming off as nagging. She didn't bite. Perhaps some wine would get her talking. He grabbed two glasses and met her on the couch.

Kicking off her slippers and running her fingers through her hair, she stretched and said, "Okay."

"Okay?"

"I'll tell you, but I want you to keep an open mind and just listen. It's... complicated."

"Got it."

As he twisted the corkscrew into the bottle, his phone pinged. He exhaled, knowing his open mind would have to wait.

There must have been a full moon as Colin raced from patient to patient, welcoming them in one minute, catching their babies the next. As soon as one room emptied and was cleaned and remade, another woman was huffing and puffing and ready to push.

Trent arrived to help when two labors stalled, and both babies began to struggle, requiring C-sections.

As the morning brought the first lull in hours, Trent followed Colin into the staff lounge. "What did Liz think of Cami?"

"Sorry, man." Colin grabbed his phone from his locker and sent Liz a good-morning text. "We haven't had time to talk."

"She makes me feel alive for the first time in years."

"Are you selling me or yourself?"

"I don't know." Trent massaged his forehead, rubbed his eyes, and yawned. "I saw another bus of patients scheduled for today and tomorrow. How many are we supposed to take on?"

Colin read Liz's *good morning* in reply and left the room.

Trent followed him into the hall. "Why aren't you answering?"

"Because you won't like the answer," Colin said, stopping by room 812W to wait. He held his hand up to quiet his partner.

When the contraction subsided, Colin entered the room to find Selena comforting a young woman. No, not a young woman. A child, really. Colin introduced himself and looked at the chart. Age eighteen, it said. It had to be a lie.

Back in the hall, he followed Selena to her station.

"What are you doing here?" he asked. "I thought you were off today?"

"Liz is covering the baby basics class for me."

"Right. She did mention..."

"You don't think it's too soon?" She chewed her lower lip.

"Nah, she'll be fine," he said, wishing Selena would have taken the class.

"I figured she would. You know Liz."

"She's a rock," he said, watching Selena tap at the keyboard. He thought of their young patient. "Did you call social services?"

"Yeah."

"How old do you think she is?"

"Twelve."

Colin nodded.

"Her mom claims she was raped somewhere in Honduras."

"What do you think?"

Selena made a face. "During a contraction, she called out for her husband."

"I don't get men like that."

"Degenerates," Selena whispered, as the girl's mother opened the door holding a pink water pitcher.

Selena left to get more ice chips, and Colin waited for her to assist in the exam. The baby was quite large and, based on their best estimation, two weeks overdue.

Out the window, Colin saw a man pacing in the parking lot and wondered if he was the degenerate. Another contraction began.

"You're doing fantastic," Colin said as the girl's terrified eyes locked in on his. "That's good," he said, breathing deep and slow with her. "Breathe in... and out." She nodded and breathed, keeping rhythm with him.

He knew the damage done to this girl was far from over. Based on the baby's size, he had to weigh the chances of causing her more harm by continuing or cutting her open. He wondered how she would cope with the recovery at the shelter. Then he thought of Gerrard Coffey and the hospital's board of directors. Taking on patients for money, no matter the risks—like a twelve-year-old delivering a fourteen-pound baby that was two weeks late. They'd leave that to Colin.

His mouth watered, and he thought of his apartment, then of Liz seeing him there. He wondered what she had been trying to tell him.

When the baby's heart rate dropped during the contraction and didn't bounce back, he nodded to Selena. She calmly but firmly explained that they needed to deliver the baby. Now.

10
Colin

The young mother just barely pulled through. The baby was brought to the NICU. Time would tell.

Colin found Trent in the staff lounge, rifling around in the fridge.

"Rough day," Trent said. "Did you bring me a piece?"

Colin looked at the container with the slice of chocolate cake that Liz had handed to him after the party. He'd forgotten it was there.

"You can have it." Colin stretched and leaned back in the new recliner, which had both heat and massage.

"Why is it cut like this?"

Colin looked over and laughed. "Liz cut it to be, and I quote, 'the most aesthetically pleasing shape for my cake-eating enjoyment.'"

"You are the weirdest couple I've ever met."

"Watch it," Colin said, holding up a fist as he closed his eyes.

"No, it's nice," Trent said. "Nance and I were never like that, and Cami just wants to talk about expensive handbags."

"Handbags? As in, you're buying her expensive handbags?"

"Go to sleep," Trent said, shoving the cake in his mouth and leaving the room.

Colin's break ended as the ebb and flow of the delivery floor began to flow more than it ebbed. At one point, Trent had five patients arrive in the same elevator, all ready to deliver. Colin managed two while Trent raced back and forth among the others.

The day continued into night, and just before and after midnight, twins were born on separate days, attracting the attention of local media. It continued into the early morning hours, when two drunk fathers had to be sobered up. Another passed out just as his girlfriend was beginning to push, resulting in six stitches to the back of his head.

Morning finally came, and Colin texted Liz a sunrise emoji. He dashed down the stairs to his office for routine appointments. Then he raced back up to deliver a baby and finally returned downstairs to see more patients.

By lunch, the staff were all overworked and frazzled. Tensions were high. One of Trent's nurses swore a bit too loudly under her breath as she left a patient's room. They all needed relief.

Colin ordered pizzas, cheesy garlic bread, salad, a huge tray of cannoli, assorted cookies, and an extra-large pan of tiramisu.

The food and sugar revived the unit. They grew calmer and found a steady rhythm. Soon, they were busy laboring and delivering. New mothers and babies were sent upstairs to the recovery ward.

Trent hurried through his office appointments. Selena clocked out for some much-needed rest. This left Colin with the staff nurses scheduled to help with the remaining patients.

When the rooms were finally empty, Colin exhaled, walking into the lounge to rest.

"Haven't had enough pain for one day?" he said, seeing Selena's head poke back into the room.

"Have you heard from Liz?"

Colin checked his phone. She hadn't responded to his text. "No, why?"

"She didn't show up to the baby basics class yesterday. It's been so crazy, I only just now listened to the message from the coordinator. I tried to call Liz, but it just went to voicemail."

Colin tried Liz's number. Straight to voicemail for him as well. "Her phone must be dead. You're sure she didn't show up?"

Selena called the coordinator and shook her head.

"It was probably too much after..." Selena dropped her phone in her purse. "I'm worried about her."

Me too, he thought, looking at his phone again. He knew she should have taken some time off after the miscarriage. She needed a break. Colin did, too. Trying to lighten the mood, he said, "Let's hope those patients don't go into labor before then, or they won't know the first thing to do with their babies."

"Haha, you're so funny, Doc. Tell her not to worry about the class. I rescheduled."

As the day calmed and the rooms emptied, Colin checked his phone. Nothing new from Liz since the morning before. He called again. The phone went to voicemail. Between a young patient in labor with her first baby and an older patient scheduled to be induced, Colin ducked out to run home.

Liz's car sat in the driveway, but the house was quiet. He pulled out his phone and swiped around.

His mother-in-law's small, cheerful voice answered. "Hello."

"Hey, Anne. Did you have lunch with Liz yesterday?"

"I did."

"Have you heard from her since then?"

"No. She had some class. Why? Is everything okay?"

"I'm sure it is." His phone vibrated. He checked if it was Liz. It wasn't. "Her phone's going straight to voicemail. I need to ask her something."

"Maybe she dropped it in my car." He could hear Anne moving around, her keys rattling. "I'll go check."

"You picked her up for lunch?"

"Yes. Now, let me see. Not on the floor here..."

"Did you drive her home after?" he asked.

"Not under the seat. No, she took a cab to her class. Sorry, Colin. I'm not seeing it."

"Thanks anyway. Oh, Anne? Would you mind calling me if

you hear from her?"

"Did something happen between you two?"

"No. Everything's fine."

"Are you sure? At lunch, she seemed a bit... fired up."

"Fired up? In what way?"

"You know Liz. Forget I said anything."

Colin's phone vibrated again. He checked it, hoping to see Liz's name. It was his office assistant. Another busload of patients had arrived.

Anne kept talking. "On second thought, I was meaning to stop by your office—"

"Sorry. I have to go."

"Colin?"

"Yes?"

"We should talk. It's important."

11
Owen

"Have you tried litter box training them?" Lika asked, opening a cage.

"Like a cat?" Owen had heard of training rabbits. He hadn't bothered.

"I'd be happy to help out with these little ones too." She cradled a tan Holland lop in her arms, running her fingers from the tuft on the top of his head through to the thick shock of fur on his back.

Owen smiled, squishing the bunny's cheeks. "Oh, I couldn't ask that much of you. For being so small, they certainly produce a fair amount of waste."

"Really, I don't mind at all."

The rabbits climbed and hopped at the edge of their cages, vying for their morning food.

"Sixteen." Lika counted them, her delicate finger pointing at each one. "Did you know two rabbits can produce over a hundred thousand in five years?" She set the little boy back into his cage. White scratch marks lingered on her arms.

"Don't worry, I keep them separate. The black cage for the boys, the white for the girls." He opened a white gate and pulled out a tiny speckled black-and-brown one. "Those cages over there are for mothers with newborns... when I do let them mate."

"And that cage? It must be for an Irish Wolfhound." She pulled up the plaid throw blanket that was draped over the rusty frame.

A sound came from outside the door.

"She'll be looking for her tea and cookies," Owen said, and sighed. "I'm meant to call them biscuits now, not cookies." He turned the key in the door and opened it to find Sarah standing outside the room, staring at a family photograph on the wall.

"Is Sheena home?" Sarah asked. "She has to get ready for ballet." A look of worry filled her eyes.

Lika passed by, patting Owen's arm. "I'll put the kettle on."

"Who's she?" Sarah asked. "Are you Sheena's new babysitter? Where's Sheena?"

"I'm just about to drive Sheena to ballet, dear," Owen said to calm her nerves. Taking her hand in his, he led her back to their bedroom. "You need to rest. Come on." He settled her in the armchair, tucking a blanket over her legs. "I'll put on a Poirot."

"His little gray cells," Sarah said.

"That's right." Turning on the TV, Owen smiled at the random bits Sarah's mind would recall.

Owen handed Lika the key, leaving her free rein in his usually locked room. With a few final directions, he left.

The weather felt crisp and sunny, a surprise to Owen. He'd always thought Ireland would be rainy and dreary. Even Sarah's aunt, who sold up and moved to Florida, had mentioned the need for vitamin D supplements to get through the long, dark winters. Owen thought the weather all year round in Ireland felt like fall in Chicago—which he loved.

When he arrived in Westport for his break, he stopped in at the bookstore for a look around. Owen enjoyed being around books and people who liked books. They were either interested in talking about books or minding their own business.

Up a narrow, creaky staircase, Owen found the art and school supplies. He never stopped by for anything in particular, just liked to have a look around. It reminded him of when the kids were young, and the back-to-school sales flyers arrived in the newspaper. Notebooks, pens, glue, crayons, and wipes. The smell of the wipes. That was what he remembered most. Such a happy time. He held a notebook and inhaled. Fresh paper. He smiled.

If only he could smell those wipes again. The ones he used to buy in Chicago. Wipe down the cages and have that scent floating through the hall instead of the smell of death. Death. That was what he thought about every night as he lay next to his wife, wondering when she would die so he could return home. It wasn't a pleasant thought, but it was the truth. Sarah had wanted to move to Ireland. He'd owed it to her for everything he'd done; he knew that. But how long would he have to wait?

The bell chimed as someone entered downstairs, pulling Owen out of his own thoughts. He checked his watch. Time to take the 450 out to Achill.

"Good afternoon," Owen said with a smile. "Where to?"

His fingers tapped the buttons. The ticket to Achill Sound printed for a lively woman in new walking shoes and layers of clothes. She'd obviously read the guidebooks.

"Lovely day," she said.

"'Tis. Take your ticket." Owen ripped the paper off and handed it through his plexiglass shield. She smiled and lifted her tote to the first seat behind him as he closed the door and started out of town. Darting his eyes from the road to his newest traveling companion, Owen chatted.

"Where ya from?" He yielded for a young girl in braids to cross the road.

"Originally Cobh, but I've been a teacher in San Francisco for the last twenty-eight years. What about you?"

"Born and raised in Cleveland," he lied.

"So, you're not from here?"

Owen knew the tone, knew what it meant. She wanted to know if he belonged, if he had a right to be living in her country. A country she herself had abandoned to build a life, always planning to return, irritated by any blow-in staking claim to her homeland.

"My wife's from Westport. We raised our family in Cincinnati. She always wanted to return." He drove across the river, passing the church out of town.

"Oh, that's lovely. I've always planned to return, but—"

She rattled off the usual excuses: family obligations, salary that could never be matched, just plain comfortable with the life she'd built. He heard the same story over and over. Sometimes from the Ireland-born who'd emigrated as children or for work. Other times the Americans with at least one grandparent—enough to stake claim to their citizenship. He and Sarah were a sort of unicorn amusement when they arrived. Young and healthy enough to enjoy a few good years.

"Visiting family in Achill?" he asked, changing the subject.

"No one in particular. My friend mentioned it'd be a nice trip on a sunny day. I thought, why not?"

"You only paid to the Sound."

"Won't that be far enough? My friend recommended a café by the post office."

Where is this idiot friend of yours? "Trust me," he said, "you'll want to go at least to Keel. At that point, you might as well loop around and see all you can."

"Really?"

"Oh yes, dear." Some nosy woman—who'd been leaning forward, eager to jump into Owen's conversation with his new friend—was now standing in the aisle, giving her advice. "It really is quite special driving from the Sound to Dooagh."

Owen's friend met his eyes in the mirror, and he sighed, then gave a curt smile. If she didn't have the sense to trust his advice alone, he wasn't so sure he wanted to be friends with her after all.

As her fellow passengers disembarked along the way, the woman held her phone out, snapping photos and complimenting his wisdom.

He pulled into the turnaround across from the pub and parked. "We have twelve minutes before we make the return. Have a stretch and enjoy the view. Don't worry, I won't leave without you."

From the window in Lourdie's Pub, he watched her wander away, down the path toward the water. Had they become friends in the way he'd hoped, he would have continued beyond the final stop to the most beautiful location on the island.

Oh well, he thought, watching her take pictures on the shore as he started the bus, closed the door, and drove away.

12
Colin

Liz's parents lived in the house where they got married. The brick outside stayed strong over time, but the inside had changed a lot. Two years ago, a deep freeze burst a pipe under the kitchen sink, leading to a complete remodel.

"Come on in." Anne locked the door and, standing on tiptoe, peeked out the window. "Have you heard anything?"

"No." Colin loosened his tie and slung his suit coat over a dining room chair. "Is Daniel home?"

"No, he's off to Home Depot. I thought it best we speak alone."

"Okay." He nodded and started to head up the stairs. "I'll just be a minute."

In Liz's childhood bedroom, a hospital bed had replaced the bunk she'd shared with her twin sister.

"Hey, Emma." Colin knocked on the doorframe. The door was always open for visitors.

Flipping through a trade catalog of wigs, she tapped a blond bob with thick bangs, number 294037.

"Let me see." He held the picture next to Emma's face. "No. No good at all. Your hair is far too beautiful to cover with this sad excuse. What is this even made from?" He flipped the pages. "Recycled plastic bags?"

Her lips didn't move, but he could see the smile in her eyes, that subtle squint she used to communicate.

"I made coffee," Anne said from the door. "Emma, I have to talk to Colin right now. I'll be up soon."

Colin kissed Emma on the cheek, then pressed his cheek next to hers for a moment. He could feel her push into him.

"How's she been doing?" He pointed up the stairs as Anne handed him a mug.

"Same old," she said, following Colin into the living room and taking a seat next to him on the couch. She lowered her voice. "I think it's my fault."

"What is?"

"Things got a bit heated at lunch." Setting her coffee on the table, she walked back into the kitchen. Colin could hear the oven door open. Other than during the construction months, he couldn't remember a day he'd been to their house when there wasn't bread baking.

"What happened?" he asked as Anne returned to the living room.

Her eyes watered, and she blinked to hold back the tears. "I know about your agreement with Liz."

"What agreement is that?"

"I know you expect children from this marriage."

"Expect?"

"She told me about the conversation you had on your first date."

"I wouldn't say I told her I *expect* children from our marriage. It was more a conversation to be upfront and say that I wanted children. I didn't want to date someone for five years before finding out it wasn't going anywhere. I don't have that kind of time, and I don't think it's fair to her either."

She smoothed her skirt and topped off Colin's coffee.

"I don't want to upset you. It's just what Liz told me."

"Fine. What does this have to do with things getting heated at lunch?"

"Would you like some bread with honey?"

"No, thank you. What's going on?"

"It's just that all this... it's too much pressure."

"All what?" He set his cup on the table.

"This desperate need to have a baby. You don't realize how stressful that can be on a woman. The sorts of things she'll put herself through to give you what you want or else risk losing you."

"Liz never said... Losing me?" Colin leaned back and spread his hands. "She said that to you?"

"Well, no. Not in those words. I could tell she wasn't happy, and I put it all together. It must be this unrealistic pressure you have her under."

"Okay, Anne." She'd done this before, working out details that seemed only to exist in her imagination and then thrusting her conclusions on those around her. "If you hear anything, please call me. I have to get back to the hospital."

"You'll take a slice of bread to go?"

"Sure."

She left the room, and Colin looked around at the photos arranged around the television. Baby pictures and school portraits, Liz and Colin's wedding photograph mirroring the one of Daniel and Anne. Not a single one of Emma since the accident.

Anne handed Colin a hearty chunk of bread wrapped in a paper towel.

"It's probably best to keep this within the family," she said, her hand lingering on his arm. "Don't you think?"

He hadn't thought of handling the situation in any way, so he didn't know what that meant. His face must have shown his confusion because Anne clarified.

"There's no need to call the police."

"Of course not." Colin pulled his arm away. "Why would you even suggest... It's not like that."

"Don't worry. I'm sure she'll turn up," she said.

"She will."

In the car, Colin's phone pinged with a message. Still not Liz. He called the hospital to say he was on his way back. First, he planned to stop by his apartment, place his usual order, and relieve the anxious pressure building in his chest. Then he could think straight.

At Valparaiso, he pulled out his second phone and apartment key from the car's doorframe and dropped in his real phone and keys. Then he stopped, seeing the tracker on his keys, and pulled out his phone, feeling stupid. He hadn't thought to track her phone or keys. He wasn't the only one who would lose keys—he just let her make jokes at his expense—but Liz was the one who'd turned him on to that tracker keyring.

He entered the app to track her phone. Nothing. It didn't show up at all. Then the app for the key tracker. He saw his own location, notated as a green dot on the map. Liz's was a blue dot. He saw it on the map. Her keys. The dot showed they were at home.

Pulling a U-turn, Colin drove right back.

Her car was in the garage. The house was quiet. He ran up and down the stairs, calling out her name. He looked out on the back patio, then followed the tracking app to the kitchen. He opened the junk drawer. Her keys were there, under a Chinese menu. Guilt gripped his thoughts as he thought of his apartment. It didn't make sense. Even if she'd taken a cab and her mom had picked her up for lunch, why wouldn't she take her house keys?

His phone pinged. The hospital again.

He looked at Liz's keys in his hand and began to laugh. *She probably forgot them since she wasn't driving,* he thought, then said aloud, "You need sleep, you idiot."

As he drove to the hospital, he thought of Anne's assumptions about his desire for kids. He knew if Liz had any issue with their plans, she was certainly the type to speak up.

She'd turn up by the evening. He was sure of it.

"I'm really proud of you, Mara," Colin said, holding baby Kyle for a picture. He'd been born at twenty-six weeks. Finally, after months in the NICU, he was heading home to his family.

"Thank you so much, Doctor. I owe you my life."

That was true. He had saved her life. He'd saved many lives over the years, mitigated bad situations, made everything better. Yet he still knew, still held in the forefront of his thoughts, the real possibility that at any moment, he could be sued. Even by someone who'd just thanked him and smiled for a photo.

So, it was no surprise when Gerrard Coffey called him into his office.

Taking steps two at a time up to the top-floor administration suite, Colin speculated which patient had filed a complaint.

"Did you call social services on Gabriela Menendez?" Coffey asked before Colin could even choose between the two leather chairs opposite his desk.

The twelve-year-old who almost died giving birth? he wanted to say. "I followed protocol." The best answer.

"Yes, I know."

"What is this?" Colin didn't like the look on Coffey's face.

"Only a few buses of migrants, and you're already saying, 'I told you so.'"

"Has something happened?" Colin crossed his leg and bumped the desk.

"Look, when it comes to the migrants, we're going to need to live by a slightly less... rigid protocol." He nodded his head as if pleased with himself.

Colin stayed silent.

"Dr. Clarke, in order for this program to work, there will need to be different guidelines for our newest patients."

"What does that mean?" Colin asked, slipping his hand into his pocket to find his phone. He tried to press record without looking down as he recognized the disaster brewing. It was bound to blow up. The last thing he needed was to be Coffey's fall guy.

"Look, let's handle any issues that arise... in-house." Coffey pushed his chair back. Colin thought of his mother-in-law wanting to avoid involving the police. Keep it within the family. He wondered what else Anne might be hiding. "Before calling DCFS next time, give a call up here." Coffey stood to show the meeting had ended and that Colin should leave.

"Sir, with all due respect, Gabriela Menendez couldn't be more than twelve years old. Her baby weighed almost fifteen pounds. She could have died."

"All the more reason to keep us running the migrant program." He walked around his desk to Colin and patted his shoulder. "You're a hero, Doc. Take the win."

Colin's phone pinged. He hated to leave so many things unsaid.

"I'm telling you now, this is a bad situation and will only get worse. In the last six hours, we've seen several cases of unmanaged gestational diabetes. There were also serious bruising and wounds on multiple women. Plus, three women experienced preeclampsia."

"Keep up the good work."

What began as two emergency C-sections turned into nine before Colin could take a breath and grab a coffee. His phone pinged like mad with news of more women in labor. *One of those days,* he thought, trying to remember what day it was.

He called Liz again and left a message, wishing she'd call or text to let him know she was all right. He thought of Liz's mom and questioned again whether he'd been pressuring Liz to have a baby. No. She wanted one, too. That wasn't it. Whatever it was, they could work it out. He thought of Anne's words. *No need to call the police.* Surely that wasn't necessary.

Then, as he slipped into the staff lounge to pour another cup of coffee, his phone pinged with a new text message.

It was from Liz.

13
Colin

Took a contract in Phoenix. Sorry. Need time to think. Love you.

A contract in Phoenix meant Liz would be gone for thirty days. *Sorry. Love you.* He looked at those words again and knew something was wrong.

Swiping around at his screen, Colin dialed Anne.

"Did she mention she might take a nursing job in Arizona?"

"Arizona? Oh. No, not that I recall. Is that where she went?" A timer beeped on Anne's end of the call. Colin waited for her to give Emma her medicine. "So, you've heard from her."

"She texted, but—"

"What is it?"

"You know how Liz is. Well— Here, let me just read it to you." With the phone on speaker, he flipped to the text and read it out loud.

"Hmm."

"You see what I mean?" He knew Anne understood Liz in a way that other mothers never seemed, or wanted, to know their own daughters.

"That does sound strange. As she said, she needs time. And like I said, you don't realize what sort of pressure trying to have a baby can put on a woman—"

"Sorry, that's my phone," Colin said, desperate to get off the phone. “I have to get back.”

Hanging up, he flipped to the text. *It's all right, Liz,* he entered in reply, then paused, trying to think of something more to add. *Sorry, too.* Her response to that message would tell him everything he needed to know.

With the influx of patients, Colin ran up and down the stairs, juggling prenatal appointments and deliveries. As soon as things settled and most of the rooms cleared out, he checked his messages. Nothing new from Liz.

It wasn't the sort of thing many people could understand, but in that short exchange, Colin knew something was wrong.

The morning air was heavy with dew as the sun rose and Colin drove home. Squinting into the rays, he felt in desperate need of a few hours of sleep.

The message ran through his mind. The strangeness of it all. He couldn't let it go. He remembered the first time he'd apologized for some stupid thing he'd said to Liz. She responded with something about real friends never needing to apologize. He didn't understand her reasoning back then. He still didn't. Same with saying, “I love you.”

Perhaps it was the lack of sleep and the strain of taking on an insane number of new patients. Maybe he just needed an hour at his apartment with his usual ritual to get things right in his head. As he drove, when he meant to turn south to go home, he couldn't stop himself from merging into the right-hand lane instead, heading north to the airport.

“Spence, reschedule all my morning appointments,” he said, leaving a message on the office voicemail. “I'll be back in time for Jill Wilson's induction this afternoon.”

As the plane touched down, the Phoenix sun radiated off the tarmac. The flight attendant handed Colin a plastic cup with water. He rubbed his eyes and looked around, unsure for a moment where he was and which patient needed him.

"Sir, please, this way." She gestured to her colleague, who was waiting at the door of the plane.

"Sorry, sorry." He grabbed his bag from the bin overhead, his impromptu flight plans returning to him.

"Sorry, thank you so much," he said to the man checking his watch at the door. Colin hated to be *that guy*. The drunk straggler hindering the crew's schedule, their ability to get on with their lives.

Grabbing a double espresso on the way to the line of cabs, he switched airplane mode off and checked his phone. Nothing more from Liz.

Stucco houses lined the street. Everything looked plain yet perfect. He remembered the first time he flew out to see Liz. She lived in a house with several traveling nurses. They were always coming and going. Coordinating schedules. Missteps leading to awkward roommate situations. Some ending up with fun, lifelong friends, others happy to never return.

He rang the bell, then wished he'd just knocked, not knowing what sort of schedules people were keeping. By the looks of the drawn curtains, he knew he'd just woken the entire house.

"Hello?" A man with disheveled blond hair and Scooby-Doo scrubs squinted into the sun. A dungeon of darkness lay behind him.

"Ian, right?"

He blinked his eyes and tried to focus, then opened the door wider. "Liz's husband..." He snapped his fingers.

"Colin."

"Right, Colin. Come in."

"Sorry to wake you." Colin looked around the entryway and into the living room. As his eyes adjusted, he could see the house looked just as it had when he'd last seen the place. Beige and basic. A simple suite of furniture but, like any other crash pad, devoid of personality. "Is Liz here?"

"Here? No, is she coming out?" Ian's tone perked up as he

led Colin to the kitchen.

"She took a month contract."

"That's odd. I'm on bedroom assignments for the next two months, and I don't have her— Oh, are you two staying at the Marriott? Is she coming over?"

Ian was looking more and more confused, and Colin knew he must be as well.

"No."

Perhaps he had misread the text? He flipped through his phone. No. Phoenix. Colin inhaled and shook his head.

"Is everything all right?" Ian asked, handing him a cup of coffee.

"Yeah, sorry. I'm an idiot. I wanted to surprise her. I must have mistaken this contract for her last one here a few months ago."

"A few months? No, Liz hasn't been here for at least a year." He leaned over the desk built into the cabinetry by the fridge and pantry. "Let's see," Ian said, flipping through a large calendar marked with a rainbow of highlights. "Thirteen months ago." He pointed to Liz's name and room assignment. "Wow, time flies. It does feel like just a few months ago."

"Yeah, that's it. I need a vacation."

"Don't we all?"

"Can I use your bathroom before I go?" Colin asked.

Splashing his face from the sink to wash it, Colin felt his mouth begin to water. He wondered if he had time to rent a room at the Marriott, order some Chinese, and get a release to clear his mind. Then he'd be able to wrap it around whatever was going on.

He didn't have time. He knew that. He'd never missed a patient's delivery, and he wasn't about to start by missing Jill Wilson's.

No time, he thought, looking into his eyes reflecting back at him. No time for whatever Liz was playing at. He'd told her on their first date that he didn't have time to mess around. He knew what he wanted—he wanted a family, and if she didn't want the same thing, she should tell him. Be honest. Simple.

He knew what he'd seen in her eyes that very first delivery together. He thought of the story of the scorpion promising to behave if only the frog would let him ride across the river on his back to safety. As soon as they made it across, the scorpion stung the frog. "What did you expect? I'm a scorpion." *You stupid frog*, Colin thought, looking at himself, *you knew you'd get stung.*

14
Owen

"Owen." A fellow bus driver pointed his thumb at the back office. "Michael's looking for you."

Owen had expected a gentle reprimand after leaving that lady stranded at the end of the line. Instead, a formal complaint had been lodged. He'd have to be on his best behavior to get back in the boss's good graces.

Luckily, his situation at home had improved with the hiring of Lika. She had turned out to be the best caregiver they'd ever found for Sarah. Plus, she was an excellent housekeeper, even neutralizing the rabbit smell.

After a warning from his boss, Owen promised to be more thoughtful. He began his shift, wishing it was already over so he could see Lika.

Daydreaming along the route, he was surprised when he pulled the bus into the airport lot. He'd arrived on autopilot. He parked alongside the bus shelter, then wandered off to stretch his legs and use the bathroom. In the upstairs lounge, he bought two sausage rolls and a Fanta. Leaning on the counter by the window, he watched passengers file out of a plane and down the stairs onto the wet ground. He didn't like sausage rolls and wasn't quite sure what they even were. There didn't seem to be any sausage in them. *Perhaps the doughy wetness is sausage broth?* The dry outer pastry flaked like a croissant, making a mess. They weren't awful for a snack. Sarah said they were meant for kids. She'd eaten hers with nostalgia in her eyes when they first arrived to close on their house.

A young woman, covering her head with a scarf to shield it from the mist, left the plane. She paused at the top of the stairs and looked out at the sky awash in smooth, gray fog. Owen hoped she'd take his bus. He quickly wiped away the crumbs on his lips with a napkin before running back to open the bus and wait.

As he printed out tickets for a mother and two kids, an elderly couple, and a group of teenaged boys with oversized duffels, his hopes were dashed.

A few minutes later, the rain beat down as he picked up speed on the N17. The sky had turned dark, with no light peeking through to the fields. "It's what makes Ireland so green," some guy commented, trying to find the silver lining.

Owen didn't mind the rain or cold in Ireland. He thought of all those Chicago winters filled with snow and ice. Waking up at four in the morning to shovel was hard work, but it made him grateful for the milder weather now. "Heart attack snow," they called it. Snow kicking into his boots, making his ankles raw. By the time he'd arrive home from work, the snow and wind would have made it look as if he hadn't even bothered that morning. Before he could take off his boots and eat his dinner, he'd have to shovel again.

He didn't miss the snow.

After a break in Westport, Owen walked along the queue of passengers waiting outside his bus door. He eyed each one, finding just the right new friend.

"I'm going to the Valley House," she said, taking off the rose marl hat that matched her fingerless gloves. Long, slender fingertips intertwined as she folded her hands together on the ledge beneath his plexiglass screen. He could touch those delicate fingers if he wanted to. He hoped she'd forget to take her ticket as it printed out. She did.

Owen watched her walk away to the emergency exit row. She dropped her bag next to the window as she tucked her hat inside and ran her fingers through her blond-highlighted hair.

Stepping down from his seat, Owen motioned for the rest of the line to wait. He ripped off the ticket and walked down the aisle to her seat.

She looked up, confused.

"Your ticket, Miss."

"Oh, thank you," she said, smiling and looking around with embarrassment at the other passengers.

"Wouldn't want you to get kicked off for not paying." He winked and returned to his seat, irritated by the remaining line. He longed to get driving and watch his new friend in the mirror.

By the time he pulled off at her stop, the bus was almost empty. The rain fell steadily on the windshield.

"I hate to leave you to walk in this weather. Valley House is two hundred meters down the way." He pointed to the right at the intersection. "I'd drive you there if I could."

"It's no problem. I'm happy to walk."

Good girl, he thought as he watched her exit, wished her a good night, and motioned for her to cross in front of the bus. Without the loud sigh of a woman two rows back, he would have waited a bit longer. He wanted to make sure his new friend found the right path to her destination.

Later that night, after Lika left and Sarah fell asleep—thanks to two extra sleeping pills—Owen drove to The Valley House on Achill Island. His new friend was perched there in the crowd, drinking and laughing with some silly boy who looked like he could use a shower and a haircut.

Owen returned to his car and waited.

Back home, he locked the rabbit room door and remembered his setup in his Chicago basement. He had hired a handyman from the church bulletin who ran water, electricity, and gas to the hall closet and installed a stackable washer and dryer. This way, Sarah wouldn't have to carry laundry to the cold, damp basement that leaked when it rained. After that, Owen had the spacious basement all to himself.

In Ireland, his hobby had been reduced to a spare room not much larger than a closet. So small. Hardly large enough for a man to really enjoy himself.

He spread the plaid blanket over the cage Lika said was big enough for an Irish Wolfhound. Then, he checked the locks. Finally, he turned to his morning chores. Three scoops of food for the boy bunnies, three for the girls. He would pick up a head of lettuce and a cucumber for them on the way home from work.

Lika had set up litter boxes and was cleaning them daily, but for now, she wouldn't be allowed in that room. He emptied the liners into a bag.

A scream pierced the silence of the morning. Owen locked the door. With the key tucked firmly against his chest, he ran to calm Sarah. The extra medication seemed to bring on night terrors. A small price to pay for a few hours of freedom and normalcy.

As he helped Sarah to her armchair, the front door opened.

"Good morning." Lika hung her coat and scarf on the empty hook. It had been Sarah's. She rarely left the house anymore; it seemed silly to leave the coat there to get dusty.

"Sarah's ready for breakfast." Owen slipped his foot into his loafer, wiggling to coax the heel up. "Have a good day."

He had barely pulled away when the call came from Lika. She was looking for the key to the rabbit room.

"I'm sorry, I'm so used to keeping it on me, I must have forgotten. Well, don't worry about them today."

"Too bad—I picked dandelions for a snack."

"You're meant to be caring for Sarah."

"I know, I just—"

Don't you dare talk back. "I'm running late," he said before ending the call and dropping his phone beside the rose marl glove on his passenger seat.

15
Colin

With one last text to Liz asking her to call back, Colin switched to airplane mode and closed his eyes. Three slow breaths, and he fell into a deep sleep.

The plane touched down in Chicago, and he watched droplets of rain wriggle down the window as they taxied to the gate. The woman next to him gathered her things in her lap and unbuckled her seatbelt.

Colin stretched and found his phone, switching airplane mode off. It made a series of pings as messages shuffled up the screen. Multiple from Selena, Trent, and Spence. One from Liz's mom. Then Liz.

Leave me alone. I need time, her text read.

He checked his voicemail.

He held the phone tight to his ear. The fasten seatbelt light switched off. People squeezed into the aisle. He listened, hoping to hear her voice.

"Colin, it's Selena. Jill Wilson just arrived."

"I'll be right in."

At the hospital, Colin checked on Jill. With her Pitocin drip started, questions answered, and nerves settled for the moment, there was a bit of free time. He knew he should eat something healthy and try to rest. The draw to stop by his apartment for a binge grew too strong. He hated it, but he needed it. He deserved to have a little relief.

Colin reached his apartment. He sought a moment of relief but was left feeling disgusted and disappointed in himself.

He went home.

The photos around the living room told the story of their idyllic life together. He thought of the text from Liz and the one he sent back to test his fears. Then what he'd received today.

Love you. Colin had never known love. He'd tried, but he couldn't open himself up. Then he'd met Liz. During their first delivery together, he saw it in her too. He knew he wouldn't have to fake the emotion of love. Love as an appreciation and concern for another human being? Sure. But passionate desire and love? No. With Liz, that was okay.

He'd recognized the difference between himself and other people toward the end of high school and then in college. He'd had a happy childhood with his adoptive parents and older brother, Mikey, never feeling the need to rebel or give them any trouble. They were proud of their little boy, who was turning into a good man.

But then, in college, his mom called to say his dad had died of a heart attack, and before Colin arrived home, she was dead too. "Died of a broken heart," Mikey said.

Colin went through the motions, mirroring Mikey through the wake and funeral. He didn't feel anything. Couldn't feel anything. He knew he'd been broken before his parents adopted him.

The grandfather clock in the corner chimed, bringing Colin back to the present. His eye caught a photo of him and Trent in college together. When Colin returned to campus after his parents' funeral, Trent became his new family, and he appreciated being taken in as a brother. Being saved.

Colin worked hard to become a strong, accomplished doctor. To give back. To save others. To build a picture-perfect life. To prove to his biological mother that she'd been wrong to let him go.

His phone rang. He wanted to see Liz's name, but worry took over. Did she abandon him like his biological mother? Like his adoptive parents when they died? Or like Trent, lost in his midlife crisis?

"Hello, Dr. Clarke, this is Vivian Shepherd. I'm returning your call."

He forgot that after leaving the Phoenix nurse house, he'd sent a message to the coordinator of traveling nurses at Jagger Medical Staffing.

"Yes, thank you for calling me back. There seems to have been a bit of a mix-up, for which I am completely to blame. We'd requested a nurse from your agency, but it seems Elizabeth Clarke was put on our schedule? This doesn't make any sense to me since, as you know, Liz is my wife. I know she's already taken a one-month contract elsewhere." He hoped Vivian would just so happen to mention, *Oh, yes, Liz went off to such-and-such a place...* She didn't.

"I'm sorry to hear she ended up going with a different agency. I was hoping after the baby came, she'd come back to us. Even for weekly contracts here and there."

"A different agency." His tone toed the line between questioning and stating a fact. He hoped she'd finally take the hint and give him something. Still, nothing. He tried to think on his feet, wondering why Liz had lied to him. And how long had she been lying? "Sorry, that's right, the last contract she took with you was, oh, a year ago in Phoenix?"

He could hear her tapping at a keyboard. "Sharp memory. Now tell me, do you need a nurse scheduled?"

Seeing as he had no idea where Liz was or if she planned to return to work, he figured he might as well lighten the load. "Make it two. Thanks."

After hanging up, he scrolled through their conversations

over the last year. Full of inside jokes and movie lines that could, if taken out of context, have painted a pretty messed-up picture. Then there were texts of the highs and lows of their pregnancies and subsequent losses.

Texts from her contract in Phoenix three months ago.

Just arrived in AZ.

What are people talking about dry heat being a good heat? It's unbearable here!

Is a scorpion in the kitchen lucky?

Now, he knew those had all been a lie. Where had she been three months ago, and where was she now?

Scrolling further, he found texts from when she'd taken a six-week contract in Austin. He didn't have time for another flight out of town to check if she was there. He called his hospital.

"How's Jill?" he asked Selena.

"She's ready. The baby's a bit shy."

"Good, I'll be back soon."

"Colin?"

"Yeah?"

"Is everything all right? I still can't get ahold of Liz. Is she mad at me?"

"No, no. She took a contract in Phoenix."

"Oh, okay." She didn't sound convinced. Colin didn't know what else he should say in the situation.

He texted Liz. *I know you're not in AZ. Call me ASAP.*

As he ran through all sorts of crazy possibilities of what she could be up to, the one thing he couldn't imagine her doing was cheating. It just wasn't something either of them considered a worthwhile pursuit. If she began seeing another man, it made sense for her to let Colin go. He deserved a shot at the family he always wanted. Right?

Lights started blinking, signaling a train, pulling Colin from his thoughts.

"Ugh," he said, slamming his palms on the steering wheel as he sat watching it pass and checked his phone. No response. He wanted to scream; he wanted to force Liz to call him back.

The release he'd felt from his earlier binge had already worn off. He needed more. He needed it. Needed it. Hated that he needed it.

Colin saw a sliver of sunlight peek through the crumpled blackout curtain in the staff lounge. Just then, his phone pinged. News about Jill Wilson's baby.

Her delivery was quick and uneventful, the way every delivery should be.

"Congratulations, Jill. I'm so proud of you. What a beautiful boy," Colin said, holding the baby in his arms and smiling for a picture. Closing his eyes, he saw the baby from the dumpster and tried to shake the thought. But he was haunted by that boy left for dead, then the idea of Liz running off and leaving him for dead. He needed to go to his apartment, open an envelope of pills, order some food, and never return.

He smiled for another picture and handed the baby to Jill. "Well done. Get some rest."

Entering the staff lounge, he took a breath. He could feel his face, red and warm. Now he was alone again. The tears came as he leaned on the table, hands shaking. His phone pinged. He cleared his throat as he dried his eyes to read the text.

Hi, Colin, it's Trina. I don't know what's going on, but it'd be great if you could get your wife to leave me alone. Thanx.

16
Colin

Trina? Colin thought, reading the text over again. It took an internet search of her phone number and several minutes piecing things together to figure out who had just texted him.

Trina Scott—the IT professional from last year's medical conference in Sarasota. It was the same week Liz left for Phoenix—the last time she had really been in Phoenix for a month-long nursing contract.

After two full days of seminars at the conference, Colin flew back to Chicago to deliver Monique Simmons's daughter. He returned to find a quiet spot in the hotel bar. He'd ordered a very neat, very pretentious martini.

"Mind if I join you?" a woman asked, pulling out the chair across from him and sitting down before he could reply.

"Ms. Scott, right?"

"Yes." She nodded and held out her hand. "Call me Trina."

"Making the rounds?" Colin pointed at the brochures for her company's medical records services.

She smiled and held up her rum and Coke. "I'm off duty."

"Good. Besides, I already signed up."

They discussed food and travel. Then, they spent a long time comparing U.S. and European ski slopes. It was a nice change of pace and a great way to end a long day.

That was over a year ago, he thought as he dialed her number.

"Hey, Trina. I got your message. I don't understand—"

"I didn't want to say anything, but this is getting creepy."

"What is?"

"I'd rather talk to you in person. Can we meet up?"

"I can't really get out of town right now."

"I live in Chicago," she said.

That gave Colin pause. With the conference being held in Florida, he'd just assumed she lived there.

When he didn't say anything, she continued, "I'm free in an hour."

Trina had the same carefree smile. Her hands still moved rapidly as she spoke, an extension of her words. But her eyes were full of concern.

"I don't know what's going on with your wife, but I won't be a homewrecker," she said. The host guided them to a small table on the patio of a local bistro. He handed them menus, then left.

Colin set his down on the table without looking. "I have no idea what you're talking about. Slow down and tell me what happened."

Pulling her phone from her back pocket, she pressed her thumb to the screen and handed it over to Colin. "I was out for a run when I got that first one, and it's been nonstop since."

Colin swiped and swiped and swiped through an endless stream of messages from Liz.

Trina? the first message said.

How could you do that?

He doesn't care about you.

You're so gross!!!

The responses from Trina were all similar:

What do you want?

I think you have the wrong person.

Who is this?

Liz eventually responded, making things perfectly clear. *This is Liz Clarke. Colin Clarke's wife.*

Colin looked up at Trina. "I don't know what to say."

"Did you read the last one? 'I've made you my project.' What does that mean, Colin?"

He shook his head.

The waiter arrived at the table to take their order. Colin couldn't eat. He just asked for a glass of water.

"She's been under a lot of stress," he said, trying to make an excuse. "She— We just suffered our fourth miscarriage."

"I'm sorry, but—"

"It's taken a toll. I'm sorry." *I didn't notice... I didn't want to notice how hard it was on Liz*, he thought.

"It doesn't give her the right to just start stalking me out of nowhere."

A few weird messages were hardly stalking. "I know. Again, I'm sorry."

"You need to get her some help and tell her to leave me alone."

The waiter placed two waters and a pitcher of margaritas on the table.

"We didn't order this," Colin said.

"It's on the house," he said, pouring a glass for them both.

"I don't want—"

"Friends?" Trina asked, holding up her drink.

"Sure," Colin said, clinking his glass to hers, trying to make sense of it all.

"So." Trina bit her bottom lip. "How have you been?"

"I'm good." He'd be much better just as soon as Liz came home and they talked everything through. "Don't worry. I'll talk to her and get her to stop. I'm sorry she dragged you into this. Like I said, she's been under a lot of stress, and I'm sorry I missed the signs."

"Signs?"

"Obviously, she's had some sort of mental break. None of this sounds like her." He didn't bother to mention the strange texts between them as a way to explain.

"Is she dangerous?"

"Oh, gosh no. Why would you say that?"

She ran her fingers through her hair. "I don't know. I thought I'd show you the messages and you'd say, 'Oh, it was all some prank,' or some explanation. I haven't heard from you in a year. I guess I just thought there'd be some reason other than..." Her voice trailed off as she bit at her straw and took another sip.

"I'm really sorry. I don't know how she got your number or what's going on. I'll get her to stop."

"Please do, or I'm going to the police."

"Whoa. That won't be necessary, Trina." He laid his hands out on the table, open.

Crinkling up her nose, she sighed and placed her hands in his.

"It's good to see you," Colin said, giving her hands a gentle squeeze, looking deep into her eyes. "How've you been?"

"Other than being stalked by some guy's crazy wife, I can't complain."

In the car back to the hospital, Colin tried to make sense of his wife's actions. First, she'd disappeared, then she'd lied about taking a nursing contract. Just when Colin had started to think perhaps Liz was cheating, she'd started hounding a woman Colin had had a drink or two with at a convention over a year ago.

Enough's enough. Call me now. He sent the text to Liz, and he couldn't help but imagine their perfect life together vanishing.

17
Owen

There's a strange noise coming from the rabbit room, Lika texted Owen.

He'd just passed the church at Bunnacurry on Achill Island. He knew the rules. Bus drivers weren't allowed to text while driving. A coworker had just been fired for that same reason when an annoying passenger recorded the driver tapping on his phone. The bus swerved in and out of oncoming traffic. "For the safety of the passengers," they were told.

To hell with their safety. He looked in the mirror to see if any would-be hero was watching and, seeing no eyes on him, texted back.

Letting a few fraternize. Hoping for some grandbunnies in the near future. Never mind them. How's Sarah?

His eyes darted from the road to the phone. He waited to see those dancing dots, a text back to say she wouldn't try to get into the room. What else could he do from there?

A dense fog moved in over the island. Owen loved the melancholy feel as houses peeked out of the mist, white ghosts dappled through the landscape.

A sheep stood in the road, head-on in front of Owen. He beeped his horn. The animal didn't move. He inched forward, slowly, beeping again. Forward some more. The sheep remained resolute. Owen stopped the bus and waited.

He might have ignored the texting rule from the bus company, but he knew better than to interfere with the sheep on Achill.

"I'm surprised we don't see more dead sheep by the road," said a man in a khaki hat and vest. He held two walking sticks as he spoke to his companions.

More sheep appeared from the bog, following their leader. Owen gave two sharp beeps and inched forward again.

"Are we supposed to just wait on them?" another man asked as his wife ran up to the windshield to take a picture.

Owen checked his phone and inched forward, pushing the sheep along and off the road. He drove through Dugort, passing the beach. A woman in a bikini came out of the cold ocean. She skipped to a man in a coat and scarf, grabbing a towel and a snuggle. Winding up and around the tightly spaced houses and art gallery, Owen tried to see Slievemore Mountain. As usual, it remained hidden in the clouds.

His phone vibrated, and he looked down to read, *I might be able to pick the lock if you want me to check on them. I can't see anything through the keyhole.*

He had to act. He couldn't just turn the bus around and return home to stop her from breaking into the room.

He called a cab company. Then Lika.

"I completely forgot to mention, Sarah has an appointment in Castlebar today. The cab should be there any minute."

"Oh, okay. What about the rabbits? There's some really strange sound coming from them. I didn't think rabbits made any noises."

"Actually, rabbits make fourteen different sounds."

"Oh, I didn't know." She laughed.

"It's quite fascinating..." he said, then entertained her by acting out each sound several times and rattling off random rabbit facts, talking over her when she'd try to speak.

"The cab's here," she said, raising her voice. "I have to get Sarah. Where's her coat?"

Owen knew it wouldn't take long for Lika to realize Sarah didn't have an appointment. He waited for the call.

When it came, he said, "Sorry. I had it marked that she did. Must be next week. Oh, well, since you're out, you might as well take her to the forest for a walk. The fresh air will do her good."

Looping back to Westport, Owen was disappointed in Lika. She'd shown such potential but, like all the rest, had proven too nosy for her own good. *Doesn't anyone know the expression "curiosity killed the cat?" It seems it'd be a universal truth.*

After faking illness to go home early, Owen let out a sigh of relief to find Sarah and Lika still out when he opened the door. Pulling the key from around his neck, he raced down the hall. The excitement of when he was young and had just started acting up. The fear of getting caught. Concocting elaborate lies he would tell, wild stories he'd create to explain himself if the truth was exposed. He almost enjoyed the fear of getting caught more than his little hobby.

He never knew if his lies were any good or if anyone would have believed them because he'd never had to lie. All the times he'd thought he'd been caught, and nothing happened.

One night, he'd crushed a few sleeping pills into the spaghetti and waited for Sarah and the kids to fall asleep. He'd been out longer than expected that night. By the time he came home, Sarah was up and roaming the dark rooms.

He could still see the look on her face as she stepped down the stairs into the basement. It had been raining, and a trickle of water streamed in from outside, down the wall. Pooling in the low spot near the old kitchen table where Owen stored their tax returns, keeping them up and out of the water. Sarah stepped in the puddle. He could tell the coldness of the water startled her as she stared at him, open-mouthed. He had his explanation on the tip of his tongue. It sounded perfectly plausible in his mind. Sarah pursed her lips, then turned back to the stairs and returned to bed.

By morning, the basement was scrubbed clean, just in case

she'd waited to confront him in the daylight. Instead, she poured him coffee and cracked eggs in the pan. When the toaster popped, she said, "Lovely day." Owen agreed and unfolded the newspaper.

Now, as he unlocked the door to the rabbit room, he thought of what a good woman he'd married. The smell of urine and sweat, heavy and thick, filled the room. The plaid blanket had shifted. Disappointed that he hadn't had any more time with his new friend, he opened the cage and dragged her out to the palm tree.

With things back to normal, he hid by a laurel hedge a few houses away. Rubbing his aching lower back, he wished for a nice hot Epsom salt bath.

The cab arrived. Lika helped Sarah to the door. Owen sighed—another excuse gone unused.

18
Colin

Colin checked his phone for a reply from Liz. Nothing. He called over and over, hearing her voice directing him to leave a message and saying she'd call back.

He'd leave another message. She wouldn't call back.

The lack of response infuriated him, but new life would not stop while he waited for her. Pushing everything to the back of his mind, he knocked at room 838W and entered.

"Good morning, Doctor," Laura Zalinski said, catching her breath as Colin walked in. Her eyes were bright with anticipation.

He leaned in for a hug and shook Stan's hand.

"I am so excited for you both. I know this has been a long time coming." Laura and Stan had been together for more than twenty years.

"It has, but I think we're ready." Laura smiled and squeezed Stan's arm.

"I still think we waited too long," Stan said. "I feel too old to be starting all over."

Laura and Stan had been high school sweethearts, welcoming their first baby the summer after graduation. Stan had taken a job with the city while Laura worked as a teller at a bank. They struggled along over the years, supporting each other's dreams. Stan worked all day, then went to law school at night while Laura held down the house. After he joined a busy corporate law firm, Laura quickly finished college and grad school. She found a great job at an accounting firm just two blocks from Stan's office. They'd always planned to have more kids once they were financially secure. Before they knew it, their baby drove off to college himself. One day over lunch they said, why not?

Colin saw himself in Stan and found encouragement in their excitement and confidence. Still, he worried that he too had waited too long.

As another contraction took hold, Stan pressed on Laura's back and spoke soothing words, reminding her to breathe deeply. Colin quietly let himself out and closed the door.

"Colin," Selena whispered from the staff lounge.

"What's up?"

"I was just about to ask you the same thing. The police are looking for you."

He looked back at the nurse station. Two plainclothes officers stood there, feet planted and hands on their hips, waiting.

"What's going on?" Selena asked.

Colin inhaled and rubbed his forehead. "I don't know." Hopefully, it had to do with one of his patients. He had a bad feeling, though.

Trina had agreed not to go to the police, but Liz must have kept on texting. Without her calling him back, Colin couldn't get her to stop. He checked his phone to see if Trina had warned him or if Liz had responded to any of his pleas. For a moment, he worried something had happened to Liz and the police were there to notify him. He shook the thought from his mind.

There was a new message from Liz.

"Tell them I'll be right there," he said to Selena and ducked into the bathroom.

When he opened the text, he saw a photograph. A photograph of Colin and Trina. Colin and Trina in bed together. "What the hell?"

"Dr. Clarke?" An officer knocked on the door. He fumbled with his phone, blacking out the screen and slipping it into his pocket before opening the door.

"I'm Detective Philomena Green," the woman said, holding out a card. "This is my partner, Eddie Fazio."

Colin looked at the card. The picture on his phone flashed before his eyes as he tried desperately to focus on the embossed words. He followed the lines of a star, a police shield, with the words *Chicago Police Department* written in blue.

"Sir, do you know why we're here?" Green smoothed her navy blazer and shifted her weight from one foot to the other.

"No. How can I help you?" He led them to the staff lounge and held the door. "Please, have a seat. Can I get you a coffee or water?" The longer he could delay the inevitable, the better.

He knew the routine. Knew what they'd ask. He didn't want to have to lie, but he didn't want to have to tell the truth either. Still, he held out hope they were simply there to talk about a patient.

"Sir, where is your wife?"

"My wife?"

"Yes, Elizabeth Clarke? We've been trying to get in contact with her."

"I'm not sure."

"You're not sure?"

"No. She texted that she had taken a traveling nurse contract in Arizona..."

"Okay?"

"I guess she didn't."

"So, she's missing?"

He wanted to laugh it off. Start over. Try to explain. That would look inappropriate. Wouldn't it? "I wouldn't say *missing*."

"This is typical behavior for her, then? To say she's one place when she's really somewhere else?"

Colin checked his phone. "I'm sorry, I have a patient in labor. I really— What is this about?"

"There's been a report filed. It seems your wife is stalking a woman. I suppose you wouldn't know anything about that either?"

He nodded. "Yes, I heard. Trina."

"She tells us you advised her not to go to the police."

"I didn't advise— Look, my wife just miscarried for the fourth time. It's been tough on her. She went away. She needed some time. Then Trina showed up with these text messages. I'm not sure what's going on."

"What is your relationship with Trina Scott?"

"We don't have a relationship."

"Okay. How do you know her?"

"We met at a conference last year."

Detective Green leaned back in her chair, her dark eyes never leaving Colin's.

"Let me see if I have this straight, because I wouldn't want to put words in your mouth. You're saying your wife suffered several miscarriages, then disappeared and began threatening some woman you had an affair with last year. You have no idea what's going on, yet you advised your mistress not to go to the police. Is that what you heard, Eddie?" She looked at her partner, then back at Colin.

Eddie nodded.

"No. That's not at all what I said. Trina and I did not have an affair. She is not my mistress. Liz is not missing in the sense of missing as you understand the term."

"How long has she been missing... in the sense that you understand the term?"

Colin tried to think of what day it was. "A few days."

"Your wife's been missing for a few days. That doesn't worry you?"

"It's not unusual when she starts a new contract to—"

"You said she didn't take the contract."

Selena's head popped into the room.

"I'm sorry, Doctor. We're not getting a heartbeat on Laura's baby."

"I have to go." Colin stood to leave.

Detective Green grabbed his arm. "As soon as you're done, come to the station."

He agreed and left.

19
Colin

Colin thought of Laura and Stan's stunned faces. The first twenty-four hours in the NICU would be the hardest. No matter the outcome, their lives would be forever changed.

Outside the police station, he took one last look at the photo of himself in bed with Trina. He knew it wasn't real, but something about it seemed familiar. Still, holding the image in his hand, he felt guilty. Hitting delete, he went inside.

"I hope everything turned out all right with your patient," Detective Green said, leading him to an empty room.

Colin shook his head.

"I'm sorry, this shouldn't take long." She opened a file and shuffled a few papers to make them straight. "Why don't you start at the beginning, and we'll see what's what."

Colin tried to explain Liz being there one day, then gone the next. All he could see was the look on Laura and Stan's faces. He hadn't done anything wrong. Bad things happened. He knew there was nothing else he could have done, and yet, he felt guilty and ashamed to have failed them. The guilt showed on his face as he spoke to the detectives. He could tell.

"And what about Trina? How do you know her?" Green asked, barely blinking as she watched him.

Colin shook his head. "I told you. We met at a conference. She gave some talk on protecting patient records from hackers. We had a drink in the hotel lobby. No, two. We had two drinks and called it a night. I'd just flown up and back to deliver a baby that day."

"In the middle of the conference?"

"Yes."

"Okay. Let's go back to what happened after the drinks... before you called it a night."

Colin frowned and shook his head. "There's nothing to tell."

Green looked at Eddie. "Is it because I'm a woman, you think? He doesn't want to say? An old-school gentleman."

"Maybe." Eddie shrugged.

Green spread her hands and leaned back, looking at Colin. "Pretend I'm one of the guys you're telling the story to. Over a poker game and a few beers. Maybe some wings. No, that'd be too messy, right? Wings and cards? Scrap the wings. Just tell me the truth."

"It'd be the same story. I don't act one way for some people and another way for others. And I don't cheat on my wife."

Green nodded. "The last time you saw Liz, did you fight?"

"No."

"Would you say you have a happy marriage?"

"Yes."

"Did she know about Trina?"

"There's nothing to know."

"Could your wife be having an affair?"

"I doubt it."

"You doubt it?"

Colin shrugged. "I don't think so. You never can really know anyone, right? Still, I doubt it."

"Okay. Let's say I believe you. Let's say I believe all of this. Tell me, what's your best guess of what's happening here?"

Colin's eyes flitted from Green to Eddie and back. "Liz is an incredible woman. She's also very proud. I think she might be far more upset about the miscarriages than she let on. My best guess? She's in a hotel somewhere running through all the deliveries we've worked together. You're a cop—you know what we see." He looked between them again, then continued. "I'm sure you have cases that stick in your heads. Images you wish you could erase. Our first delivery together was the worst I'd ever experienced, and I've had some bad ones." He rubbed the back of his neck and crossed one leg over the other. "You see women having half a dozen babies and throwing them away or abusing them, as you try desperately to have just one yourself. It's hard. I thought... she's so strong. I thought she could handle it all."

"Has she had mental health issues in the past?"

He shook his head. "I should have paid more attention."

They sat in silence for a moment.

Detective Green cleared her throat. "Why haven't you contacted the police?"

"I'm sorry?"

"When you discovered she wasn't where she said she'd be, and she wasn't responding to your calls. Why weren't you worried? Has she done this before?"

Colin took a breath. "Honestly, she's an adult. She doesn't ask my permission and run everything by me. I just... I don't know. I'm busy. Most of my shifts last twenty hours. My life's a blur. I don't know if you've heard my phone? It hasn't stopped vibrating this entire time. This"—he held up his phone—"this is my life. It's all a blur."

Detective Green looked down at her file.

"Can I see your phone?"

Colin wished he hadn't mentioned it, but he handed the phone over to her.

She swiped around.

Nudging the phone over to Eddie, Green asked Colin, "Where's the picture?"

"Picture?" His voice cracked. He cleared his throat. They knew about the picture. There was no point playing dumb. "I deleted it."

"Why would you do that?"

He didn't answer.

Green handed Colin his phone and picked up a pen. "Did you

see her when you went to Phoenix?"

"No. I already said she wasn't—"

"And you spoke with a roommate? Who was that?"

"Ian Bradshaw—no, Broderick? Something with a B."

"Okay." She scribbled in her notes and clicked her pen.

"Eddie, run a check on her credit cards. We'll see if, as Dr. Clarke has suggested, she's checked into a hotel."

"I'll get on it," Eddie said, and left the room.

Green looked at Colin. "We'll find her, tell her to leave Trina alone, and be on our way." She closed the file, looked at her watch, and folded her arms. "To be honest, Dr. Clarke, we see this all the time. You hit a rough patch, have a roll in greener pastures, wife finds out and lashes out, then everyone moves on. I'm sure once she meets someone new, you and Trina will be able to live happily ever after. Until then..." She stood up, clutching the file and holding out her hand to Colin. "The texts are hardly threatening, so there's really not a whole lot we can do."

He wanted to correct every false assumption she had made. He knew it was useless. "I understand."

"If anything else comes up, you'll let me know." She held out another card.

Back in his car, Colin flipped through the new messages. Laura and Stan's baby hadn't made it. He inhaled deeply, counting to ten and holding the breath in before slowly exhaling and starting his car. The image of their baby boy overlapped with the image of the baby found in the dumpster. He thought of the parents of both babies. Desperate and distraught but for vastly different reasons. Both baby boys, so fragile and vulnerable. Colin had done all he could, and it wasn't enough. He'd failed them. He'd failed Liz.

At his apartment, he dialed the number. Hating it and needing it. Hating that he needed it.

"Three orders of beef and mushroom, two shrimp pad Thai..."

20
Owen

It was an unfortunate turn of events. Owen had such plans for Lika. If only she'd known to mind her own business. To be like his wife, all those years ago, as he was working out the details of his little hobby, getting the hang of things. There would be mistakes. Of course, there would be. A good woman should know her place.

A disappointment. That was what Lika was. *Such a disappointment*, he thought as he opened the door the next morning. Her smiling, joyful face—such perfect cheekbones, delicate by nature, strong by nurture.

A disappointment.

"I forgot to mention, I'm off today," Owen said, leading her to the kitchen and pouring two cups of coffee as he took his morning pills. "Looks like a lovely day to take Sarah out to Achill."

"Really?" Lika looked out the window at the clouds. She rubbed her arms.

"Forecast says it's meant to clear up soon. By the time we get out there, I bet it will be perfect. Get your coat. We'll drop you at your hotel after."

The drive out was far quicker than when he drove the bus. The weather hadn't changed much. Clouds hung low, allowing only the smallest patches of sunlight to shine through onto the hills.

"I thought it'd be nice to go to the place I proposed to Sarah," he lied, looking at Lika in the rearview mirror.

He turned off the R319, and the road took a sharp incline and an even sharper turn. A haze of mist surrounded them.

"I don't think this is safe." Lika gripped the back of Sarah's seat. Sarah just stared straight ahead.

"Most people go to Keem," Owen continued, ignoring her fears. "They say it's the best view. They're wrong. From up here, you can see all of Achill and Blacksod. The bridge we just passed over and Clare Island. All the beaches..."

"We won't see anything in this fog."

Exactly.

At the top, Owen and Lika held Sarah on either side, slowly trudging through the spongy ground up to the top of Minaun Heights. Down below, he could hear the ocean's waves raging against the rocky cliffs.

"They used to be called Cathedral Cliffs," Owen said. "Used to have natural stone pillars. I wish you could have seen them."

"That's okay."

Lika slipped, her foot twisting on a rock. "Maybe we should come back another day," she said, pausing to favor her ankle. "I can't see anything."

"Trust me, the clouds are going to part. Everything will be made clear. We're halfway there." The wind forced them over toward a steep drop-off to their right. "Try to stay on the sheep path."

Lika was pretty. Determined. He wanted to give her a chance, but he knew taking a chance was the last thing he should do. They'd been in Ireland for years before all the rumors of why they'd come had finally died down, and they were able to live in peace. He couldn't take the chance. No. *Oh, what a disappointment*, he thought, looking at her as they reached the statue of Mary at the top.

He helped Sarah to the bench.

"Is that bench safe?" Lika asked.

"Sure it is."

Owen walked around the statue, looking out in the direction of the hidden view, veiled by the cleansing white of the clouds. He was right, though—the sun peeked through. They could see Clare Island. The wind picked up, pushing the clouds inland.

Bills Rocks and Keem Bay came into view as well, then Dooagh and Keel. The base of Slievemore Mountain. The curving road with tight-packed houses and the colorful art gallery. Bunnacurry and the gas station. The bridge. He looked back again to Sarah on the bench and Lika. Her eyes filled with awe at the view. Owen kicked his foot around in the mud, dislodging a rock. He picked it up.

"It's incredible," she said, turning in circles. "You were right."

"No, I wasn't."

The rock made a sharp, wet crack as it gashed the back of her head. She fell to the ground.

"No... Sarah, please help," Lika begged, trying to crawl away. "Help me..."

Two more blows to the head. Then silence.

"Owen?"

He turned to see Sarah inching around the statue. The look in her eyes seemed more lucid than he'd seen in months. Tossing the rock, he wiped his hands on Lika's jacket, then helped Sarah back to the bench and sat down beside her to enjoy the view.

"I love it here," Sarah said. "Did you cut yourself?"

Owen looked down to see the blood splatter on his pants. He took her hands in his. "Nothing to worry about."

As they sat, looking out over the islands, Owen thought what a shame it would be if someone came along and disturbed such a pleasant moment with his wife.

"Where are the kids?" she asked. "I don't want them getting too close to the edge."

"Don't worry, love. The kids are safe." He put his arm around Sarah. She rested her head on his shoulder. He kissed her. A moment of bliss—it made their moving to Ireland all worthwhile.

The next morning, as Owen started his car, a man knocked at his window.

"Owen Ryan, is it?"

"Yes?"

"I'm from the council. There's been a complaint."

Owen turned off his car and stepped out.

"What sort of complaint?"

"Noxious odors. Do you have pets, sir?"

"Yes, I have rabbits."

"How many?"

"Well, I—"

"Do you mind if I have a look?"

"Of course."

Owen considered his options, readied his lies, and showed the inspector into the rabbit room.

With notepad in hand, the man paced the room. Then, lifting the plaid blanket with his pen, he dropped it and stepped back.

"What is—" He vomited in the middle of the floor. When he finished, he pushed his way past Owen and pulled out his phone. "What the hell?" He looked back at Owen as he waited for someone to answer his call for help.

"My wife thinks they're her children," Owen said, trying to look sympathetic.

"Some are dead."

"Yes, well... my wife—"

"They're eating the dead ones."

All part of the process, he thought. "She won't let me remove— She has a problem."

"I'd say." The man heaved again.

Out on the lawn, the inspector breathed the fresh air. His supervisor arrived and introduced herself to Owen.

"We've been through so many caregivers," he said. "They just take my money and sit on their phones all day."

“I know it’s a hard decision to put her into care. There are day programs. You could drop her on your way to work and pick her up after. I can get you the phone numbers.”

Owen bit his lip and rubbed his hands together to calm his shaking nerves.

“I’d really appreciate that. Thank you so much.”

“Oh, love... Hang in there. In the meantime, I’ll have to issue a warning. You have one month to get this cleaned up. My recommendation would be that you have no more rabbits until you can assure their safety. I wouldn’t want you facing charges.”

“Thank you so much.” Owen mirrored the supervisor’s sympathetic head tilt and nod. “I will do everything you’ve said. And please, I really would be grateful for those numbers.”

Once they were gone, Owen looked to the sky, the sun shining, birds singing. His excuse had worked. What a lovely day.

21
Colin

The words of Detective Green looped around and around in Colin's head. The narrative she'd created—it irritated him to be lumped into such a cliché. After all the years he'd spent foregoing the frivolities of youth, taking life seriously while others were drunk and high and blowing off steam. Building a life—a respectable life, the kind of life parents dream of for their children. He'd always been careful to ensure that any action he took would be viewed as good.

Now this.

He undressed, removing his suit—the skin of perfection and success—and replacing it with a grubby T-shirt and jeans.

The detective was right, even if she wasn't right about the details. He had hit a rough patch, and instead of fixing it, he'd created a secret series of additional problems to keep the facade beautiful.

He looked around his apartment, the stains of food and sweat on the couch. The bathroom stank of bile no matter how many disinfecting wipes he used.

Checking the microwave's clock, he saw that it was time to begin the ritual. Everything would be better soon.

He opened a manila envelope and counted out ten pills, then added five more for good measure.

When the doorbell rang, he was still holding them in his hand. He grabbed some cash from the cigar box on the counter and opened the door.

The delivery driver looked in over his shoulder. "Wow, you having a party here?" The same old joke about the huge order for one person.

Colin handed him the money and grabbed the bags.

The food, spread out in order. A fork in hand for the initial bite. Everything in place. Then he thought of Liz, and just before he could remind himself that he shouldn't think of her, he thought of the picture she had sent.

There was something familiar about it. He'd seen it before, but it couldn't be... *Can you recover deleted texts?* he wondered as he picked at a piece of beef with his fork. He searched for the perfect slice of tender meat and the right-shaped mushroom, both glistening in the brown sauce.

He hadn't needed to delete the picture. The police already knew about it. The only thing it had done was make him look more suspicious.

He held the food to his lips, smelling the garlic and ginger. His mouth watered; the pills were kicking in. Warming him. Cradling him in comfort.

The picture. He thought of the picture and the texts from Liz. The wording. Her telling him sorry. She needed time. *Sorry.*

She never said sorry. It was one of their inside jokes. It didn't make sense.

Love you. Again, she never said "love you." They'd talked about that before, another inside joke between them, a stupid joke. Most people wouldn't understand.

The detective had asked if Liz could be cheating. Colin laughed as he picked around with the fork. Cheating was another inside joke. He knew neither of them would cheat, yet he had wondered about that himself. Nothing made sense.

He couldn't explain any of it to the police. They'd never understand that a message of Liz apologizing and proclaiming to love him was the strangest part of the entire situation. That a wife saying, “Sorry. Love you” was all wrong.

He couldn’t turn on Liz like that. He couldn’t out her for what he knew she was all along. What he saw in her and took advantage of. He knew with a woman like Liz, he could build a perfect life without having to say things like “Sorry,” like “I love you.”

Colin felt responsible. She’d obviously had a breakdown, and it was all his fault. He hadn’t paid attention. She’d been trying to tell him something, and he kept brushing her off for his patients. He didn’t know what to do.

He couldn’t go back to the police.

Colin lifted the fork again. A mushroom touched his lip. The tip of his tongue tasted the salty sauce. He sucked it into his watering mouth. Craving it, needing it, hating it, loving it.

The memory of the picture of him and Trina popped into his head. He had to see it again to understand.

A beautiful life crumbling around him. He looked at the full spread of food piled high on the coffee table. The delivery drivers always commenting on the amount—”Enough to feed an army,” “You’re keeping us in business,” “Meals for the month?”

Standing up, he swung his arms. He craned his neck and paced the room. He didn’t know how to get Liz to talk to him. He didn’t know how to fix everything.

He did know where he could start, though. It was time to stop.

In the kitchen, he found a roll of black trash bags. Loading up all the Chinese food containers and stacks of pill packets, he threw them into the dumpster out back. With a bucket of Lysol, he let lemon scent fill the apartment. He scrubbed away his shame and opened all the windows to let in air and light.

It felt good. The pills helped. In the bathroom, he tried to vomit those up, but without the entire ritual, he couldn’t.

In his car, he reread the texts from Liz yet again.

“What are you trying to tell me?” he asked out loud as he drove. “Is this some clue or joke?” He couldn’t stand the silence. He had to do something to get her to respond. He couldn’t think of anything. Nothing angered Liz enough to get a rise out of her.

Nothing scared her. What could he threaten that would force a response?

And what about the picture? He hadn't responded to her before deleting it. Perhaps she was waiting on him. She had to know it wasn't real. But he had to see it again to confirm his suspicions before texting back. Having had no luck in recovering it, he swiped on his phone.

Hi, Trina. It's Colin. Could we meet up? he texted and waited to see the dots moving around. They danced, then stopped. No text came.

He texted again. *I'm not upset you went to the police. You did the right thing.*

The dots began to move again.

Her text came. *What the hell is with this picture?*

He didn't know how to explain in a text. He called her phone.

"What the hell?" Trina asked.

"I am so sorry. I have no idea what's going on. It's obviously fake."

"How—"

"I don't know. Can we please meet?"

"What for?"

"I deleted the picture, but I need to see it."

"You've had it for a year, and now you go and delete it? You should be happy I'm not calling the Sarasota police too."

"Trina, please, it's not—"

"Did you drug me, then sneak into my room when I was asleep? You're a creep. No, you know what? I'm deleting it too."

"It's not real," Colin yelled.

"How do you know?"

"What do you mean how do I— Don't delete it. Please."

A Mustang pulled alongside his car, and the driver motioned to ask if Colin was leaving his parking spot. Colin waved him off.

Trina didn't say anything.

"Please," Colin said.

She still didn't respond. He listened to her breathing.

"I'm sorry you've been dragged into this. I swear to you after we had our drinks, I went to my room and went to bed." How could he get her to believe he wasn't interested in her in that way?

"I'll think about it," she said, and ended the call.

As he drove back to the hospital, his phone began to ping and ping and ping. He pulled over to read the texts as they appeared.

You betrayed me

You ruined us

I hate you

You broke my heart

I loved you and you dragged me through the mud

Ten, twenty, thirty texts and counting.

Another text pinged. *The second I was gone, you ran to her.*

He threw the car in park and typed back, *Who is this?* He hesitated to hit send. Then he erased it and typed something else. *Come home.* He deleted that one too.

Looking through the texts, nothing seemed right. His head was spinning. The pills had kicked in. He tried again to vomit. He couldn't. *I shouldn't be driving*, he thought, as his eyes darted up to the road to be sure he hadn't stopped and parked in the middle of the intersection.

Outside his car, he sat on the curb and considered pulling the garbage bag of food from the dumpster. Beginning the ritual again. He couldn't think straight. He pictured the bag of food, then the baby in the dumpster. The baby in the Chinese food in the dumpster. Nothing made sense.

He remembered the story he'd been told.

It had been snowing for days, and Mikey Jr. was out shoveling neighbors' sidewalks with a couple of buddies from the basketball team. Five bucks a house. They worked quickly, clearing the snow and moving on to the next door, knocking before the owner picked up a shovel. Mrs. Sullivan gave them hot chocolate.

A deep freeze was in the forecast. Their parents were yelling out to them—time to call it a day. Mikey walked home, dragging his shovel. He saw his dad in the alley, standing by the dumpster for the apartment building behind their house. He was holding something in his arms. Mikey ran to help.

Bloody paper towels were all that covered the baby to protect him from the cold. If he hadn't been found, Colin would have frozen to death overnight.

Now, as he sat on the curb, his phone kept pinging and pinging, dragging him from his memories to the present. He hung his head and tried to think. He'd conditioned himself to think best after a purge. He couldn't do that anymore.

Looking at his phone, he started to type, even as her messages kept coming.

I'm sorry I couldn't fix... He deleted the text and started again.

I love you and I will find you. He hit send.

Colin stared at his phone as the tidal wave of messages from Liz stopped. He read the words he'd written to her. Over and over. It sounded so right in the moment. After twenty rereads—high on pills and sitting on a dirty curb—it started to sound like a threat. He read it again through the eyes of the detective. Detective Green. He meant to be more careful this time. To do everything right. To say all the right words. To act exactly as a man should act when his wife goes missing.

He turned the detective's business card in his hand. Flipping it around, feeling the paper, running his fingers over the embossed blue ink. He wondered why the card was in his hand.

Surely, any innocent man can seem like a terrorist, drug addict, or wife killer. It all depends on how his texts and actions are framed.

It's just the pills, he thought. If only he could find Liz, the detective would understand.

He needed help. Who could he call? Scrolling through his contacts, he thought of his distant cousin, Felix, with all the tech businesses and other start-ups. Finding his name, Colin sent him a text.

22
Colin

Waking up in the hospital parking garage, Colin checked his watch. His mouth felt dry and hot. He was still wearing his binging T-shirt and jeans. A security guard tapped at his window.

"Feeling better?"

"Yeah, thanks," Colin said, wondering what day it was.

"Man, you might want to swing home. Shower, shave..."

"Yeah, yeah."

After going home, Colin returned sober and refreshed. The same security guard gave him a thumbs-up as he entered.

Downstairs, in his office, the rooms were full of patients waiting for him to start taking appointments. Just as he knocked on the first room and opened the door, his phone rang. Felix. Poking his head inside, he said, "Sorry, you'll have to excuse me."

"I've been waiting over an hour in here," the patient yelled.

In the hallway, Colin answered the call.

"Can I ask you a favor?"

"Anything, cuz."

"Could you trace a phone?"

"Theoretically? No problem."

Colin frowned. "Never mind."

"Whoa, whoa, I'm just joking. Who are you looking for?"

"My wife," Colin said, lowering his voice.

"Sure. Yeah, anything you need. Damn, what happened?"

"No, nothing." Colin didn't like Felix's tone. The pity in his voice. Worse, the hint of excitement for some drama. "I'm an idiot. Liz is a traveling nurse. You know, right?"

"Yeah, you mentioned."

"Well, about a year ago she switched agencies. I must have been too busy—I wasn't paying attention. Now she texted that she wants me to swing out for a visit. I tried calling her agency to chat with the coordinator and find out—"

"And Liz would never know you weren't paying attention. Oh, man. See, this is why I play it casual with the ladies. Never have to listen to anything they say."

"That's a good policy. So, could you?"

"Sure, we're family, right? I'll get right on it and send her location to you tonight."

A room opened down the hall—another angry patient looking for Colin. He waved, and the door closed.

"Great, thanks."

"Happy to help, cuz."

Ending the call, he took a breath before facing his first patient.

At home, Colin's phone rang.

"Hi," Trina said, crying. "Could you come over?"

He rubbed his eyes and looked at the clock. Just after 3 a.m. He'd been home for only an hour, but his sleep felt so heavy, he thought he'd been home for days.

"Trina? What happened?"

"I'm sorry, I didn't know who to call. The police are no help. Sorry... I shouldn't have called you."

He sat up in bed. "No, it's okay. Tell me what happened."

"I was asleep, and there was a knock at my door. Some guy saying I invited him over. He said we'd been talking on some dating app." Colin could hear ice cubes clinking into a glass. "Liz signed me up on a bunch of sites, and she's giving out my address."

"Did you call the police?"

"Yes." Her tone seemed harsh. Colin felt bad for asking—she'd already said they weren't any help.

"Okay, I'll get dressed."

23
Colin

They talked for a few hours, Colin apologizing repeatedly while they tried to come up with some way to make it all stop. The best he could think to do was call the police again, which seemed useless.

"Maybe I should move," Trina said, opening the curtains. The sun was already lighting the sky. "Change my number and email. Start a new life. Coffee?"

"Sure." Colin stretched, checking his phone.

Trina went into the kitchen. When Colin finished scrolling through messages from work, she still hadn't returned. He started to worry but found her asleep at the kitchen table and let himself out, double-checking that the door had locked behind him.

At home, he showered and shaved as he made a plan to help the detectives find Liz. He'd approach it systematically, starting with the last person to see Liz, her mom. Then he'd work backward and forward from there. He thought of the last night they were together. Liz had wanted to tell him something. She'd been working on something.

Dropping two pieces of bread in the toaster, he turned the dial all the way up. Well done, with extra butter. Liz preferred hers just barely warm.

Did she know that night that she was leaving? he wondered.

Is this what she was working on? What she tried to tell me?

There was a knock at the door. He lowered the toaster dial down to two, thinking it was Liz, home to make a disgusted face and laugh at his burned toast.

Detectives Green and Fazio were standing on the stoop. Other officers were milling about, chatting in the driveway.

"Is she okay?" He couldn't understand why the detectives looked serious while all the other officers seemed so casual. "Did you find her?"

"No," Green said. "It's been a slow morning. I thought we'd swing by and have a look around. That is, if it's all right with you?"

"Oh. I was just... Of course." He held the door open. Green waved the search crew over.

"Is this because of the guy from the dating site?" Colin asked.

"Guy? Did your wife meet someone?" She turned to her partner. "Have them hold up." Then she looked at Colin. "Have you heard from her? She's met someone and moved on?"

"No. Just more weird texts. Nothing threatening. Trina called. She got a message from a guy on a dating site," Colin said. He wondered if Green was pretending not to know or if Trina hadn't really contacted the police.

"We'll look into it," she said, motioning for everyone to get on with the search. One officer waited near them. "Can I see any computers, tablets, anything your wife uses?" Green asked.

"Sure."

"And her passport? It's here?"

"Yeah," Colin said. "It's in the safe."

Colin watched the officers move through the rooms. They opened and closed drawers and cabinets with their blue rubber gloves. They barely disturbed any of his things. He expected to see papers flying, the entire pantry tossed on the floor, broken statues and glasses. *Isn't that how they search?*

"Do you have a second set of keys for your wife's car?" Green asked, following Colin into the kitchen.

"Here," he said, handing her Liz's keys. Green flipped

through the keyring and frowned.

"Are these hers? Her house keys?"

"Yeah."

Green flipped back through the keys. "Does she usually leave her keys when she takes a cab?"

He didn't know. He didn't think so. It did seem strange to him.

"Is her purse here, too?"

"I haven't seen it."

"Not her wallet? Nothing?"

"No."

"Honestly, if it wasn't for the texts from her, Dr. Clarke... I'd be more concerned about her plans." She let her meaning sink in.

He'd thought the same thing, and he nodded.

"My mom took her own life right after my dad died." Colin had never admitted that to anyone except Liz. He'd always said she died of a broken heart. Which was true.

"I'm sorry to hear that." Green handed the keys off to another officer. "I am really busy right now, and there isn't much we can do. I'll do what I can. I'm sure she'll walk through that door any minute."

"I hope so." Colin noticed the toast had popped up and gone cold. Still white, feeling like stale bread. Just as Liz liked it. He put it on a plate and sat at the kitchen table, nodding to another chair for Green to sit. His phone pinged, and he responded to the message.

"The office. I told them I'll be a bit late."

Green pulled her notepad from her back pocket and clicked her pen.

"Has she had any run-ins with Erwin Jones over the years?"

"Erwin Jones?" Colin shook his head. "I don't know who that is."

"Eddie!" Green shouted. "Grab the file from the car."

Eddie soon returned, handing over the same folder Green had at the station. Looking through it, she found a few pages and handed them to Colin.

"Your wife has a restraining order against a man named Erwin Jones. Sometimes goes by Rex Martin. Marty Rex. Rextin Marti..." With each name she said, Colin felt her eyes looking at him for acknowledgment that he knew what she was talking about.

He scanned the document. "Aaron Townsend?"

"No," Green said. "That's not Erwin Jones, that's a statement from her friend. You know Aaron, right?"

Colin looked at the detective.

"Okay," she said, taking the papers back.

Colin felt stupid. "She doesn't talk about her past."

Her face softened. "You know something, Dr. Clarke, maybe fifteen years ago I wouldn't have believed you. But I've seen a lot since then, and the only thing I'm certain of is that people never fail to surprise me."

"Have you questioned this Erwin guy?"

"We'll look into it." An officer nodded to her, and she stood up. "Looks like there's not much to see here."

Colin was glad to watch the officers packing up to leave. Eddie stood in the entry as Colin walked Green to the door.

"Thank you," he said, not knowing why he was thanking her.

"You didn't sound like yourself on that message yesterday. Having a look around was the least I could do."

Colin tried to keep a neutral face, but his eyebrows drew desperately into a furrow. He remembered thinking about calling her as he sat on the curb, holding her business card in his hand, feeling the embossed ink. The blue embossed ink. He hadn't called. He must have. She said he did.

"I know you have patients to see, so if I could just get the keys to your apartment? We can have a look around, and someone will drop them off to you as soon as we're done."

My apartment?

Colin swayed, feeling lightheaded.

24
Owen

As he cleaned out the cages and buried the dead rabbits, Owen regretted using Sarah to cover up his ways.

She'd always been understanding of him. He hated to use her like that, to risk having her removed from her home and taken into care. Rumors would start again about their family, just when they had died down. It wasn't fair.

It was that girl, Lika. Something about her. The symmetry of her face. Her sweet, delicate nature. So pure. He'd wanted to have her, to possess her. He lost focus. That was all. He knew he had to control his urges. It was the only way. The right way to live—control and focus.

He thought of Lika as his bus crossed over Achill Sound. He waited for a car to pull out of the diagonal parking spot across from the grocery store. A little boy looked up at his father, telling him something important as they carried their groceries.

At the bus stop, Owen saw familiar faces—and three young women. New women he hadn't seen before. They were giggling as they waited their turn to board the bus.

"Keel, please," each said in turn, paying the fare and pocketing their tickets.

The third one seemed more serious, more mature. He could tell. She hadn't been giggling, only laughing blithely. He could tell she was mature and understood life in ways the other two would never grasp. She'd seen things, he felt certain.

"What brings you to Keel?" he asked, clenching her change in his fist.

"Work at..." She looked to her companions to help answer. Her cheeks blushed.

He knew she knew the answer. It was only her English that had failed her. It couldn't be helped. He understood and nodded. "You'll be here for the summer then?"

"Summer? Yes." She smiled, and he handed over her change.

As he passed the turn for Minaun Heights, he imagined Lika's perfect face and wondered how long it would take for her to be found. It was surprisingly easy to hide a body there with all the ridges and deep, boggy mud pools. Sure, some turned up when hikers ventured off the sheep paths, but that didn't happen often.

On the return to Westport, the bus was empty. Rain blew in sideways. He flipped on the wipers and the radio. A country song. It made him laugh as he remembered the first rabbit he'd bought in Ireland. The man at the pet store assuming Owen was Canadian because he didn't sound like some rootin-tootin cowboy from down yonder. He laughed again and switched on the blinker to pick up a woman who was flagging him down.

"Hello, there," he said, turning off the radio.

Pulling her hood off and looking up at him with her round blue eyes, she said, "That rain came out of nowhere."

American, he thought. "Can't be helped. Best to dress in layers." His fingers hovered over the ticket keypad, waiting. "Where to?"

"Oh, sorry... Westport," she said with a smile, her eyes fixed on him. "I was surprised to hear your American accent. I'm from Chicago. Where are you from?"

Owen knew her type—Americans clamoring to become fast friends with any fellow American they met abroad. Nosy. Always nosy. Yeah, he knew her type.

"Kearney, Nebraska," he lied.

"Wow, what brings you here?"

He closed the door and drove as she sat in the seat just behind him. He steered the conversation to tales of the West of Ireland. Things he'd heard and read. Things he'd make up. When she circled back to personal questions about his past, he hoped for another passenger to wave him down.

Turning on the radio, tuning her out, he yelled, "I love this song."

She said something, but Owen couldn't hear. She tried again, then gave up.

In Westport, Owen flagged down a fellow driver to swap routes. Settling into his new bus, the 440 to Knock Airport, he was relieved. Then, as passengers boarded, he saw her again, waiting in his queue. When their eyes met, she smiled and waved. Old pals from the motherland.

The bus filled up with passengers, most of them heading to Castlebar. The American bought a ticket straight through to the end of the line. Another hour and a half with his clingy friend.

He was glad to see that all the seats behind him were full. She'd have to squeeze in the back. He glanced in the mirror. She watched him. *What a pushy woman*, he thought. *So off-putting*.

The bus unloaded near the cemetery in Castlebar. The American inched her way up and settled in a new seat, just four rows behind him. He looked straight ahead at the Tesco, then checked the mirror. Her eyes were on him. Constantly.

At Claremorris, the remaining passengers disembarked at the leisure center.

"Thank you."

"Take care."

"Cheers."

The American remained, her eyes fixed on Owen in the mirror.

When she said Chicago, did I make a face? he wondered.

Could she tell I was lying when I said Nebraska? He focused his eyes on the road. There had been rumors and questions. Gossip in Chicago. That was all. Just stupid gossip. A few pictures in the newspaper. Nothing to get worked up about.

His eyes stayed on the road to the airport. The parking lot gate wouldn't open fast enough. He parked at the bus stop and opened the door.

"Knock Airport," he said, looking into her eyes through the mirror. "Safe travels."

She walked to the front of the bus and hesitated. Owen braced himself. He could see from the look on her face—she needed answers.

25
Colin

Detective Green had Colin cornered. She knew about his apartment and had already sent her team on ahead. She also knew Colin was late for appointments. It wouldn't look good when they arrived to search the place. He was sure it would still reek of cleaning products, not to mention the couch covered in stains. What else could he do?

"Of course." He went to his car to get the key and returned. "She never goes there—it's for out-of-town guests. If you think it might help..." He handed her the key, trying to sound casual.

In his car, he flipped through his recent calls. Not only had he called Detective Green while he was high and sitting on the side of the road, but he had also left a two-minute message.

What the hell did I say?

He texted his assistant that he was on his way to the office.

Rushing through his appointments, Colin tried to look engaged as he kept checking his phone and listening at the front desk. Waiting.

As the day went on, he knew they wouldn't be coming with his keys. Surely, they were doing a more thorough search there than they had at his house. He wondered if he'd thrown away all the pills. That didn't matter; they probably would search the dumpster. He knew it looked like a crime scene. Guilt, embarrassment, and shame washed over him. He thought of all the times he'd sworn he'd stop.

Trying to hold it all together, he took a breath and knocked on another exam room door. Entered. Tried to focus. Tried to listen. Pretended to listen. Nodded, mumbled, made some notes.

He was in no condition to be seeing patients.

"Dr. Clarke, they're here," Spence said, catching him in the hall.

Colin squared his shoulders and prepared to see Detective Green.

In the waiting room, he didn't see the detectives or any officers. No one to haul him into the station.

"Spence? Where are they?"

His assistant pointed to the door as it opened. Women filed in and took their seats.

"Don't worry, Dr. Clarke. I have a system to get them registered in no time." Spence passed by with a pile of clipboards. "Did you need something else?"

"No. Thank you." Colin checked his phone as it started to ping repeatedly. Messages from Liz.

I love you, but I can't do this anymore.

You should have thought about that first.

I would die for us.

Did you think of that?

I thought you were smarter than all this.

I was wrong.

I should have taken your mother's lead a long time ago and left you.

Colin reread the last one. Which mother? The one who threw him in the dumpster or the one who killed herself? Did it sound like Liz could be suicidal? He wasn't sure. Maybe her mother would understand.

Slipping into an empty exam room, Colin swiped around on his phone and closed the door.

He tried Anne, but she didn't answer. Then he tried her house. Liz's dad picked up.

"Hey, Daniel," Colin said. "Anne's not answering her cellphone. Is she home?"

"How you doing, Colin? No, she's off at the outreach center."

"I'll try her there."

"Sounds good," Daniel said. "Tell Liz I said hello."

Colin didn't know what to say—he just hung up. He dialed Anne's cellphone again, planning to leave a message.

Instead, she answered on the first ring. "Hello."

"Hi, Anne. I need to talk to you."

"Good, because I need to talk to you."

"What happened?" he asked.

"Are you having an affair?" she whispered.

"What? No. Why would you say that?"

"The police came around. Thank God Daniel was out."

"I just talked to him. Why haven't you told him what's going on?" Peeking out the window, he watched two hospital employees vaping in the parking lot.

"I didn't think I'd have to. I was sure she was just upset about the babies. Now...I just don't know what's what."

"Neither do I. Can we meet? I'd like you to read these texts from Liz and tell me what you think."

"Texts? So you've heard from her?"

"I'm not sure."

"What does that mean?"

"Please. Can we just meet, and I'll explain?"

"Not at home. Daniel's there."

Colin's phone pinged, and he looked at the message.

"Could you meet me at the hospital?" he asked, fixing the blinds and leaving the room.

Colin checked on his patient, Leticia Unger. A seemingly healthy twenty-five-year-old. Married for three years, having just finished law school and scheduled to sit for the Illinois Bar Exam next week. Everything had been going as planned until, at thirty weeks gestation, she started leaking amniotic fluid.

He couldn't think straight and felt exhausted both mentally and physically. Chances were high any doctor would make mistakes in his situation. He'd usually ignore the voice in his head calling for a second opinion. He also knew Leticia had finished top of her class at The University of Chicago's Law School and was already working for one of the top firms downtown. He wouldn't be that foolish.

"You look like hell, man," Trent said, opening his locker and loosening his tie.

Colin could say the same about him and wondered if they should get a third opinion. He waved him off and poured a cup of coffee.

"Is everything all right?" Trent asked.

"I need your help."

26
Colin

In the parking lot, he slid into Anne's passenger seat and reclined the chair.

"Here." He handed his phone to her and closed his eyes.

"You need to get some sleep," she said. He could feel her staring at him.

"I don't have much time. Please read them."

She scrolled and mumbled, then gasped and tsked her tongue.

"What on earth is all this, Colin?"

He sat up and turned to Anne. "I was hoping you could shed some light."

"Me? What would I know about all these texts?"

"That they don't sound like Liz."

Her eyes scanned the screen. "They're from her phone."

"I know." He'd never had a close relationship with Liz's family. They were nice and all when they gathered for holidays or invited each other over for the odd barbecue in the summer. Still, there had always been a bit of distance.

"Liz is not the most... emotional, right?"

"She's just practical." Anne handed him his phone.

Practical? That wasn't the word. "When Liz told me about the accident—how Emma almost died—she told the story so...

matter-of-fact."

"She's told that story so many times. She's desensitized."

He pushed. "I have seen every single one of my staff choked up at least once or twice. Never Liz."

"What are you saying?"

Colin lay back on the seat and rubbed his eyes. There was no way Anne didn't know what he was talking about. "I don't know. The texts don't sound like her."

"Sure they do." There was a wavering in Anne's voice. Colin opened his eyes and looked at her. Tears streamed down her face as she pulled an embroidered handkerchief from her purse.

In silence, they sat watching a white Lexus back in and out of a parking spot too small before giving up and driving away.

"No. You're right," she said.

"This doesn't look good. I'll have to call the detective." Colin knew he should have reported her missing from the beginning.

Anne held out her hand to see Colin's phone again. Her thumb scrolled up and down through the messages several times. She sucked in her bottom lip and ever so slightly shook her head.

"Anne, I have to call the detective. I think someone else is texting from Liz's phone."

"Daniel," she whispered.

"What? Daniel's texting from her phone?"

She shook her head more and wiped her eyes. "The police. They'll tell Daniel. It'll be in the news."

"So what if he knows?"

"It'll kill him."

Colin did his best to comfort her. His phone pinged, and he glanced at it.

"They need me back upstairs."

"Wait." Anne grabbed Colin's wrist. He was surprised by the strength of her grip. "Wait until I've had a chance to tell Daniel myself."

"Seriously?"

"Please."

Colin saw the security guard making his rounds.

"Okay. Tell him today." He stepped out and stood in the parking lot, holding the door open. "And one more thing. What happened with Erwin Jones?"

"Who?"

"What about Aaron Townsend?"

"Who are these men? Is she with them?"

Colin took some comfort in knowing he wasn't the only one in the dark about Liz's past.

"I don't know, but I'm going to find out," he said, closing the door.

As he was crossing the street with a group of residents, a patrol car pulled up and stopped. Colin recognized one of the officers who, only hours ago, had been opening and closing his kitchen cabinets, lingering on the knife drawer.

"Dr. Clarke?" He pulled over in a no-parking zone.

Colin closed his eyes and inhaled.

"Sir, Detective Green asked me to drop off your key."

Colin opened his eyes and held out his hand. The metal felt cold and heavy.

The officer didn't say anything else. Colin didn't ask. He turned to the door and exhaled.

Back in the office, Trent agreed with Colin's assessment. Leticia was put on bed rest, and steroids were given to help the baby's lungs develop in a hurry. An early delivery was probable. All they could do was wait and hope for the best.

With fifteen minutes until another bus of new patients arrived, Colin ducked out to his apartment. He parked out back in his assigned spot—something he hadn't done in over a decade—and grabbed the mail. The pills went straight to the trash with all the others he'd thrown away before the police arrived.

Whenever he imagined the investigators in the apartment, he worried. The strong smell of lemon disinfectant might lead them to think Colin was hiding a crime scene.

But the apartment didn't smell like cleaning supplies. It looked just like his house, barely touched. If it hadn't been for

Detective Green's business card left on the counter, he wouldn't have even suspected anyone had been around.

Slumping on the couch, he felt his mouth water. Automatically, he reached for his phone to place his usual order. No. He wouldn't fall into that same routine. Jumping up, he ran to the kitchen for a drink of water. It'd been years since he stopped by the apartment without falling blindly into his ritual. He was glad the pills were already in the trash outside. He had to get away.

As he locked the door, his phone rang.

"Dr. Clarke, I know you're busy," Detective Green said. "I have a few more questions. If you have a minute? I just pulled up to the hospital."

"I'm not at— I'm running home."

"Fine by me, I'll meet you there."

He knew what she wanted to ask.

27
Colin

Meeting Green in the front yard, he led her through the gate to the patio. The cool breeze felt good in the shade. He offered her an iced tea, which she declined. He poured one for himself.

After sharing a few pleasantries, Green clicked her pen into action.

"Colin, why didn't you mention that your first wife also went missing?"

He'd been expecting the question and had known it wouldn't look good whether he told them upfront or waited until they found out on their own. He sipped his tea.

"She did, right?" Green nodded, clicking her pen several times fast before setting it down.

"No."

"No? Then why did I find a missing person report?" She felt around in her pockets and looked back at the gate. "I'll fetch the file from my car." She pushed back her chair.

"No, I know what it says."

She clicked her pen again, then twirled it like a baton. "Great, so we can skip the part where you deny it all."

"I won't deny it. I was working thirty-hour shifts. When I was home, if I wasn't sleeping, I was a zombie. My wife needed more."

"And, from what I read, she found it."

Colin swatted a fly from his drink and took a sip, keeping his eyes on the detective.

"Yes, she did. I found out. One day, there'd been a mix-up on the schedule, and I left work early. I saw her with a bag getting in a car with some guy. She kissed him. I followed them to the Hilton in Rosemont and just watched them."

"Most husbands would have confronted her. Why'd you report her missing?"

Colin refilled his glass.

"Tell me, Dr. Clarke. Was it for attention?"

That caught Colin off guard. No. He hated the attention. He'd always hated negative attention. He bent over backward to be the good son, the good student, the good doctor, the good husband. He'd worked so hard to build a perfect life and hide the dark, dusty corners.

"I was being...dramatic," he said, tipping his glass back for an ice cube.

"Dramatic?" She winced as the ice crunched between Colin's teeth.

"Looking back now, it sounds ridiculous. I had this brilliant idea that if she saw how worried I was for her safety, she'd realize how much I loved her, and she'd come back."

"Is that what's happened here? You know where Liz is and you're hoping she'll see your efforts to find her and come running home?"

"No. With my first wife, I was young and foolish." He rubbed his face with both hands, trying to find the words to start over with the detective. "I don't know where she is, and I'm worried."

"What are you saying?"

"I'd like to report her as missing."

"Even though she's actively texting you and Trina?"

"I don't think it's her texting us."

"Why not?"

"It doesn't sound like her."

Green looked at her phone. “Let’s put a pin in that. We’re already working on tracking her phone and financials.”

“Put a pin? Detective, I give patients bad news all the time. I can hear it in your voice. What’s wrong?”

“We’ve hit a few roadblocks.”

“Such as?”

“Our IT guy is a real whiz with phones, but he’s having trouble with your wife’s. And...I know you file taxes separately, so I don’t know how much you share, financially speaking.”

“What is it?”

“It seems your wife has been having a thousand dollars automatically deducted from each check and sent to a savings account at a credit union. Every time it arrives, she stops by and withdraws the thousand in cash. She’s been doing this twice a month, every month—for years.”

Green stopped talking, allowing reality to set in.

“She planned to leave,” Colin said.

“I’m sorry. It’s what the evidence suggests. She got some app to jam her phone and leave it untraceable, saved up a load of cash, and walked away.”

Colin thought of the texts. The words used. It didn’t make sense. “Why send all the texts if she wanted to walk away?”

Green shrugged, clicking her pen.

“What about Erwin Jones?” Colin asked. “Could he—”

“No.”

“Did you talk to him? What about—”

“We’ll keep looking into things,” she said, standing and offering her hand. “If you hear anything...”

Washing the pitcher after she left, Colin wondered if Felix was having the same trouble tracking Liz’s phone. He sent him a quick nudge to check.

Something about the way Detective Green had cut Colin off when he asked about Erwin Jones didn’t sit well. In fact, something about the way she wanted to put a pin in filing a missing person report didn’t sit well either. She seemed so quick to form assumptions.

Opening his laptop, Colin searched for Erwin Jones. When nothing turned up, he tried to remember Liz's friend's name—the guy who'd made a statement. Aaron Townsend. *Were they dating back then?* he wondered, as he scribbled down Aaron's address and imagined finding Liz hiding out there.

His phone rang.

"Colin, I'm sorry, I don't have anyone else I can talk to about this. Would you mind coming over?" Trina asked.

Feeling responsible for the harassment he'd inadvertently brought into her life, Colin agreed.

28
Owen

"Thank you," the American woman said as Owen opened the bus door at the airport. She stopped and looked him square in the face. Reading him. Her eyelids squinted around her round blue eyes. "It was really nice meeting you."

"Safe travels," he said again, urging her to keep moving.

Running her fingers through her hair, she smiled and turned to leave.

The encounter left Owen unsettled as he drove back to Westport for his break. At the vegan café, he ordered a blueberry-lemon crumble and a hot chocolate.

He'd been in that situation before. He knew how to handle himself. How to handle nosy women looking for gossip. *Rumors and gossip*, he told himself as he poked at the crumble with his fork, watching the window shoppers pass by.

It wasn't just the American he had to deal with; the council was onto him too. He knew he should ease off a bit. He wasn't an animal, after all. He'd taken it easy before. He could do it again. Find other hobbies. For the time being.

At Castlebar, outside the hospital, several schoolgirls were waiting for him. Chatting, laughing, scrolling through their phones, being loud.

Swiping their transit cards in turn, they followed each other, one by one, to the center of the bus. Owen watched each girl take her seat. He could tell which was the leader, which one wanted to be the leader, and which one would most likely fall victim.

Young girls are so easy, he thought.

"Where to?" he asked another passenger.

"Claremorris." The man wouldn't meet Owen's eye. He kept turning to look at the girls, who'd rushed off ahead of him. Hungry. Starved to get back near the group.

He paid with cash, never removing his gloves.

"Lovely day," Owen said, as if to inquire about the need for gloves.

The man nodded as he turned down the aisle.

Owen closed the door and watched him settle into a seat across from the most vulnerable in the group. The odd girl out.

The man attempted eye contact with the girl, moving and clearing his throat to get her attention.

The girls whispered when their leader noticed the man leaning over to look at them. His eyes were eager to connect with the group.

The leader-wannabe, not to be outdone, crossed her legs, her uniform skirt inching up. "Hello?"

If that man was anything like Owen, he'd be repulsed and turn away, then steal glances at the quiet, vulnerable one. The ideal victim. Not that loud, vulgar beast.

He wasn't like Owen. He blushed and mumbled a hello in return. The girls laughed, and other passengers looked over. Redness spread from the man's cheeks over his face and neck.

Owen pulled to the side of the road for a woman in a yellow safety vest.

"Lovely day," she said.

"'Tis. Where to?" he asked, his eyes darting from the woman to the man in the mirror.

"Knock Shrine, please. Have you been?"

This led to a series of questions about the Shrine's history and hours of operation. Normally, Owen enjoyed playing tour guide. Now, he didn't have the time, with a predator stalking its prey right in front of him. It felt filthy and vile to watch. A bit embarrassing too. *Has the man no shame?* Owen wondered as he noticed something in the man's hand. Squinting in the mirror, ignoring the woman's questions, Owen tried to see. He couldn't be certain, but he was sure enough.

Owen watched the man's hand drop down as he pretended to look around on the floor for something.

Not on my bus, Owen thought as he excused himself from the Shrine pilgrim and told her to have a seat.

As soon as the woman stepped out of the way, Owen left his plexiglass booth and stormed down the aisle. The girls stared, stunned, as he approached.

"Get off my bus or I'll call the police!" he shouted at the man, whose face was now more purple than red from bending over. He looked up at Owen. Still, he wouldn't make eye contact.

Owen lowered his voice as he leaned over the man. "I will drag you out myself, you pedophile."

That worked. Gathering his things, the man stood and pushed past him.

Owen had second thoughts. He shouldn't let an opportunity pass by. Reaching in his pocket, he pulled out his phone and met the man at the door. Owen refused to open it. Blocking the emergency handle, he called the police.

The man waited in silence.

"What made you think he had a camera? This thing's tiny," the officer asked Owen as he took his statement.

"There was a reflection of sunlight from his hand. At first, I thought it was his watch, but then I realized it was in his palm."

"Good eye. You wouldn't believe the creeps living amongst us. Those girls owe you a pint."

Not all the girls, Owen thought as he watched the quiet one call her mom, tears streaming down her face.

He knew how to take it easy and play it safe. And he would.

29
Colin

Trina was wrapped in a chunky throw blanket when she opened the door. Colin almost asked if everything was all right, but he knew that would only sound foolish.

He leaned in for a friendly hug, and the blanket dropped around her shoulders. She tucked her auburn hair behind her ears and draped the throw on the sofa as she passed through to the kitchen. Colin followed behind, taking in the room.

"You redecorated."

"Midcentury modern."

"Looks good."

She smiled. "Can I get you a glass?" She pointed to an open bottle of red on the kitchen counter next to two glasses. He noticed a slight stain already on her lips.

"Just one."

"Oh, because you're on call?"

"No. Two drinks got us into this mess." He thought it would lighten the mood. The words hung in the air. They'd come out wrong.

She stared and then, as if a light had turned on, laughed. He remembered that laugh. Hearty, with the right amount of sweetness. A real, honest laugh.

"Right. We had two drinks when we met," she said. "Sorry. I'm not the quickest—"

"It was a bad joke."

"I don't know if that even counts as a joke." She handed him a glass, leading him back to the living room.

"Any word from your wife? Besides these crazy texts?" Her smile faded, though her tone remained playful.

"Same old. The police aren't much help."

"I told you."

"Yeah, you're right. What'd they say about the dating apps and giving guys your address?" He still questioned if Trina had gone to the police.

"They can't prove I didn't set up those accounts."

"Have any more guys come around?" Colin watched her swirl her glass gently.

"No. I was thinking of getting a dog or a security system."

"That might be a good idea—"

"I have a better idea."

"Oh?"

She left the room and returned with the open bottle in one hand, a corkscrew and another bottle in the other.

"How about we don't talk about any of this," she said. "We can just veg out, watch a movie, and pretend everything is happy and wonderful." She topped off Colin's glass before he could answer.

He thought of Liz saying the same thing the last time he saw her. Veg out. He wanted to tell Trina he didn't think Liz was sending the texts, but vegging out and playing pretend for a few hours sounded good.

"I feel like I've been looking over my shoulder since this all started. I haven't been able to sleep," she said, folding her hands under her chin.

Colin hated to see a woman so tormented for no good reason.

"What movie were you thinking?" he asked and took a sip.

Halfway through, he felt pretty sure Trina had inched closer to him from where they'd started. His phone pinged. He was needed at the hospital. She hugged him and—perhaps it was the wine lulling her into comfort—seemed to nuzzle her cheek against his chest as she whispered goodbye.

30
Colin

After two routine deliveries and no new migrant buses or patients, Colin checked his phone. He loaded the directions to Aaron Townsend's house.

Several scenarios ran through his head as he followed his GPS's instructions. *Should I play the grieving husband?* he wondered. *What if Liz is off with this guy?* Detective Green said he was her friend, but who knew? Colin laughed to think of Liz cheating.

When he arrived at a revitalized suburb's quirky main street, he saw *Townsend Architectural Firm* etched on the main floor's window. From his search, Colin figured if Aaron wasn't at his office, he'd be upstairs in his brilliantly restored second-floor owner's unit. It had been featured on *Architectural Digest*'s website.

The office was charming and bright. Aaron's assistant showed Colin right in without asking if he'd had an appointment.

"How can I help?" Aaron said, handing Colin a green juice and crossing his leg, his flip-flop rhythmically slapping against the sole of his foot.

"I wanted to ask you about a friend of yours—"

"Let me guess, Elizabeth. Police were here a couple of days ago." The flip-flop dropped to the floor, and he picked it up with his big toe. "Expensive suit. You don't look like a cop."

"No... I'm Liz's husband."

"Oh, gosh. I'm so sorry. I thought you might be a reporter or something."

Colin never expected to drink green juice while looking at hairy toes. Still, there was something soothing about Aaron's relaxed attitude.

"We ran in the same circle," Aaron said. "You know. Minimalists."

"Minimalist? Liz?" Colin thought of her closet full of designer labels and outfits for every occasion. The sunglasses, jewelry, handbags, scarves. He frowned.

"Seriously. I might still have some of the videos."

"Videos?"

"Yeah, we'd make videos and throw them up online."

"Videos of what?"

"Living with less to connect more. Find meaning in life. All that jazz."

Colin looked around at the tidy yet not-so-minimalist office. "You're no longer... practicing?"

Aaron scratched his beard. "Minimalism helped me to focus. To see what I wanted in life. Around that time, a group of us—Elizabeth too—we were setting up conferences and traveling around the U.S. Spreading the minimalist gospel. It started out great. Then it began moving in a different direction. Becoming something elite, shallow. So many people get into thinking if they reduce everything, they'll be left with something great and meaningful."

"They're not?"

"For most people, if you strip away all their fancy suits, lucrative careers, and mansions, what do you think they have left? People find that they're empty. Scares the hell out of them."

Colin felt Aaron looking at him. Seeing him. Seeing through him. He shifted in his seat and smoothed his tie.

Aaron continued, "Then there are those who look at it as a numbers game. One hundred possessions, fifty possessions, ten.

The funny thing you notice is, you get down to a few possessions, and you think, what now? How low can I go?"

"Zero?"

"Right. But that doesn't work. The most committed minimalist will set the number to something low. Say twenty possessions. What would those twenty be? I'm telling you, it's crazy. Twenty possessions, and the minimalist elite get so arrogant. Owning just one pen. But it's no longer a pen. It's a *writing instrument.* They give you a sixty-thousand-dollar diamond-encrusted pen. You almost drop it, and they laugh. You've never held such a heavy pen before."

"Liz did that?"

"Oh, no. Not Elizabeth. No. She was great."

"Oh." Colin shifted in his seat. "I'm sorry, were you and Liz...?"

"No, no, no. Just friends."

Colin ignored the tone he thought he heard. "What about Erwin Jones?"

Aaron threw his head back and laughed. "Rex Martin, he went by. His videos are still online, if you're interested?"

Colin nodded. Aaron grabbed his laptop and sat next to him, finding one and pressing play.

"Hey folks, this is your Minimalist Mentor to Mankind, Rex Martin..." The man's eyes sank into his angular cheekbones. His clavicle jutted forward, tugging his skin as he spoke.

"This guy was the one stalking Liz?" Colin asked.

"Crazy, crazy guy. Super legalistic with minimalism. Always pushing others to be *more* minimal. Quite the oxymoron." Aaron laughed again.

Colin looked at his watch.

"Sorry," Aaron said. "It's been a while since I thought of him. So, yeah. He'd hang around our group, more on the periphery. One night, he showed up at Elizabeth's place, broke in while she was sleeping, and piled all her possessions in the middle of the room."

"Oh..."

"Yeah. When she woke up, he was standing over her with a knife, saying he'd chosen her."

"Chosen? For what?"

"He was going to mentor her to be a better minimalist."

"Better?"

Aaron's office door chimed as someone entered the waiting area. Colin shifted again in his seat.

"There had been a reflection in one of Elizabeth's videos. Something she didn't mean for people to see." Aaron waved his hand as if it was nothing important. "A pile of stuff on the floor behind her."

"I see."

"Yeah, well, he didn't want her preaching minimalism if she wasn't living it. I swear to you, compared to most people, she was hardcore."

"What happened?"

"She's smart. You know that, right? Sure, you do."

Colin smiled.

"She agreed with him and convinced him to leave to go get his camera gear. She was going to let him reveal the lie she was living. He was so excited to team up with her, he ran right home. Left the knife on the counter. Fingerprints and all."

"Just like that?" Colin's eyes were wide.

"Yep."

"Wow, quick thinking." Colin couldn't help but be impressed by his wife.

"She left everything and ran. Never looked back. Kind of like now... Sorry."

"It's okay." Colin was thinking the same thing. "Do you know where she went?"

"I saw her at the police station and offered her one of my tiny houses at cost." He pointed to a picture of six houses lined up in a field.

"You design tiny houses?"

"I did. Back then I was designing them, but city ordinances—an uphill battle. Then I went on to..." He walked to a rendering hanging behind his desk. "Have you ever seen a Japanese business hotel?"

Stacks of coffins to sleep in? Colin thought. "Little cubbies for rooms?"

"Exactly. I thought, why not take the tiny houses, make them super luxurious, and stack them in interesting, artistic ways? That way, you'd have loads of likeminded people living in beautiful, efficient homes. The overall building would be big enough to get past the red tape."

Colin followed him to the framed architectural rendering on the wall. Hundreds of tiny homes winding upward like a corkscrew, encircling a full selection of amenities.

"Studio apartments reimagined," Colin said.

"Yes."

"And the shape, it's like a—"

"Beehive." Aaron's hand swept past the name, written in calligraphy. "Elizabeth named it."

"I'd love to see it in person."

"We were trying to get funding for it when Elizabeth ran off. And like you said—with a much nicer tone—it's basically just studio apartments, so... no dice."

There was a knock at the door.

"I'm sorry," Aaron said. "I've got an appointment."

"Thank you so much for meeting with me," Colin said, following him to the door. "You mentioned you might have some of her videos?"

"Oh, yeah, for sure. She'd send a few for advice every now and then. They'd be on an external hard drive. I'll have to look around."

Colin passed by another man in flip-flops, holding two pickleball rackets and waiting outside Aaron's office.

"Aaron," Colin said, his hand on the front door handle. "You wouldn't happen to know where I could find Erwin?"

The newcomer laughed. "Rex Martin? Don't tell me you're going minimalist again, Aaron? I swear I can't. I just can't deal if you—"

Aaron laughed. “Don’t worry, Lee.” He turned back to Colin. “I might have an address on him. I’ll let you know.”

Colin walked out to the sound of Lee ranting about expensive writing instruments.

31
Colin

Every time he went home, Colin felt uneasy. He could still hear her chatting away in the kitchen as she rolled meatballs in her hands or crushed graham crackers for a pie crust. Key lime pie with meringue, sweet and light on your tongue. She'd call him over to tease him with a taste, then shoo him out of the kitchen with the flick of a towel.

In the shower, he thought about her living as a minimalist. It was hard to imagine. Just a phase. Everyone had their phases.

And Erwin. He'd violated her space, and she'd held her own. Colin couldn't help but feel proud of her for keeping her cool—convincing a crazy man with a knife to leave her home.

Then she'd disappeared.

Really, it seemed the smartest thing to do when faced with a stalker. Colin knew that once a stalker got fixated, a restraining order was just a worthless piece of paper. He'd seen his fair share of women in labor needing to call the police when the wayward father appeared in violation of such orders.

Liz had disappeared back then. That was what Aaron said. Never looked back. Left all her things. Left everyone. Left them wondering if and when she'd return.

After drying off, he wrapped the towel around his waist and walked through Liz's closet. It was larger than their smallest bedroom. Larger than Colin's childhood bedroom.

His fingers ran through the hanging clothes. The fabrics cool and smooth. A stack of folded cashmere sweaters. Her shoes lined up on display.

Her keys left in the kitchen.

Left everything and never looked back, Aaron had said.

"She's gone," Colin said out loud. The sound of his voice felt jarring in the dead stillness of their house. He couldn't accept the truth.

He looked at his phone. The texts from Liz hadn't stopped.

I loved you, and you betrayed me.

You ruined my life.

You're rotten.

You're trash.

Fine, he thought, then typed a reply.

You left. You're gone. Then BE GONE. Stop texting me. Stop texting Trina. YOU made YOUR choice. GO. If that's what you want, Liz. GO.

He looked at the words. Read them over and over. He still couldn't help feeling it didn't sound like Liz. But what did he know? He hadn't known anything about Aaron and minimalism. She'd never mentioned a stalker. His finger hovered over the send button. The little dots began to dance. He waited. A new text appeared.

Oh? What's that? Cat got your tongue? Say whatever's in your heart. I'm all ears, dear, cheating husband of mine.

He pressed send and pulled on a pair of shorts.

On the back patio, he twisted open a bottle of beer and remembered the beautiful life they had built. He imagined Trent introducing his newest girlfriend, Cami. Her tantrum, only playing at being a big girl, trying to fill the void of Nancy. *What an idiot Trent was to let Nancy get away*, Colin thought, then laughed at himself for letting Liz get away too.

Trent cheated, and Nancy left. What did I do? Colin wondered, opening another bottle.

Looking back into the kitchen, he tried to imagine Liz into

existence. He checked his phone for a reply. Nothing.

Three beers later, it rang.

"Colin, can you come over?" Trina sounded drunk. He knew it wouldn't look good. He knew it didn't feel right to go running to a drunk woman calling on him for his protection.

"Sure," he said.

Trina had graduated from wine to whiskey. Colin found a glass in the cupboard.

"There's a new Harlan Coben series."

"Sounds good." Colin tossed a pillow to the armchair and sank into his usual spot on her sofa. It felt cozy and safe.

"I could go for Chinese," she said, holding a menu. "What do you say?"

"I don't eat Chinese."

"Who doesn't eat Chinese?"

"Really, I never eat it."

"I don't believe you."

Conversation with Trina was light and fun while they ate pizza and speculated on who was behind the fictional mystery. When the last episode ended and their pizza went cold, they couldn't avoid the inevitable.

"What happened this time?" Colin asked, not really wanting to know.

She handed over her phone, and he read the text. *I hope you die.*

"Isn't that a threat?" Colin didn't know anymore what was what. "Did you call the police?"

Trina moved closer to Colin and finished her drink. "What can they do?"

Colin rolled his eyes. She was right. "You should report it. To have a record at least."

"I thought you didn't want me to go to the police?"

Maybe it was the booze or the stress of it all. Colin didn't know what to think. He didn't know if hoping for someone's death was worth calling the police. All he did know was that he'd ruined his perfect life. He also knew, as he looked at Trina, that she'd moved closer.

"I'll call Detective Green tomorrow," she said, resting her head on his shoulder.

His phone rang. He hoped it wasn't the hospital.

Looking down, he saw that he was in luck.

"Felix, how's it going?" Colin stood and walked to the back door, signaling to Trina he'd be just a minute as he stepped outside.

"Hey, cuz, sorry it took me so long. I'm at a loss. Your wife's phone is as good as gone. Did she buy a new one?"

"What? No." He didn't know what to say. "Never mind."

"Anyway, it's these damn crime shows that make it look so easy."

Colin thought of the one they were watching. "It's not that easy?" He laughed.

"See? You civilians really think it is, don't you? And why is that?"

"Movies?"

"Exactly. Damn movies," Felix said. "There are firewalls and cybersecurity measures, not to mention counter-cybersecurity measures."

"Counter-cyber—"

"Exactly. Listen, did you get a chance to look at the updated dossier for the facial-recognition software I sent you?"

"The one the Department of Homeland Security is using?"

"Yes, well, we're still in talks. Anyway, it's something to consider. I'd love to keep my best businesses in the family, if you know what I mean."

"I know what you mean."

"Speaking of family, are you coming to the next meetup?"

"I don't think so."

"Don't be discouraged. I'm sure she'll turn up one day."

Colin wasn't sure if Felix meant Colin's mom or his wife. At this rate, he wasn't sure either would.

He hung up and found Trina in the kitchen, pouring a bowl of cereal.

"Liz never cooks either," he lied. *Why did you lie?* he asked himself. Perhaps the whiskey was doing the talking. Yeah, the whiskey. A dumb excuse.

"Are you serious? I love to cook." She shrugged in triumph. Triumph over Liz.

Of course you do, Colin thought, kicking himself for giving Trina a small win over his wife. He felt like an idiot, but he couldn't take it back. "I should get going."

32
Colin

"That's it, push," Colin said, then nodded to Selena.

"Okay, easy, Minnie. Breathe, breathe. Don't push."

From the ultrasound, Colin knew what to expect. He'd seen it before. The baby's intestines had grown outside his belly through a hole near his belly button. Gastroschisis. Colin and Selena were prepared, but there was no way to really prepare parents for the sight.

"One more push now, Minn," Colin said. "That's it. Good job." He gripped Minnie's little boy in his hand, assisting Selena in clearly separating the umbilical cord from the intestines.

Selena held out the scissors to Minnie's husband, Frank.

He hesitated, making a fist. "There's so much." His eyes remained fixed on his son's insides. "I don't want to cut..."

"Go ahead and take the scissors," Colin said and handed the baby to Selena. Carefully, using his own hands, he shielded the baby's organs, and Frank made the cut.

Colin looked at the stunned parents, the worry in their faces, as Selena tended to their boy, Frank Jr.

"How will they fit all that back into his tiny body?" Minnie asked.

"It's swollen right now," Colin said. "It'll be all right. I'm proud of you, Minnie. You did incredible. Congratulations."

"Thank you, Doctor." For a moment, the worry eased from her eyes, and she smiled, the tension of the moment broken. Frank leaned over and kissed Minnie. Then the tears and wonder started. The usual euphoria. Too powerful to be ignored.

"He'll be okay," Frank assured her.

Minnie nodded, and they both looked over as Selena wheeled him out to the NICU.

"The pediatric surgeon will be up shortly to check him out." Colin prepared them for the next step, then left Minnie to rest.

Selena found him a few minutes later, dumping coffee grounds in the staff lounge trash.

"How ya doing, Doc?" She opened a box of pastries and picked around for something good.

"Fine." He knew she wanted to talk about Liz. What could he say? How could he explain the stream of texts that he'd felt vibrating on his leg during the entire delivery of Frank Jr.?

"Could you do me a favor?" He had to change the subject and get away, so he sent her off to the gift shop for Minnie.

"Sure, Doc. She'll love it."

Flipping through the newest barrage of texts, Colin caught an update from Detective Green tucked in the middle. *Nothing new to report on my end. We're still looking into it. Let me know if you hear or think of anything.*

A text pinged from a new number.

Still looking for the videos. I found Erwin's contact info. Not sure if it's current but worth a try. Good luck. Aaron.

The next text had Erwin's address and phone number.

Colin scrunched his forehead and frowned. He knew the address. Pulling the blackout curtain to the side, he let the sun stream into the room. Dust motes scattered. Colin squinted, his eyes adjusting. His heart sank, and he felt sick. His hands trembled. Colin could see Erwin's house.

All that time... *Did Liz know he lived so close?* he wondered. *Was he watching her... watching us?*

The police had been to Aaron's office to interview him.

Surely, they talked to Erwin too. Colin willed himself to move. To leave the room. To go to Erwin.

In the middle of the block, he stopped in front of Erwin's house. It was the third in a row of three-bedroom raised ranches—the same kind of house Colin grew up in. The grass had gone to seed. A windchime hung, silent. He rang the bell but didn't hear a chime. He knocked.

"Can I help you?" A woman in burgundy scrubs opened the door, holding a plate and towel in her hand.

Colin followed her just inside the door to the living room. There he was. The famous Minimalist Mentor to Mankind. The man who'd once been nothing more than skin draped over bone, on the verge of starvation and death. It looked like he had rebounded, overshooting the goal. Now he was confined to his bed, several hundred pounds overweight.

Colin had heard it before—anorexia being the opposite side of the obesity coin. The same disordered thinking working in the opposite direction. Never had he witnessed such a precise example.

"Let me guess, you think I've got Elizabeth tied up in my basement?" Erwin said, with a hint of a laugh. It grated on Colin to hear the man who'd once terrorized his wife utter her name in jest. He didn't know what to say. It was obvious Erwin couldn't have done anything to Liz.

Colin smiled. If there had been any room to walk, he would have paced the floor. He mused that minimalism and hoarding must be opposite sides of some other coin.

"What's so funny?" Erwin's tone was sharp.

"Just thinking about how Liz fooled you into leaving so she could escape."

"Escape? She begged me to help her. I was doing her a favor." He struggled to adjust himself higher in the bed.

"I'm sure she did." Out of spite, Colin wanted to mock him, but he knew the nurse was just around the corner in the kitchen and she'd be listening. "Have you had any contact with her?" he asked, though he knew he hadn't.

"Like I told the other detectives, no. I haven't seen or tried to contact Elizabeth since she went psycho on me, flipped out, and then filed a restraining order. She's completely crazy. Don't you guys share notes?"

The image of Colin's apartment flashed in his mind. He couldn't help but pity the man imprisoned before him. Knowing it was a dead end, what more could Colin ask? "Is that when you stopped being a minimalist?" He spread his hands, looking at pile upon pile of books and papers. Magazines coated in dust. Yogurt containers stacked, toppling against the wall.

"No." The slight laugh returned. "I'm still a minimalist. All this"—his hand swatted back and forth at his wrist—"is my mother's. I moved in to take care of her a few years ago. I tried my best to convince her to let me clean things up. Clearing things out should have made her feel better mentally. I thought that might improve her condition."

"She wouldn't let you?"

"No. I did it anyway. Cleaned out this room."

Colin looked around at the mess.

"She pulled everything from the dumpster and arranged it just as she'd had it. Exactly. Then she died the next week. I couldn't bring myself to throw anything out again."

"Sorry to hear that. Thank you for your time," Colin said. He turned to leave, then stopped. "You said Liz went psycho. What did you mean by that?"

Erwin closed his eyes, shaking his head. "Just a look about her. Something off, you know? The way she talked to me, agreeing with me. Just creepy. When she mentioned I should go get my camera equipment, I was happy to get the hell out of there. Mark my words, she's certifiable."

"Thank you." Colin opened the door.

"Wait!" Erwin yelled. "You didn't leave your card in case I think of anything else."

Colin patted his pockets and shrugged. "Sorry, fresh out."

"That's all right. The other detective left hers."

Walking back to the hospital, he scrolled through the latest stream of messages from Liz. He hoped Detective Green would find something soon.

One message caught his eye.

For what it's worth, I would never kill myself.

33
Owen

"Mr. Ryan?" The supervisor from the council tucked her hair behind her ear as she stood at Owen's door.

"I thought I had more time?" he asked, stepping outside.

"Yes, I'm sorry. You do." She smiled.

Owen remembered her name from her business card. Saoirse. He couldn't remember how to pronounce it. Sarah would have known, but she hadn't had a lucid moment since their last trip up the cliff. The poor thing.

"Have you had a chance to call those day programs?" She smiled again and gestured toward his house.

"Oh, yes. For my wife. No, no, I've been busy with work and cleaning things up around here."

"It's all right. I don't want you to worry about that right now. I'm sure you'll manage. Truthfully, I've seen far worse."

"Oh, all right then."

"I've had an idea, and I was hoping... As you're aware, I'm sure, we've taken in many refugees recently."

"I've seen it in the paper."

"Then you've probably read about the lack of housing."

"Sure." He watched her lips quiver, then form into a smile. "You said something about an idea?"

Saoirse's eyes turned toward her car. Owen followed her

gaze to see a young woman sitting in the passenger seat.

"We've appealed to holiday homeowners to offer up their empty houses, but we're still in need. We're looking to anyone with a spare bedroom. I noticed you had two. Of course, one's for the rabbits, and I don't expect you to— Anyhow, I thought it might be a good fit. Darina has experience with dementia patients, and—"

"Sarah wouldn't have to go off during the day."

He eyed Darina. The sun reflected off the windshield, hiding most of her face.

"Why not?" he said with a smile. He had to be good for a while anyway. Why not be a good Samaritan, too? Take the poor refugee in, in exchange for experienced care for his wife. Keep himself on the straight and narrow for the time being. "Sounds like a win-win situation."

Saoirse waved the girl over.

"Hello," Darina said, her cheeks flushed from nerves.

Upon further inspection of the delicate creature, Owen admitted to himself he'd made a giant misstep in agreeing. He sighed. A lose-lose situation. He'd never be able to control the desire with her.

After watching Saoirse's car drive out of sight, Owen found his lodger in the kitchen, filling the kettle. She offered him a cup. *What a good girl.*

Darina looked too perfect. She was his.

On the bus, Owen chatted more than usual, asking questions and sharing stories. When the bus was empty or any stragglers were all the way in the back, he played music. He listened to the words, spelling them out in his head. Filling his imagination with anything to keep from thinking of his delicate new pet.

"Hiya, Owen." Sissy McGovern boarded the bus. She'd grown up with Sarah and remained pen pals throughout the years when Sarah's family moved to the US. At first, Sissy had been thrilled when they moved home. Of course, she hadn't been around much since Sarah's dementia took a sudden turn and she couldn't remember her old friend. *Too hard*, she'd said. Owen understood.

"Good morning, Sis. How's John?"

"Grand. Jay and Tommy are in from London. How's Sarah?"

"Just fine. We've got a new carer for her. Someone experienced with dementia."

"That's what she needs. I've been meaning to stop by."

He closed the door and pulled from the curb. "You know where to find her." He knew the tone felt a bit too sharp. "Sorry."

Reaching her hand in through the plexiglass opening, she squeezed his arm.

His break was an hour-long daydream of Darina. Replaying every word she said, every move her lips and hands made. How she ran the cold water first, running the stream over her fingers before filling the kettle. He wanted to swing home to check in, see if she needed anything to make her stay more comfortable. Surely, she'd been through so much. Comfort was what she needed. Comfort and security.

He thought of the cage.

No.

He thought about stopping by his house just to check in. Back in time for the 450 to Achill. He knew he had to behave, and he would. Instead of driving home to be tempted, he drove to the pet store.

"Those just arrived this morning," the man said, adjusting a water bottle. His uniform T-shirt inched out of the back of his jeans as he reached.

"Can I hold that one?" Owen asked, pointing to a tan-and-white bunny.

The guy hesitated. "We're not supposed to. Unless you're serious about buying?"

"I've always wanted one. You're right. Probably just wishful thinking."

"Okay. My supervisor's at lunch." Sliding the cage open, he reached in, picked up the rabbit, and handed it to Owen. "My name's Michael. If you do end up buying one someday, you'll mention I helped you, yeah?"

"Yes, of course," Owen said, wishing the man would get moving so he could enjoy the few precious moments he had with the dear little creature. Owen held him close, tiny nails prickling his chest as it climbed up to his neck. He brushed his cheek against the rabbit's plush fur and thought of Darina.

34
Colin

Navigating the language of childbirth could prove quite tricky. Colin had learned that the hard way thirty-one hours into his first thirty-six-hour shift as a resident.

A woman at twenty-eight weeks gestation had been held overnight for observation when she experienced a headache with aura. Making his rounds, Colin rattled off words from her chart to sound smart, full of book knowledge and inexperience. It did not go well when he very proudly announced that she'd had two prior abortions. The woman, exhausted and afraid for her own health and her baby's, broke down in a hysterical fit of sobbing.

He always remembered the nurse's face as she explained that a miscarriage is technically an abortion, but people see it differently. He knew that. He wanted to tell her that he knew, but she walked away.

Colin had felt stupid, but he'd learned a lot about how to guard his own tongue and allow his patients to choose the words.

Adoptions and surrogates, donor eggs and sperm, complicated family dynamics—all potential landmines to be tiptoed around while providing the highest level of care.

"Here he is," Selena said, already in the room when Colin arrived to examine Joanna Frasier. The twenty-year-old ballerina had gone to Cancun for spring break. She drank a bit too much and came home with an unexpected souvenir.

"Joanna," Colin said, shaking her hand and giving a wave to her mom, who was seated in the corner.

"Can I talk to you?" Joanna's mom stood up and pointed toward the door.

"I'll meet you in a minute," Colin said. The air in the room felt off. He looked at Selena. She didn't send him any signals to explain.

He examined Joanna and asked, "Is there anything I should know about?"

"I don't plan to hold it," Joanna said. "I don't want my mom to hold it either."

Colin knew the plan. Joanna had decided everything by their second appointment together. She'd reached out to an adoption agency and chosen a couple, deciding to make a clean break. She'd shut herself off from the baby, imagining she was a surrogate for the couple. She said it was the best way she could cope. Colin understood.

When he went out into the hall, Mrs. Frasier was wiping her tears. Colin could tell the strain of the last few months had taken a toll. She had begged Joanna to keep the baby. She'd offered to help. When nothing worked, she'd offered to raise the baby as her own. Joanna refused. This was her last chance.

"Doctor," she whispered, standing close to Colin. "The people adopting her are out of town. If the baby comes before they arrive, who will hold her?"

"Mrs. Frasier, you have to understand. It's Joanna's decision. I'm sorry. She's decided that if you can't accept it, you'll need to leave."

Colin hated being the bad guy. To his surprise, though, Mrs. Frasier surrendered and, with her head hanging low, returned to her daughter's side.

As her labor progressed, the adoptive couple called for an update. They'd been able to find an earlier flight home. But at the rate things were moving, Colin didn't think they'd make the birth.

Back out in the hall, Selena handed him a phone. "The

adoptive mom wants to talk to you. Maybe you can pause Joanna's labor until they arrive." She winked and walked away.

"Dr. Clarke." Another woman in tears, pleading with Colin. "I've read about the importance of skin-to-skin contact right after birth, for the baby to bond. What if this moment is lost forever and it affects her for the rest of her life? What if she's never able to bond with us? Or anyone, for that matter? All because she felt rejected at birth."

"I'm sure..." There wasn't much he could say. "Joanna's mother would like to hold her. Maybe you could convince Joanna?"

She was quiet.

"Dr. Clarke?" A man's voice had taken over. "This is a difficult situation. I don't know if you remember me. My name is Charles Fitzgibbons. You delivered my kids from my first marriage. My wife—"

"Jan."

"Yes. Do you remember after our second was born, Jan couldn't stop throwing up? You had me recline in my chair and tuck my son under my shirt on my chest?"

"I do." It was something Colin had recommended anytime the mother couldn't hold the baby immediately after birth.

"Doctor... would you hold her?"

"That's highly—"

"Please."

A scream came from the room. He could tell it was time. Ending the call, he went back into the room to prepare. During the delivery, the request stayed on his mind. When the baby was born and taken away, he felt particularly sorry for the eager grandmother.

In a room far from Joanna's, Colin wheeled in the bassinet, removed his lab coat and vest, and unbuttoned two buttons of his shirt. Tucking the newborn under his chin, he reclined in the armchair, which sat next to a freshly made bed. He listened to her breathing and looked down at her eyes opening for a peek at the world, then closing. Her back rose with every inhale and lowered again. He rubbed her back with one hand.

He imagined she was his. He didn't mean to. Yet after all the stress and confusion, the years of wanting this moment for himself, Colin gave in fully to his imagination.

He looked at the bed and pictured Liz, smiling and looking back at him. Their eyes met as if to ask each other, *Where did she come from?* Their perfect little miracle.

Colin could feel the baby's lips rooting around, hungry after her arduous journey. He regretted not stopping in the nursery first for a bottle and knew his fairytale moment would be short-lived.

Thinking of Liz's message, her saying she wouldn't kill herself, infuriated him. He wanted to reply. What could he say to get her to come out of hiding and face him? Still, every time he thought of the messages, he couldn't help but think how nothing sounded like Liz. And the detective, with her standard "We're looking into it," that left him with little confidence.

Rubbing the baby's back again when she started to whimper, he thought of how perfect miracles could come out of a trip to Cancun.

Cancun.

The picture of him in bed with Trina. He knew it had looked familiar.

Handing the baby off in the nursery, Colin took out his phone and dialed Detective Green.

35
Colin

"I'm glad you called, but I wish you would have called sooner," Detective Green said. "I didn't know she was still texting you both."

"Trina didn't call?"

"What happened, Dr. Clarke?"

He didn't know what to say. *Why would Trina lie?*

"I could use a cup of coffee," she said. They made a plan to meet up, then ended the call.

When Colin arrived at the café, he found her sitting in a booth, looking out the dirty window.

"Just a coffee," he said to the waitress, handing back the menu.

Green scrolled through the messages on his phone. None would be considered threatening. She asked questions to clarify what some might mean.

"I don't know."

"What about this one? Is it some inside joke?"

"No. But we have plenty," Colin said. "That's what's so strange to me. None of these are our jokes. And the last one, about killing herself..."

"Let me get this straight." Green set the phone on the table and turned it around, sliding it to face Colin. "Her saying she wouldn't kill herself makes you think it's not her texting?"

"Yes. I'm sure you've heard many people swear their family member wasn't suicidal after they committed suicide. But Liz is... different."

"Different how?"

Colin ripped open a sugar packet and watched the crystals rush into his coffee. He liked the sound they made.

"Dr. Clarke, if you're not going to be forthcoming, I don't know how I can help."

"She said once that people who commit suicide are overly emotional."

"Okay?" Green made a face trying to connect the dots.

"She couldn't understand it."

"Suicide is hard for most people to understand."

"No. See, that's the thing. She could understand the idea of suicide. She couldn't understand the emotion behind it."

His phone pinged repeatedly, vibrating across the table.

"May I?" Green asked, picking up the phone and reading. "Wow. Okay, this one might be something." She handed Colin the phone. He read the message aloud.

"You don't deserve to live."

"It's not exactly a threat, but the general tone of the messages seems to be escalating," Green said.

"Here's another." Colin gave the phone back to the detective as it pinged again.

"What does this mean? 'Why'd you kill us?'" She held the phone up for Colin to read. "Dr. Clarke, this seems to be a whole lot of the same old, same old. You cheated on your wife, and she's pissed."

I didn't cheat. "Do you have the picture of me and Trina in bed?"

"The one you deleted from your phone?"

He ignored her accusatory tone. "Yeah."

Green pulled out her phone and swiped through to a

screenshot she'd taken of Trina's. "Here."

"You see the mark on my chin? Liz and I were down in Cancun on vacation when a patient went into labor. I flew back up to deliver her son, then back down to Liz. I was starving and exhausted when I returned—I ate a bowl of guacamole and woke up in the morning with it on my face." He pointed to the dried-up glob on his chin.

Green enlarged the photo.

"You asked if any of those were inside jokes? *This* is our inside joke. And I assure you, Trina was not there."

"Right. So, it's photoshopped. But why?"

"Something else." He tapped the screen. "This picture was only on my phone. Not Liz's."

"Your phone's been hacked," she said, sipping her drink.

"What's happening here?" Colin leaned back, looking out the window. Nothing made sense.

"I'll look into it."

"Can I say something?" Colin asked, cupping his mug in his hands.

"Sure."

"I'm worried I went about this all wrong. I kept thinking she'd walk through the door, and I'd look foolish for wasting your time. I should have come to you right away. I'm telling you, there's something going on here. I don't think this is my wife texting us. If it is, she's had some major mental break. Either way, she needs help."

"I asked you if she had a history of mental illness, Doctor." She waved off the waitress's attempt to top off her coffee, her eyes not blinking as they stayed fixed on Colin's.

"She doesn't have a *documented* history."

Green blinked. "I'm sorry. There isn't much to go on. I'll keep looking into it. If anything new comes up..." She finished her coffee and motioned for the bill. "Until then, you should get some rest. You look wrecked."

"Yeah," Colin said, looking at his phone. "I have to get back to the hospital."

Outside in his car, he read through the most recent messages. Another appeared. It was from Aaron Townsend—he'd found the videos from Liz's minimalist days.

In his office, downloading and watching between patients, Colin saw his wife as a complete stranger to the woman he'd known.

The first video was a day-in-the-life vlog. Liz's alarm rang as she faked an exaggerated yawn and stretch. She opened the curtains, and the morning light flooded in. The room looked stark and empty. It felt even more bare as she rolled up the yoga mat and blanket. She tucked them into the closet and proceeded to dust the hardwood floors with a rag on her hands and knees. First dry, then wet.

The next video had been labeled "All That Remains," and in it, Liz tallied up her possessions—one hundred in all.

A bus of new patients arrived, interrupting the videos. Colin clicked for the final three to download while he worked his way through fifteen pregnant women. With every patient visit he finished, he'd think of the videos and pray one might give him some clue to follow.

He sneaked to his office after the bus left but before his next appointments. There, he watched the next video. Liz paring down to fifty possessions. As for clues, he saw nothing. The next video was titled "What I No Longer Buy as a Minimalist," which, it turned out, was everything except soap. Even then, she used one bar for her hair, body, dishes, and laundry. He thought of all the products lining their shower and bathroom sink and laughed.

The Liz from the videos seemed like a completely different person. Had it happened again? Had she morphed into someone new yet again? This time from the Liz he'd met and married into the jealous, bitter woman from the texts?

If only she would talk to him, he could understand.

In the last video, Liz had filmed herself and friends at a minimalist conference. Aaron was there, chatting with an older woman, motioning to a table piled with books for sale. Aaron picked one up and signed it for her. Erwin's skeletal frame walked by, and for a moment, Liz panned the camera to follow him. Colin watched every person, every face. He tried to see something that would give him a clue. And finally, it appeared.

Liz began play-interviewing Aaron.

"Tell me, Aaron Townsend," Liz said in a serious reporter voice, "what brought you to this wonderful world of minimalism?"

"You," he said, spreading his arms and smiling, his big white teeth shining through his chestnut beard.

"Me?" She laughed.

"I love you," Aaron said.

Just friends, Colin thought, *sure*.

36
Colin

"I love all of you," Aaron Townsend continued in his interview with Liz. "All my fellow minimalists. You encourage me, challenge me, support me."

"You got that right," Liz said, laughing. "Like a support group for the materially challenged." Liz turned the camera back to herself and signed off.

That's it, Colin thought. A support group.

Colin had called Liz's mom, the last person to see her. They'd had lunch together, and Liz had gone off in a cab to teach the baby basics class but never showed up. That was where Colin had ended his search. He hadn't worked backward to see if anything had happened *before* her lunch with her mom.

Liz had gone to her fertility support group meeting before lunch. Maybe she'd said something there, or something had happened that could be useful. Detective Green had probably already checked it out, but he couldn't remember telling her about the meeting.

Colin left his office and took the stairs down. He walked through the staff hallway, behind the Emergency Room, and past Outpatient Surgery. He also passed the gift shop and cafeteria before reaching the multipurpose rooms. He'd taught classes there himself—another "exciting opportunity" from Gerrard Coffey. It was mandated by the board that all doctors and nurses teach one class per year.

The coordinator of the rooms was stacking materials for an AA meeting when Colin found her.

"Dr. Clarke, what brings you down to the dungeon? I hope you don't need to reschedule your class? We've lost a few rooms."

Looking down the hall, he wondered what all the commotion was. Then he noticed a row of beds.

"What's going on?"

"I was hoping you could tell me. Something about Labor and Delivery overflow." She shrugged and heaved a case of water bottles onto the table.

"Great," he said, rolling his eyes. "Let me help." Lifting another case, he ripped open the plastic wrap. "I was wondering, who runs the fertility support group?"

"There's no real leader, per se. Hannah is the contact for new attendees. She started the group. If you have a patient who could benefit..."

He nodded and took Hannah's contact information.

When he got to his car, he left a message for Trina to call him back. He tried Hannah. Straight to voicemail, so he left a message.

Then Liz. He didn't know why he bothered calling. When he did, he felt disappointed that her phone too went to voicemail. He left a message.

"Liz, I don't know what this is. I've gone to the police. The truth is going to come out. It's out of my hands now." He could feel his old dramatic self returning as he said the words. That same jealous man who had followed his first wife and her lover to a hotel. Instead of confronting them, he'd gone home and planted evidence, then called the police to report her missing.

His phone pinged with a new voicemail.

"Hi Dr. Clarke, this is Hannah. Sorry, we seem to be playing phone tag. I'm currently off on maternity leave. If you'd like to swing by my house, I believe we're practically neighbors."

She texted her address and, sure enough, they lived in the same neighborhood.

Dying for a hot shower first, Colin texted that he'd be by in an hour and drove home.

Every day, their house seemed stiller, darker, and void of life. He wondered when that would stop, and life would begin again.

Closing his eyes, the warm water soothing his worn body, Colin tried to think. The only way he could ever really deal with a complex problem was after a purge. He reminded himself that he wasn't doing that anymore. It was time to be just as perfect behind closed doors as he appeared for the world to see.

The phone rang. He closed his eyes and turned the water hotter and hotter until his skin prickled red. Then he rotated the dial all the way to the coldest level.

His breathing quickened. The sudden change made his skin feel like it was on fire. Colin bounced on the balls of his feet, back and forth like a fighter in the ring. He felt invigorated and alive. Even more than that, he could think straight. A voice in the far reaches of his brain told him it was only a Band-Aid, that he'd need the binge. Need the purge. He was nothing without it. He'd hate it and hate himself, but he'd always need it.

He turned around, and the ice-cold water streamed down his shoulders and neck. His teeth chattered. The phone rang again.

Tucking a towel around his waist, Colin grabbed a second one, swinging it over his shoulders to warm him up.

There were two messages, both from Trina, both asking him to come over. The second sounded more urgent than the first. He looked at the time and texted Hannah an excuse to reschedule, feeling rude. Then he dressed and drove off to see Trina.

"Thank God you're here." Trina's eyes were wild as she shoved a duffel bag in Colin's arms. "Look at this. Look."

The zipper was halfway open. He looked in the bag, then reached inside.

"Where'd this come from?"

"I found it under my bed."

Colin held up a package of zip ties, then dropped them back in.

"Did you call the police? We shouldn't be touching this." He dropped the bag to the floor. Trina looked scared and small. Her eyes were puffy from crying.

"Did you call the police?" he asked again.

"How did she get in?"

"That's what the police will figure out," Colin said, pulling his phone from his pocket.

"Wait." She grabbed his hand.

"What do you mean, wait? They said to call if there's a threat." He kicked the bag. "This, right here? This looks like a threat to me."

The tears streamed down her face. "You don't understand."

"I don't understand? What don't I understand? There was a bag with zip ties, gloves, and a hammer left under your bed."

"She was probably just trying to scare me." Trina walked to the kitchen sink and flipped on the faucet, splashing water on her face.

Setting his phone on the counter, he walked over and handed her a towel.

"Thanks."

He followed her to the living room.

"You don't know what it was like to tell the police I was being stalked by the wife of a man I'd only had drinks with. The look on their faces like I was guilty. Then that picture. I thought maybe something did happen, and I didn't remember it. I was embarrassed, and they just brushed me off like some crazy mistress." She folded the towel on her lap and pulled at a loose string.

"I'm sorry." Colin was sick of saying sorry. "I don't know why you were dragged into this. But that bag, under your bed—"

"I know. Why leave the bag and not do anything?"

Colin leaned back, rubbing his face. His phone pinged.

"I don't know. Maybe you scared her off." He didn't want to

say what he thought. Didn't want to imagine that the bag had been left to be conveniently used at a later time.

Trina leaned back against Colin, her hair brushing his arm. "Will you just stay for a while?"

Looking in her eyes, he felt responsible for the fear he saw. He nodded. "Okay. I'll stay for a bit. We have to call the police."

"I will. Thanks." Jumping up, she walked to the kitchen. "I don't know about you, but I could use a drink. What can I get you?"

She turned around. Colin was already standing behind her. He picked up the duffel bag, zipped it shut, and stuffed it into the pantry.

"I just need to check my messages," he said, leaning on the counter, swiping his phone on. He read the new message.

The color drained from his face.

"I have to get home," he said, running to the door. "Lock your door, and call Detective Green about the bag."

37
Owen

Owen drove to the pub after his shift. He planned to be good, and he would be good. The only way to ensure he'd be good was to stay out long into the night. Returning home to find the lights out, he'd go straight to sleep.

Fumbling about in the dark when he got home, he tried to be quiet as he untied the knot in his shoe. He tripped and bumped into the umbrella stand, slamming his hip against the wall. He held his breath and listened for movement in the house. Nothing.

Walking slowly down the hall, he slid into their bedroom. Sarah's head drooped as she slept sitting up in her chair. He turned off the TV and pulled the blanket up to her shoulders.

After undressing in the bathroom down to his boxers, white T-shirt, and socks, Owen turned on the shower. On second thought, he turned it off, reminding himself to go straight to sleep.

He meant to walk back to his bedroom, but it didn't seem the hospitable thing to do. To pass by without checking on their new guest? That would be rude. Especially with it being her first night. He stood by the door, left slightly open. Certainly, a sign she was available for visitors.

He knew it was all moving too fast. Happening too soon. The

door creaked open. Without another thought, Owen stood over Darina. He could hear the steady inhale-exhale rhythm. Her eyes moved gently under her eyelids.

For a moment, he remembered the time back in Chicago, all those years ago. Home late from work, Sarah pretending to be asleep. Owen had sneaked down the hall to watch their daughter. His perfect, delicate Sheena. She'd been such a joy from birth—happy and calm. He'd hold her on his lap as he watched the evening news. She'd bury her face in his chest and cover her ears to block out the bad stories. He could still smell the baby shampoo. His perfect angel.

Darina rolled to her side, bringing Owen's thoughts back to the present. He watched her settle. Her breathing returned to the deep rhythm of sleep. Pulling the blanket down around Darina's knees, he smiled to see the subtle curvature of her narrow hips. Her hand moved, reaching for the blanket. Not finding it, she crossed her arms and rolled to her other side.

Owen reached out his hand to touch her skin, feeling with his imagination as his fingertips ran up and down her back. Almost touching. Almost. *Sound asleep in a stranger's home*, he thought, pleased.

She rubbed her arm and rolled onto her stomach, her shirt riding up on her waist. Owen licked his lips. Then he noticed. The tattoo on the small of her back. The pure canvas defaced. His lips pursed tight as he pulled the blanket up over her head and turned on the light. She struggled awake and sat up, pulling off the blanket.

"What are you doing?" She scurried up to the headboard, hugging her knees under her chin.

"You have one chance to explain yourself, young lady." He slammed the door and crossed his arms.

"What do you mean? I didn't do anything."

"Don't play games, Sheena. I saw your tattoo."

"Sheena? Who's Sheena? I'm Darina. It's me, Owen. Darina."

"Does your mother know? I bet she brought you to get it.

Didn't she? Come on." He grabbed her arm and dragged her to the door. Swinging it open, he stomped down the hall. "I won't have you talking about your mother behind her back."

Darina dug her heels into the carpet and twisted her arm free. Before Owen could catch her, she ran back to her room, slamming and locking the door.

Leaning against the wall, he exhaled and frowned. There was no way he'd be good with Darina living in his house. He had to get rid of her. It had to be this way. He'd promised himself he'd be good, but he couldn't.

He walked past her room, listening to her cry. Such a delightful sound.

"I'm sorry," he said, leaning on the door. "Wouldn't you like to come out and have a cup of tea?"

All he heard in reply was more sobbing.

"If you'd just open the door so I can explain." He waited, considering whether or not he should go get the key and open it himself. "You can't hide in there forever."

Sitting outside the door, he called Saoirse at the council and left a message.

In the morning, Owen's phone rang, waking him. Disoriented, he looked around the hallway. Darina's door was still closed. His phone rang again, and he answered.

"Hello, Owen," Saoirse said. "I just got your message. I'm so sorry—"

"I'm sorry," Owen said. "I should have mentioned my PTSD. I feel just awful. Sometimes I sleepwalk and think I still see my daughter. I must have thought Darina was her. I got confused and hollered at her. What did I do—"

"Take a breath," Saoirse said. "Can I talk to her, please? She isn't answering her phone."

"She won't open her door. Oh, ma'am, I don't blame her. I probably scared the life out of the poor thing."

"She's been through a lot too. I'm sure she'll understand. Tell her I'm coming to talk to her."

He stood outside the room, listening to Darina's cries. He liked the sound. *It would be nice to comfort her,* he thought, knowing it'd be better if she left before he gave her too much comfort. With a gentle rap on the door, he said, "Darina, again, I'm sorry. The lady from the council will be here soon to collect you. I'm leaving for work now. You won't have to see me again."

He wanted to hold her on his lap. For her to nuzzle against his chest and hide from all the bad news. To be his pet.

The day was sunny but felt bleak as Owen greeted passengers excited to explore the island, their phones scanning the scenery as he drove. With a cursory glance, he watched a young woman in the mirror. Even her eager face did nothing to soothe his spirit. He hated being good.

Arriving home that night, Owen saw the light on in the living room. Two figures were sitting on the sofa. He readied an excuse and dragged himself inside.

"Hiya, Owen."

"Sissy," Owen said, letting out a sigh of relief. "How nice of you to come visit." He kissed Sarah on the head. "You look in good spirits, sweetheart."

Sarah looked at him with vacant eyes. He heard a noise in the kitchen.

"Is John here too?" he asked.

"No, he's down at the pub."

Owen stepped back into the hall as Darina came around the corner holding a tray of tea things. She hesitated, then squeezed past him into the room.

"Would you like a cup of tea?" she asked Owen.

He stared for a moment, confused. "No. No, I think I might meet John for a pint."

"That's a great idea," Sissy said, spooning sugar into her tea.

Owen sat at the pub, half-listening to John prattle on about something, all the while wondering why Darina hadn't run for her life. Realizing Saoirse had convinced her to stay, he ordered another pint. He couldn't be good. Saoirse would see the truth.

Cracking his neck and massaging his stiff back, he walked home.

38
Colin

Colin slowed at a red light, looking both ways before inching through the intersection. He held his phone up, only partially watching the road as he reread the text from Liz.

We can work this out.

I'm coming home right now.

See you soon.

Three lines of text. Colin recited them in his mind as he drove at almost double the speed limit, swerving into oncoming traffic when the cars backed up at the donut shop. He tried but failed to beat the train, texting back that he was stuck. He'd be there as soon as possible, and he agreed they could work it out. Everything would go back to normal.

As the train cars rolled by, one pulling the next, he thought about telling her. If she was open to it, he wanted to forgive and forget everything that happened. The sooner they could sweep it under the rug and get over the initial awkward hump, the better. He thought of the babies they'd have, completing their perfect family, erasing the whole mess. He was glad he hadn't told more people what was going on. It would embarrass Liz if Trent had known.

The train gate started to lift. He slammed the gas pedal down, skidding on the tracks. His phone pinged. Another message from

Liz. A photo. Their foyer. She was home.

He pulled to the curb and ran into the house—still blanketed in that uncomfortable silence left by her absence—calling out her name. His voice sounded sharp, biting. He wanted to sound gentle and welcoming. He stopped and took a breath. Tried again.

"Liz?"

Taking the stairs two at a time, he raced to the top. Into their bedroom. The bathroom. The changing room.

"Liz?" *What the hell?*

Back downstairs, he returned to the entry, comparing the photo to the odds and ends on the side table. Other than his keys, it looked the same.

"Liz?" The sharpness returned, its echo piercing his ears. "Enough. Where are you?" He checked out back on the patio. Nothing.

His phone pinged with a message. Liz.

Sorry, babes! Love ya!

Another ping. A new picture.

He looked at the photo of himself and Trina, sitting at a bistro table outside, sharing a pitcher of margaritas, Colin's hands reaching out to Trina. Trina's hands resting in his.

Colin fell to his knees, shaking his head. His mouth watered. His hands shook. He needed just one little release. *Dear God, just something real*, he thought, feeling stupid to have been set up. His mind raced with questions. His phone pinged again. Liz.

How's Trina? I hope she's safe...

Colin's eyes grew wide as he thought of Trina. The duffel bag. His fingerprints. He grabbed his keys, dialing her number as he started the car. No answer.

Racing back to her house, he dialed over and over. He imagined he'd find Liz there, crazed and obsessed, holding Trina captive. He'd do anything to protect his wife and the life they'd built together, but Trina was an innocent bystander. *What a mess*, he thought as he pulled up in front of Trina's house.

Banging on the door, he tried to control his breathing. No answer. He leaned over the railing to see in the front window. The curtain was drawn. He could see the flickering of the television. Knocking again, he paced, wondering if Trina had listened when he told her to lock the back door when he left.

"Hi." The door opened.

"Are you okay?" he asked, imagining Liz behind the door, holding the hammer from the bag.

"I'm on my second bottle, so yeah... can't complain." Trina laughed and swung the door open.

Colin looked up and down the block, then hunched over, hands trembling as he gripped his knees and gasped for air. Trina led him inside the house to sit down.

"What happened?" she asked.

"Hold on. My phone," he said, sinking into the cushions, checking the newest message. The text was urgent. Leticia, his patient whose water had ruptured at thirty weeks, had started contracting regularly. It wasn't ideal. Colin hoped the steroids had helped the baby's lungs prepare for life outside the womb.

He dialed a number.

"Hey Trent," Colin said, trying to sound casual. "You remember Leticia?"

"Yeah, I heard. She's on her way in."

"Would you mind doing me a favor?"

Colin had asked many favors of Trent over the years. Never this. He'd never missed one delivery. Not for anyone. Not even when Liz was pregnant for the first time and called to say she'd started bleeding. Nor the next three times, when she had to have the remains of their dead babies sucked out of her uterus so they could try again. Or when Liz had to get a ride home afterward while Colin returned upstairs to be hailed the best doctor in the world by his patients. *Liz said she understood*, he thought, feeling like an idiot.

"What the hell is going on?" Trent asked. "Where's Liz?"

"She took a contract in Phoenix."

"Really? Because Selena said there was something weird going on and that some detectives came asking about you and Liz—and some chick you met at a conference..."

"It's not like that."

"I hope not, after all the crap you gave me about Nancy."

"Can you cover me or not?" Colin watched Trina twist a corkscrew into her third bottle. He shook his head at her to say no.

"Yeah," Trent said. "I'm already on the floor."

"Thanks."

Trina stood with the bottle of wine in one hand, the cork in the other, her lips pressed into a pout.

"You have to go?" she asked.

"No. I need something stronger."

They talked late into the night about anything other than their reality, trying to find a moment of peace in a situation without answers. Colin kept laughing. It felt wrong but good. He enjoyed a few more drinks and had a few more laughs. *Hiding out in my mistress's house*, he thought, reflecting on what Trent had said. Laughing some more, he poured another drink.

"What did you think of me?" Trina's fingertip traced the rim of her glass.

"What do you mean?" He knew what she meant but hoped she'd back off and say never mind. She didn't.

"In Florida, when I asked if I could sit with you and have a drink."

"I thought you seemed nice and had a great smile."

"I thought you were nice too."

The liquor heightened his exhaustion. His arms and legs felt like lead. He didn't want to move. He didn't want to talk. He just wanted to be still and pretend for a moment that it was all some crazy dream.

Trina moved closer to him on the couch.

He thought of a joke—something to ease the tension that had built. His brain was awash in a whiskey haze. She leaned in and gently touched her lips to his.

He turned away.

"Sorry," she said, backing up.

"No. It's my fault." He stood up and swayed, staggering to the bathroom. His phone pinged.

"Liz?" Trina asked, turning on the TV.

Colin nodded as he opened the text.

"It's another picture."

Making a face, he ran to the kitchen and grabbed a knife.

39
Colin

Colin ran out the door, down the steps, and into the street. A black BMW drove away. The cicadas droned on, pulsating in the trees. He slowed his breathing, looking up and down the quiet block. A streetlight above flickered out.

Looking back at the house, he saw Trina. She hesitated in the doorway before wrapping her sweater around her body and meeting him out on the lawn. His phone pinged again. The knife sliced into the turf at his feet.

“What is it?” Trina asked. “Show me.”

He looked at his phone, then turned to scan the houses across the street. “I have to go.”

“No. Come back inside.”

He couldn’t move.

“Come on,” Trina said, putting her arm around his waist, leading him in.

Colin locked the door, then watched the neighbors’ houses for movement as he closed the blinds.

“I shouldn’t be here,” he said. “This just fed right into her claims that I’m having an affair. What the hell, Trina? Why would you kiss me?” Feeling like a jerk for blaming her, he grabbed his keys.

“Wait, Colin. I’m sorry. I’m sorry. You can’t drive like this.

Let me get you an Uber."

He stopped, holding the doorknob. "That car—it had an Uber sticker."

"What?"

He could feel her moving closer behind him.

"Colin, please. Don't leave me here. I'm scared."

"You should call the police."

"Let me see your phone. What did she say? Tell me, so I can tell the police what happened."

He handed it to her and leaned his forehead on the door, knowing it didn't look good. The photo confirmed Detective Green's assumptions about Colin.

"She was here?" Trina raced to the window, yanking the blind cord. "She was right outside my window." Swiping away the picture of them kissing, Trina gasped at the next image.

Colin turned around and, leaning on the door, slid to the ground. He'd never seen himself so deranged as he appeared in that photo—standing in the street, face red and puffy from alcohol, holding a knife. He couldn't let Trina show the detective. He couldn't let Green see him like that.

"Okay, I'll stay." He stood up and walked to the kitchen for a drink of water.

"I'll make up the couch."

"Thanks," he said, taking his phone from Trina and turning it off.

Rain pelted the window. The room was dark and stuffy. Colin's tongue felt dry. He wanted to be in his own bed. Feeling around on the table and the floor, he found his phone to check the time. Remembering he'd turned it off, he waited for it to load. He tried to remember the last time he'd turned it off. Never. Not even at their wedding.

As it came back online, the relentless pings of messages and reminders from his calendar pierced his ears. He switched it to silent and went to the bathroom.

"Good morning," Trina said, walking to the kitchen when he opened the door. "Coffee?"

"Please," he said, scratching his stubble.

Folding the blanket and sheet on the couch, he looked down at his phone. Sixty-two messages and thirty-nine missed calls.

"Shit," he said, dialing his voicemail. He dropped onto the couch as he listened to the news.

When the last message finished playing, he hung his head. Bile stung his throat, and his eyes watered. He ran to the bathroom and slammed the door.

Trina asked if he was all right. He couldn't answer. He wanted to be in his apartment. Hidden away from everyone. Safe.

Splashing cold water on his face, Colin looked in the mirror. His own reflection made him wince. He'd known disgust before, every time he binged. This was a whole new level of shame and repulsion. He took a breath and tried to pull himself together to get out of Trina's house.

Slowly, he opened the door.

"Here you go." She stood there, waiting with two mugs. "Are you okay? How much did you drink?"

He leaned on the doorframe, his hands shaking.

"Come sit down." She walked to the kitchen, setting the coffees on the table. Colin stayed frozen.

"What happened?" She returned to his side and dragged him to the table, making him sit.

"She needed me last night."

"Liz? What'd she do?"

Trina rubbed his arm, then picked up her cup and blew on it. Colin watched the steam rise and dance around with each breath.

"Leticia."

"Who?"

"My patient."

"What happened?"

"She needed me. I wasn't there."

"Is she okay?"

"She's dead."

"Oh, Colin..."

He could hear Trina's voice comforting him. Nothing she could say would fix what he'd done. He should have been there for Leticia. He shouldn't have gone to Trina's house in the first place. Leticia was dead. And Liz had real proof—not just some sloppy, photoshopped picture—of his affair... and his temper. He thought of the image of him standing like a maniac in the street. He didn't want to look. He had to see it sober.

Scrolling through dozens of new messages from Liz, he found the photo. It looked worse in the light of day. The taste of bile returned. He ran back to the bathroom.

This time, when Colin finished and came out, he could hear Trina's shower running upstairs. Grabbing his things, he left.

His phone, still switched to silent, flashed nonstop as he drove home. He couldn't answer. Couldn't hear Trent's voice. Not yet.

At home, he showered. A long, scorching shower. In the kitchen, he put two pieces of bread in the toaster as he slowly measured out coffee beans. Simple tasks.

Glancing at the front door, he saw the silhouette before hearing the bell.

"Where've you been?" Trent pushed by Colin, storming into the kitchen. "Having a nice, relaxing morning, it looks like. Where's your girlfriend?"

"It's not like that." Colin hated to see Trent—the man who'd cheated on his own wife regularly from day one—coming into his home, accusing him.

"Then tell me what it is like. Explain how my partner, who's never missed a delivery, could miss such a high-risk—"

"I don't even know where to begin."

Trent unbuttoned his blazer and pulled out a stool. "It better be good."

Trent's expression softened as Colin told him all that had happened, showing him the messages and admitting to the kiss.

"And I thought Nancy was vindictive when she caught me messing around."

"Liz isn't vindictive..." Colin said, refilling their coffees.

"How can you say that after all this... insanity?"

"I don't think it's her." He slid the coffee pot back onto the burner and groaned. "I can't stand not knowing what's happening."

"I don't know what I'd do. I'm pretty sure you're handling it better than I would." He wiped a drip of coffee from the counter. "I'm shocked. You and Liz—you've always been *that* couple. And the baby... I'm shocked."

"Me too," Colin said, offering Trent some toast. "Wait, what do you mean?"

"No, thanks."

"What did you mean, the baby?" Colin asked again.

Trent shook his head. "No. Nothing."

Colin stared. "What?"

"Just that—when I went to do the D&C, there was a heartbeat. Colin... Liz is still pregnant. She was gonna tell you..."

Colin gripped the counter. "What are you talking about? You didn't say that. You were going to have the lab run more tests, and next time, you had an idea to increase... What are you talking about?"

"I can't. I promised—"

"Promised Liz? Promised her what?"

"Look, she's my patient. You know I can't just tell you. Besides, she was worried. You know she always has low levels. For all we know, she ended up miscarrying after all. Maybe that's why she ran off. You said it yourself... it's a lot for someone to go through." Trent looked at his phone. "I have to get going."

He stood up and held out his hand. Colin shook it in a daze.

"If there's anything I can do..." Trent said.

"You've got enough with Leticia. I'm sorry."

"Unfortunately, it's all part of the job," Trent said. "In light of all this, why don't you take some time off?"

"Thanks, but I need the distraction."

Trent stopped at the door. "Yeah, well. With Leticia's death, the last thing our practice needs is you coming in distracted."

Colin rubbed the back of his neck. "You know what I mean."

"Look, take some time—"

"I—"

"Colin. Take. Some. Time. It's not a request."

40
Colin

Washing the cups, Colin replayed everything in his mind. His head throbbed. He tried to remember his conversation with Trent in Outpatient Surgery when he'd gone to see Liz. Trent had said he'd run more tests. And what about Liz? She was still under anesthesia when he went to see her. Wasn't she? Colin didn't know what to believe. Maybe Trent was right, and she'd ended up miscarrying after all. But why wouldn't she tell Colin? Instead, she'd disappeared and accused him of cheating.

He thought of the picture of himself outside Trina's house and wondered if Liz had been in that black BMW that drove past. Remembering the Uber sticker on the back window, he grabbed his phone.

It went to voicemail. "Hey Felix. Can you hack into someone's Uber account? If so, call me back."

He immediately regretted leaving the message. *No one from inside that car could have taken the picture*, he thought. He remembered standing in the street with the knife, the car's taillights two blocks away by then.

His phone pinged. He read the new message.

Just checking if you'll be coming by today? We have family coming at 2.

He'd completely forgotten to reschedule with the fertility

support group coordinator. With no other ideas or leads, he texted back to say he was on his way.

"Hello, you must be Dr. Clarke." A young woman in tennis shoes and an apron opened the door. Her hair was pulled up in a high ponytail, swinging from side to side as she led Colin through the house and out to the back patio. "Hannah, Dr. Clarke's here."

"Thank you, Stephanie," she said.

Stephanie smiled and went back into the house.

"Dr. Clarke," Hannah said, holding out one hand, the other cradling the bundle wrapped against her chest. "Have a seat."

"Congratulations." He pulled a heavy metal chair out and sat down. The fresh air and morning sun felt good.

"Thank you. This little bug has been a long, long time coming."

"You started the fertility group, right?"

"Yes. When Peter and I lost our first at nineteen weeks. Almost made it halfway." She smiled and tilted her head.

"I'm sorry to hear that."

The baby cooed and shifted, struggling to lift his head, bobbing it back down on Hannah's chest.

"How can I help you, Doctor?"

"Please, call me Colin." He wasn't sure how to broach the subject. "My wife is in your group. Liz."

"Liz? Oh, I'm sorry, I didn't make the connection." She looked confused. "Is everything all right?"

"Not exactly. Liz has gone missing." He found the words came out much easier to a stranger. "Just after your last meeting, actually."

"Oh my gosh."

"I'm just trying to retrace her steps, and I thought maybe she said something at the meeting? Or something happened?"

"Oh my, well, I wasn't there," she said, tilting her head down to her son. "I checked into the hospital the night before. Strict bed rest—tough, but worth it. You know something? I think I heard you out in the hall when I arrived. My doctor's Dr. Park. Anyway, let me call a few of the other members and see. Have you called the police?"

"Yeah."

"Of course you did." She smiled. "Sorry, I'm not thinking straight."

Colin waved his hands and smiled. "No worries. They're working on it. Still, I couldn't just sit around waiting."

"I don't blame you." She winced a little and leaned forward, bringing the baby to her lap. The little guy's cheek was red and creased from sleeping against his mother's skin.

"Can I help you?" Colin asked.

She blew out through her mouth and pursed her lips. "You're a doctor," she said as if to remind herself, pressing her fingertips into her engorged chest. "Would you mind grabbing me some frozen peas?"

Colin jumped up, happy to have something to do. To know what to do and how to help. It all felt so normal.

Bouquets of roses, lilies, and tulips covered most of the large granite island in the kitchen. Bottles were lined up, cleaned and sterilized, on a rack next to the sink.

"Hello again." Stephanie walked through with a bucket of water and a mop. "Are you looking for something?"

"Just the freezer," he said, pointing.

Stephanie moved on and opened the basement door, flipping on the light. "If you need anything, give a yell." Water sloshed around as she stepped down the stairs.

"Thanks." Colin opened the freezer and poked around. Something fell in the basement. He looked at the stairs. Stephanie was out of sight. His eyes lingered on the cork wall leading down. Closing the freezer, he walked over. A collage of birth announcements was pinned to the cork. It reminded him of the walls in his office. The light was dim. Scanning the pictures, he saw several familiar faces. Babies he'd delivered. Others he knew to be Trent's patients. A picture of triplets that Dr. Park had delivered—only one survived, and the living baby was holding her deceased siblings' hands. Colin stared, wondering if Dr. Park had that photo displayed in her office.

He squinted at another announcement. The woman looked familiar. It was too dark to make out the writing. Reaching for the picture, he pulled out the pin. The air left his lungs as he grabbed for the railing.

41
Owen

Owen drove his bus on autopilot for days, thinking of ways to avoid Darina and her perfectly symmetrical face. When she'd managed to corner him as he locked the bunny room, she'd apologized to him for that night. She didn't have anywhere else to go. Her mother had died when she was little. Her father left to fight in the war. She was willing to forgive and forget.

That only made it harder for Owen to be good. Her trusting, hopeful eyes willing him to become her protector—he knew she'd submit to everything he'd ever wanted in a pet.

Arriving home in the rain, he shook off his coat. Sissy had taken Sarah to get her hair cut and colored, just like she used to before their lives changed.

Darina sat on her bed, thumbing around on her phone.

"I'd like a coffee, please," she said, holding the phone in front of her face. A chime sounded, and she tapped around.

"Hello," Owen said. "It sounds like your English lessons are coming along."

"Yes. I'd like a coffee, please," she repeated, and laughed.

"I'm ordering some food... If you'd like to look at the menu..."

She bounced out of bed and walked to the kitchen. *So spunky and joyful.*

While they ate, they chatted about their homelands and how Ireland was both different and similar. What they missed and what they were happy to never see again.

"I'm sorry about your daughter," Darina said, spooning her curry over rice. Her eyes remained focused on her food as she asked, "How did she die?"

Owen picked up his napkin and wiped his mouth, then folded it twice and held it tight in his fist. "That was long ago, but still, like yesterday." He shook his head as tears filled his eyes.

"I'm sorry," she said, picking up her plate. "I shouldn't pry."

"No. Please, sit down. I'm not used to talking about her. It's good for me... She was only eight when she died. Before that, she was so full of life. Then a monster... he killed her. In her own bedroom."

Darina looked up at Owen, seeming unsure what to say.

"I'm sorry again about the other night," he said. "You remind me of her in many ways."

"Do I?"

"Yes. Almost too much like her. That night, I thought you were her. I was happy for the first time in years."

"You're a bit like my dad. The way you work so hard and care for your wife. Trying to do it all on your own."

Owen smiled as Darina squeezed his hand.

"It's fate bringing us together then, isn't it?" Owen said, taking his evening pills. He imagined Darina being notified that her father had died in the war. She'd run to Owen for comfort. He'd hold her. Take care of her. He'd protect her. It would make up for the day Sheena was killed. He'd have a fresh start. A second chance. He hoped Darina's father would die. *Hope.*

Someone knocked at the front door. Owen left to answer while Darina cleared the table.

"Doesn't she look great?" Sissy said, helping Sarah take off the scarf protecting her blond curls.

Owen kissed Sarah's cheek. "Just like our wedding day."

"I can't stay," Sissy said, stepping outside.

That night, Owen wouldn't have to be gentle when he pulled

down Darina's blanket. He wouldn't have to hover his fingers just over her soft skin. He wouldn't need to tiptoe or try to be quiet. The sedative he'd crushed into her curry would keep her asleep. Keep her quiet. That night, he wouldn't have to be so careful.

42
Colin

"Dr. Clarke. Are you all right?" Stephanie asked, running up the stairs.

"Sorry." He backed up into the kitchen as she picked up the bags of peas and handed them to Hannah.

"What happened?" Hannah asked.

"Sorry, I slipped. What is this?" Colin asked, turning the announcement toward her.

"You found my secret board." She smiled, taking the card from his hand. "These are previous members of our fertility group. They've all gone on to have babies. It's sort of a vision board."

Stephanie left the room as Hannah handed the card back to Colin. She walked into the living room, spreading a blanket on the sofa, unwrapping her son.

"What do you mean? A vision board?"

"Maybe it's silly, but every time someone had a baby, I was encouraged to keep trying. I used to have it posted on that wall there." She pointed to the wall opposite the fridge. "Some months it was too stark a reminder of what I would never have." She smiled down at her son and stroked his bare feet. "One day, seeing them so happy, it was all too much. My husband came home and found me crying on the floor. That's when he moved it to the stairwell."

Colin reread the announcement in his hand. "What about this one?"

"Yeah, not everyone ended up giving birth. Some adopted. She's heading to China soon to pick up her daughter."

"There was a baby shower," he said, remembering that day. "Liz..."

"Yes." She made a face, turning to Colin. "Liz was there. Does that mean something?" Her eyes brightened.

Colin nodded his head. "Can I take this with me?"

"Sure. I hope it helps."

In his car, taking several deep breaths before dialing, Colin tried to make sense of it all. He looked at the adoption announcement again. *Trina Scott is excited to announce the adoption of...* He looked back at Trina's name. Then her picture. Name and picture.

Liz and Colin had been out to dinner when she remembered about the baby shower brunch the next morning. It was too late to go to any other store. They'd stopped off at the market on the way home. A bouquet of flowers, a gift card, and then Liz had said, "Why not a bottle of Clicquot? She's not pregnant, after all."

"Why not?" Colin had agreed, eyeing the latest craft beer selection. "We should have Trent over for dinner."

"I'll whip something up. Ooh, be sure he brings his new girlfriend." Liz had said it with such a devilish smile.

She'd never said Trina's name. Not that he could remember at least. Yet there they'd been, buying Trina flowers and champagne. It didn't make sense.

He snapped out of the memory, still sitting in his car outside Hannah's house. He had to know how long Trina had known Liz. Why hadn't she mentioned it to him? Her phone went straight to voicemail.

He couldn't wait. He called Hannah, watching her house as the phone rang.

"Let's see," Hannah said, the baby fussing in the background. "They joined around the same time."

"Liz has been in the group for years," Colin said.

"Yeah, that's right. Does that mean something? Do you want her number?"

He tried to thank her but couldn't speak. Liz and Trina had known each other for years.

"I texted a few in the group. I'll let you know if I hear anything back. I really have to go now."

Dropping his phone on the seat, he looked up. Terrified, he found he'd driven to Valparaiso, never knowing he'd even started the car. He continued on to his apartment.

In that moment, it was all he could think about. He hated that he wanted it so much, but it was the only thing left in his control. The only constant in which to cling.

Inside his apartment, he placed his usual order and waited. His phone pinged. A message from Felix.

Hey, cuz. Took some doing. Liz's Uber account hasn't been used in months. Hit me up if you need anything else. Happy to help.

There was a noise in the hall, and he opened the door.

"Such a big order," the delivery driver said, walking toward Colin.

He wanted to slam the door shut. He also wanted to offer the kid a few hundred for any other orders he had in his car.

"Thanks."

He closed the door and set out the containers. Three beef and mushroom, two shrimp pad Thai... He'd find a way to cram in the egg foo young this time.

Poking around for the most tender piece of meat, the best mushroom, and the right amount of sauce, he felt his mouth water. His hands shook as the anticipation built. Touching the food to his lips, he paused. His phone rang. He took the forkful into his mouth, trying to block out the noise as he chewed, setting down his fork as the call went to voicemail.

Holding the container in his lap with one hand, he scooped a handful up to his mouth with the other. His phone rang again. He dropped the pile of food back in, wiping his hand on the couch.

Trina.

"Colin," she whispered, sobbing. "We need to talk. Can you come over?"

"We can talk on the phone." His mouth watered. His heart raced, desperate for the binge to begin. He went to the sink and rinsed his hand, then craned his neck under the faucet, taking a long drink.

"Hannah just called," Trina said. "Let me explain."

"Where's all the baby stuff?" Colin asked.

"What?"

"You had a shower. Didn't you get baby gifts?"

She didn't answer.

"Liz was there, Trina. My wife. Liz. Was at your house." His voice rose to a yell.

"Please, Colin. I can explain everything."

He looked at the coffee table, disgusted by the food. He had to get to the truth. He wasn't thinking straight, standing there primed for a binge. In that moment, his mind's only concern was getting to the release.

"Okay," he said. "I'll come over, but..."

"Yes?"

"No lies."

"I promise."

43
Colin

Brown sauce dripped from his hand onto the carpet as Colin shoveled in sliced beef and mushrooms. Three containers down. The shrimp in the pad Thai were much smaller this time, making for an easier go of swallowing. He felt enormously thankful to the restaurant, as if they'd known how badly he needed to get the food in as fast as possible.

Thoughts of Trina popped into his head. He tried to make connections and think of her possible responses, the excuses she'd make. He stopped himself. He had to focus. The ritual had to be completed in the correct order. The binge first. Then Trina.

His skin felt warm, sweat forming on his forehead—drops of greasy sweat, he imagined.

"The pills," he said, looking around. He'd forgotten the pills. He hadn't ordered any more since throwing away the others. It was too late. They were the first step in the process. He had forgotten. The entire binge was falling apart. He knew the release wouldn't feel quite right.

"It's okay," he said, starting in on the egg rolls—a marathoner reaching the final few miles. He looked at the egg foo young; the finish line would follow. He cheered himself on, encouraged by the speed at which he'd inhaled the food, not feeling it backing up his esophagus. That happened every now and then. The first time, it had terrified Colin. It felt like he was suffocating himself.

He finished the egg rolls. With a deep, satisfied inhale, he ate the egg foo young.

Afterward, when it was all over, he looked at himself in the bathroom mirror. He hated himself and felt disgusted.

Splashing water on his face, he stood tall and took a deep breath. "Okay, Colin. That was the last time." He always hoped that was true.

The hot shower and loofah scrubbed away that thick, greasy feeling on his skin. Wrapping a towel around his waist, he looked at the changed man in the mirror—full of confidence and focus. He hated his addiction, but in that brief little moment, when everything felt right, he loved it.

At the kitchen table, away from the filth of food smeared on the couch and trampled on the floor, he thought about what he should ask Trina. He was no detective. He knew she'd make up excuses, claiming she hadn't realized he and Liz were married. When he met Hannah, she hadn't made the connection either. Maybe Trina didn't know?

She'd say she didn't know, and she'd apologize. It was all a crazy misunderstanding. It was possible.

No, don't make excuses for her, he thought.

She'd say, "Now more than ever, we're in this together. Liz planned everything and used us both." And Colin would believe her, feeling responsible for her being dragged into it. She'd look at him with those doe eyes and say she was scared. "Could you stay a little longer?" Trina would ask, and Colin would relent.

Nothing made sense. As a doctor, he'd been surprised by how eager women were to reveal the most intimate secrets to him, especially during labor. Never having to pry for information, he knew he wasn't the right person to question Trina. He didn't know what to ask or how to ask it.

The only thing he was sure of was that he needed help. His phone was wedged in the couch, sticky with the remains of his binge. He dialed.

"Detective Green, I think I found something."

"Okay, I'm listening."

"You know Liz was last seen by her mother at lunch? I'd forgotten that her mom picked her up from her support group."

"Okay?" Papers rattled on the phone. "Her mom said she picked her up from the hospital to take her to lunch."

"Yeah, the group meets at the hospital." He imagined all the times he might have passed Trina in the hallway, coming or going to her meetings.

"Okay. What about this group?"

"I met with the coordinator, and she had this wall of baby announcements. All members of the group who ended up having babies or adopting."

"Dr. Clarke, I'm testifying in court soon. Can you get to the point?"

He couldn't help but think it was all some crazy coincidence. Liz hadn't talked much about Trina. They probably barely knew each other, and Liz probably only went to the shower because the whole group was going. If she had been good friends with Trina, she wouldn't have waited until the last minute to buy a gift, swinging by the grocery store after dinner, throwing together whatever looked good enough.

"Dr. Clarke?"

"There was an adoption announcement for Trina."

"Trina Scott?"

"Yes."

"Lots of people come and go from support groups. Are you sure they even met?"

"They've been in the group for years together. Liz joined right after our first miscarriage. The coordinator said Trina joined around the same time. That doesn't matter. I know they know each other because the adoption announcement was for a baby shower just before Liz went missing. I remember her going to it."

He could hear a whistle of air blow out of Detective Green's mouth.

"Send me the coordinator's number. I'd like to see the

announcement myself and ask her a few questions." She seemed to be moving around and no longer talking to Colin, just thinking out loud.

"I have the announcement," Colin said.

"Okay, send me her number and a picture of the announcement. I'm late for court."

"One other thing..."

"What?"

"I'm heading over to Trina's house, and I thought I should ask—"

"Don't. If she's been lying, we need to figure out why."

"I could ask if—"

"Colin, please don't interfere with the investigation."

"Right."

"Stay home. Sit tight. I'll call you later."

After hanging up the phone, Colin couldn't help but feel like Detective Green didn't have the time for what she probably still saw as a sordid love triangle. Sending the photo and Hannah's number to her, he dialed another number.

"Hey, cuz. I'm glad you called..."

Colin couldn't get a word in and regretted reaching out. Felix hadn't been able to trace Liz's phone, and the search of her Uber account hadn't resulted in any information, as he'd mentioned. Still, Colin thought with all of Felix's tech connections, he should be able to hack into Trina's computer or phone and find something.

He listened as Felix went on about the new facial-recognition software. Colin had heard this speech many times before.

"Felix, sorry to cut you off. I have a delivery."

"Wait, I'm just about to get to the best part. Two minutes, I promise."

Colin sighed, knowing the final pitch for money was about to come. "Okay."

"Don't be mad."

"Why would I be mad?"

"Don't you see what I'm trying to tell you? I know how much

it means to you to find her. I've been using everything I have at my disposal."

"Okay?" Colin shook his head, trying to follow.

"Yeah, cuz, I'm sorry. I hacked into the ancestry site. I've been tracing your DNA to help you find her."

"My DNA? How?"

"I said, don't be mad."

Colin sighed. "What does my DNA have to do with finding Liz?"

"What? No, not your wife. I think I found your birth mother."

He imagined his mother wrapping his tiny body in paper towels and placing him in a plastic bag—twisting the bag and tossing it into a dumpster.

"Did you hear me? I haven't confirmed a current address yet, but I'm pretty sure it's her. Isn't that great?"

"Yeah. Yeah, thanks." Colin hung up the phone. His esophagus stung with bile, and he ran to the bathroom. Before he could make it to the toilet, he tasted blood.

44
Owen

"I'm sorry for your trouble," Saoirse said to Owen as they left the police station. "This won't bode well for my pilot program to place refugees in homes."

"It can't be helped," Owen said thoughtfully.

"If any reporters come by—"

"My curtains will stay closed." He winked at her as she rubbed his arm and left.

At the vegan café, he considered ordering something different. No. The blueberry-lemon crumble felt safe. *You just never know when you try something new*, he thought. He felt bad for Saoirse—her seeing refugees in need and wanting to help.

He smiled at her do-gooder naivety. *What a nice lady*, he thought as he read through his copy of the police report.

Such a shame Darina hadn't worked out. Owen told the police he'd been more than willing to forgive her when he discovered she'd stolen money from them. When his wife's friend, Sissy, called looking for her wallet and it was found in Darina's mattress, Owen agreed with everyone else—they had to turn her in. All for the best.

Too bad she'd run off before the police could arrest her.

"Probably long gone at this point," the police officer had said. "If she shows up, call us right away."

"I will," Owen said, knowing she never would.

All for the best, he thought now as he picked at the crumble and sipped his hot cocoa, watching the window shoppers stroll along. A young woman, standing in his bus queue, pulled her sweater off over her head, her midriff showing as she struggled. He'd be printing her ticket in just a few minutes. *Where are you heading?* he wondered. A bit too tall for his liking. Exceptions were sometimes made.

As he wiped his mouth, something caught his eye. A woman standing across the street on the curb, as if waiting to cross. No one ever waited. Cars simply stopped, and people crossed. She pulled forward a bit, staring at Owen. A red car stopped. She waved for the car to pass. Her hair was tucked into a baseball cap, the bill tilted down over her eyes to conceal them. He knew those eyes. He knew she was looking right at him.

Those big, questioning eyes. Gossip. Rumors and gossip. That was all it was. Yet there she stood. Hunting him. It was his own fault she was there. He hadn't been good. He planned to be good. He couldn't. She knew everything. Somehow, she knew. Soon, everyone would know.

His mind raced through every pet he'd had since arriving in Ireland. Every potential mistake. She'd need proof this time. He envisioned the resting places around his property. Out on the bog and the blue mountains of Achill.

A gray car stopped. Big Eyes stepped out into the street. He willed another car to come along and slam into her, throwing her into the side of the gift shop on the corner. *No luck,* he thought as she crossed unscathed.

Her head tilted up now, her eyes never leaving his. He wondered if she could see him or if she was simply looking at the café. Hopefully, a glare from the rising sun would blind her. He frowned as her eyes remained fixed on him.

The door to the café opened with a burst of air. Two men with cameras walked in. Another man carried equipment. A fourth man adjusted his hair in the front window's reflection. A young boy, looking like an intern of sorts, balanced a crate against the lamppost outside.

She's brought a news team, Owen thought, looking down at his hands. He'd meant to be good. He could see the blood on his hands, in his nails. He blinked. No blood. They were clean. Gossip. That's all.

"Excuse me, sir," Tousled Hair said to Owen, passing by to talk to the owner of the café.

Owen looked back at Big Eyes as she opened the door, trying to get to him, blocked by the crew and their equipment.

Owen checked his watch. This wouldn't do. He had a schedule to keep. Rushing off toward the bathroom, he left through the cramped common courtyard shared by three other businesses. Odd crates and chairs were stacked against the cement walls, with peeling paint flakes scattered on the ground.

Entering the gift shop next door, he raced through the storage room and out the front door. He didn't look back until boarding the bus and checking his mirror. He tapped an elderly man's destination into the machine. The ticket paper jammed.

"Go ahead," he said, waving the man along. "Machine's down."

Each passenger that boarded seemed to need a personal invitation to take a seat without paying.

"No. No, the machine is down," he repeated, waving them through. His eyes fixed on the woman in a baseball cap as she ran toward the bus.

"Does this bus go to—"

"Take a seat, Blondie," Owen said, waving her through.

The passenger paused, seeming confused.

"Hurry up now, we're running late," he said, closing the door and pulling away from the curb. Every passenger's head turned back and forth in shock and confusion as he left Big Eyes chasing behind. An elderly man stood up, wobbled, then sat down without saying a word. Blondie found a seat in the back.

"That's awful, the poor thing," a woman said out loud to a chorus of agreement.

"She'll catch the next one." Owen's tone told them all they

needed to know. If anyone had anything else to say, they'd risk being left behind with that poor soul.

Soon, they all turned to their phones and thoughts, leaving Owen to enjoy stolen glances as his eyes turned from the road to Blondie in the mirror. He felt bad for being so rude. It wasn't his nature. Certainly, she'd understand.

At the end of the line, to his delight, Blondie was alone on the bus.

"Eager to see Achill, then?" he asked. "I always thought it such a shame the bus line ends three miles shy of the most beautiful beach in Ireland."

Tsking, she took off her glasses and looked toward Keem. "That's too bad."

Pleading puppy eyes. Owen winked. "Just this once."

Out of Service, the bus's display announced as Owen sped past every stop. Bypassing the usual loop, he was able to make up time. As he left Achill for the mainland, he relaxed. Now he'd consider what to do about Big Eyes. Replaying the café scene in his mind, Owen realized the film crew hadn't been with her. No. Big Eyes was alone and vulnerable. He smiled at the thought.

Later that night, Saoirse called to see if Darina had turned up.

She apologized again. "Can I find you a carer from the area? I have someone in mind. She's well known in Westport. Comes from a lovely family, married to a solicitor—"

"No. No, thank you."

"I understand. I'm sorry again."

"Will you be here tomorrow for my inspection?"

"No. I saw you had things cleaned up when I brought Darina over. I'll mark it as closed. Again, I'm sorry for all this."

"Please, don't worry yourself. You never can tell how someone really is behind closed doors. It's already forgotten."

"Well, if there's anything I can do—"

Owen knew she needed to perform some small token of

penance, or she'd never fully go away.

"Actually, would you mind seeing if there's room for my wife in one of those day programs you mentioned? Perhaps the one with art therapy?"

"My pleasure."

No. You never can tell how someone really is, he thought with a smile as he untangled strands of blond hair from his fingers.

45
Colin

Rinsing the bile and blood from his mouth, Colin answered his phone.

"Dr. Clarke, have you been seeing Trina Scott?"

He rolled his eyes. "I thought you had court?"

Detective Green sighed. "Just answer my question."

"I've already told you. No, I'm not—"

"Let me rephrase," she said. "Have you been meeting with Trina Scott?"

"Yes."

"And why is that?"

"What do you mean, why? Because you weren't taking her seriously. Because she was scared and didn't have anyone to turn to. Because—"

"Dr. Clarke, you should have—"

"I know it doesn't look good. I should have called you. And I'm sure this only confirms your belief that I'm having an affair with Trina."

"Are you done?"

He didn't like her tone, like she was scolding a toddler throwing a tantrum. Perhaps he was acting like a toddler.

"Sorry," he said.

"We didn't know about the support group. You were right."

She cleared her throat. "Dr. Clarke. This is the part where I tell you flat out to stop interfering with my investigation. Let me do my job."

"With all due respect, it doesn't seem like there's been much of an investigation."

"I know it may seem that way. I assure you, I'm looking into it."

"Fine, you're looking into it. I'm heading to Trina's right now. What did you find out?"

"You're not listening to me."

Dropping his towel from his waist, he struggled to dress with one hand.

"What did you find out?" he asked again, pressing the speakerphone button and sliding his arm into his sleeve.

"I can't say."

"She's expecting me."

"Tell her you were called to the hospital."

"I'm taking some time off."

"Fine. Please stop moving around and listen to me."

Colin stood with his zipper between his fingertips. "Yes?"

"Liz hasn't been texting you and Trina."

"I knew it." Colin sat down at the table, buttoning his shirt. "Who is it?"

Green let out a breath. "It's Trina."

He picked up the phone. "Trina?"

"Yes. She's texting you and herself... pretending to be Liz."

The room started to spin. Colin froze, unable to speak. He swallowed and inhaled, shaking his head in disbelief.

"Since when?" he breathed into the receiver.

"We're still obtaining that information. It looks like the entire time."

"What does that mean? How? Does Liz— Where's Liz?"

"Dr. Clarke, I don't know. That's what I'm working on. I need you to stay put and come up with some excuse to not go to Trina's. Just send her a text so she doesn't get spooked. Colin, listen to me. I'm going to find your wife. I need you to work with me. Do you understand?"

He didn't like this new tone. This serious tone he hadn't heard before. A tone that told him the detectives had screwed up. A tone that announced things had changed.

"Yes. I understand."

"Thank you. I know it may seem like things have been slow, but once we get a warrant, things will move fast. Don't worry, the truth will come out. We'll find her. Just stay put."

"Okay."

After hanging up the call, he finished dressing and drove off, dialing at every stoplight, hanging up when it went straight to voicemail. He had to warn her.

Answer your phone, he thought as he rolled through a red light.

His father-in-law opened the door, glasses and newspaper in his hands.

"Are you all right?" Daniel asked, stepping aside to allow Colin to pass by. "Is that blood on your lip?"

Colin wiped his mouth. "Cut shaving," he said, trying to force a smile. "Is Anne home?"

"Sure is. I'll get you a glass of water," Daniel said, walking to the kitchen sink.

"Thank you."

"Oh, hello, Colin!" Anne yelled from upstairs. "Thank you for coming."

She met him in the entry and pulled him to her bedroom. Turning to her husband, she said, "I've called him to look at that rash on my leg."

In her room, Anne searched his face for answers. "I haven't told Daniel yet. You didn't say anything, did you?"

"No." Colin thought of the poor man pottering around the house, working on the newspaper crossword, oblivious to the reality going on around him. "I didn't say anything, but you need to. Now. You can't put it off any longer."

"What's happened?" Her voice was barely audible as she sat on the bed. Colin sat next to her.

"The police have found something—someone involved in all this."

"Who?"

"A friend, or... I don't know if she's a friend. Another member of Liz's support group—"

"What group?"

"It's a fertility support group. Because of the miscarriages. The woman the police thought I was having an affair with—she's a member of the same group."

"Shh, not so loud." Anne looked at the door, then back at Colin. "So, you are having an affair?"

"No."

"Then I don't understand."

Colin explained the entire story again. When she nodded that she understood, he said, "I think something has happened to Liz. I think the police think something bad has happened. Something really bad."

Anne frowned. Colin could tell she didn't believe him. Maybe it was denial.

He said, "It's time to tell Daniel. It's all about to come out, and it'll probably be in the news. You won't be able to hide it from him."

She stared into Colin's eyes, searching for something to say. Finally, she said, "Let's just wait and see what they find."

Colin's eyebrows knit tightly together. "Anne, I don't think you understand. This woman, Trina, I think she's done something to Liz."

Anne flinched like she'd been slapped in the face, and her eyes filled with tears.

"Try to think," Colin said. "When you had lunch with Liz, did she say anything about going to meet someone before teaching the class?"

"It's all my fault," Anne said, tears wetting her cheeks, her shoulders slumped down.

"You can't think like that. It's not your fault. Do you remember anything?"

Slowly, she shook her head. Colin could tell she was no longer listening to him. He rubbed her back, and she tensed, then turned to him.

"We have to find Liz."

"What?"

"If we find her, Daniel will never have to know."

"Anne—"

"Do you know how to track her phone?"

"The police are look—"

"No. We'll go to this woman and get her to tell us where Liz is. Maybe she's holding her somewhere. We can find her and bring her home."

"Anne, please. The detective said—"

"And if she did something to Liz, then I'll tell Daniel. If she's—you know—I need to be the one to tell him, not the police. You understand that, don't you?"

"I promised the detective I wouldn't get in her way. Come on." Colin stood, holding out his hand. "We'll tell him together."

"No."

"We can't keep hiding the truth. It'll only make things worse."

"No."

"Anne, we have to. He's going to find out, and it's better if we—"

"Colin. I said no. Daniel has been through enough. This will kill him."

She stood to leave as Colin's phone rang.

He looked at Anne and sent the call to voicemail.

"That was her, wasn't it? The woman who took Liz."

"We don't know that for sure. Let the police—"

Anne grabbed his wrist. "It wouldn't hurt to ask."

Colin thought for a moment. "No. I'm going to tell him."

46
Colin

Colin found Daniel beside Emma's bed. Anne rushed in behind him, grabbing his wrist, but he pulled away.

Emma's eyes sparkled with delight when they entered the room. So many visitors. Colin could see that she was wondering where Liz was.

"I hope it's not contagious," Daniel said, brushing Emma's hair.

"The rash?" Anne said. "No. It's—"

"Just a little cream, and she'll be cleared up in a couple of days," Colin said.

There was something about the way Daniel ran the brush through Emma's hair. So gentle. Barely touching the strands. As if he didn't want to inflict any more pain on a girl who'd already suffered so much trauma.

As he watched, Colin couldn't find the words to inflict more pain on Daniel either. He looked at Anne.

"I'll never forget that police officer on our doorstep." It was all she needed to say.

Daniel shook his head. "Worst moment in my life. The cop they sent over, he looked like he was fifteen years old. First day on the job. They should have sent someone with more sense."

"They mixed up the girls," Anne explained, patting Emma's

leg. "Said Liz was in the ICU and Emma was just a little bruised up."

"That wasn't the problem," Daniel said. "I can forgive that. Honest mistake. It was the way he sounded. Like one of the girls being okay should be enough for us. Like Emma was just some extra part we could do without. I just about passed out."

"Both of us." Anne nodded. "No parent should ever have to have a police officer show up at their door like that."

Colin shook his head and frowned. He wanted to get out of their house, fast. His phone rang. Trina again. He sent it to voicemail. It rang again.

"I should get going," Colin said, kissing Emma's cheek and shaking Daniel's hand.

"I'll grab my purse." Anne followed him to the landing.

"You're going out?" Daniel asked, standing in the doorway.

"Yes, I won't be long." Anne returned to give him a kiss. "Colin wants to show me the right cream for this rash. I really don't think I can go another minute."

In his car, Colin answered his phone as he waited for Anne to get in.

Speaking in a whisper, Trina said, "Tell me you're almost here."

"I'm on my way." Colin struggled to decide what to do as he drove in circles. He wanted to confront Trina, but he'd agreed to leave it to Detective Green. Anne tried to grab the phone. He pulled away.

Trina pleaded, "Please hurry—I think someone's in my house."

Sure. Colin knew he was being played. What he couldn't figure out was why. He wanted to scream. To scream at Trina for answers. To find Liz. To find the truth. *Is she alive?* he wondered as he took a breath. He had to stay calm and not screw up Detective Green's plan. Wait on the warrant. Don't interfere. He thought of the change in Green's voice. He knew she was worried.

“She’s here,” Trina whispered. “Liz is in my house.”

The fear in her voice, once a source of guilt to Colin, now grated on his nerves. She was lying. He had to hang up. He tried to say he was on his way, but he stopped himself. Was she telling him the truth? Had Liz been there all along?

“Where is she, Trina?”

“I think she’s in the kitchen. I heard the back door. Are you almost here?”

“I was in the kitchen,” he said. “She wasn’t in the kitchen.”

“What? Oh, thank God. You’re here.”

“Where’s my wife, Trina?”

“Where are you?” she asked, raising her voice.

Clenching his teeth, he asked again. Anne took the phone from his hand and ended the call.

“Not over the phone, Colin,” Anne said. “If she runs, we won’t find her. How much farther?”

“We’re almost there,” he said, steadying his breath and turning toward Trina’s house.

“I know this neighborhood,” Anne mused, and mentioned something about the corned beef sandwich at the corner deli. “I’m glad you changed your mind and didn’t tell Daniel. Thank you.” She held his hand and gave it a squeeze. “We’ll find her.”

Colin didn’t respond. He didn’t like being played by her either.

His phone rang again.

“Detective Green,” Anne said, reading the screen.

Colin answered.

“Where are you?” Green asked.

“Driving.”

“I hope you’re not driving by Trina’s house.”

“No.”

“Good. Wherever you are, turn around and get to the station.”

“Why?”

“Where are you, Dr. Clarke?”

“Why do I need to go to the station? Do you have her?”

"Pull over, Dr. Clarke. We had an agreement."

"Do you have her?" Colin slowed at a red light, looked both ways, and pressed the gas.

"Not yet. There's something I need to tell you."

Anne motioned for him to hang up as he came to another red light, where two box trucks were blocking his way.

"Dr. Clarke... Colin. Pull over. There's something you need to know."

Colin watched the lights change and waited for the trucks to move. They turned right, one after the other, slowly, the second almost clipping the tail end of a silver Camry. Colin proceeded straight. Two more blocks. A garbage truck pulled in front, cutting him off. He wanted to drive on, to get to Trina. He was too curious.

"Okay," he said, pulling over. Anne huffed and crossed her arms. "What do I need to know?"

47
Owen

It's always lovely when it's sunny on my day off, Owen thought. He sipped his third cup of coffee, watching a swarm of starlings flutter around the cloudless blue sky. *Murmuration—that's what a group of starlings is called.* He remembered this from the bird book left by the previous owner of their house.

Sarah had been awake for a few hours, staring into the abyss. He'd need to find a new caregiver, even if Saoirse managed to set Sarah up at a daycare a few days a week. He hoped he'd hear something soon. It'd do Sarah good to get some fresh air and a change of scenery. Although the doctor had mentioned that familiar sights and sounds were more comforting. *What do the doctors know?* Sarah's foot tapped the beat as Owen worked out.

When he was finished, he ejected the workout video. "What say we head to the island today? Looks like a nice calm day. Lovely, as you say." He slid the blue floral curtains open.

Sarah's eyes turned to the local news on the TV. She seemed to focus, then pointed as a woman's picture appeared on the screen.

"Hmm. Yes, she's missing," he said, sitting on the edge of the bed. The reporter requested the public's help in locating the young woman, last seen on Achill Island. Friends reported that the woman had been seeking work over the high season. Her two children, ages three and five, had been left alone with a supply of food in their Athlone apartment.

Owen shook his head. "What is the world coming to? Leaving her children alone to make a few bucks?"

Sarah's voice sounded strangled as she said, "Her... her."

The reporter continued, "She was last seen leaving The Valley House to take a walk. One pink glove, believed to belong to Zlata, was found along the road."

"Zlata," Owen said, feeling around the duvet for the remote. "That's a pretty name." He clicked off the TV. Sarah's eyes raced as she tried to speak, her mouth failing her. He knew what she would say if she could string the words together. She'd woken up that night. She'd wandered out of bed. She shouldn't have done that. It wasn't safe. He'd be sure to let the daycare staff know that she was prone to wander. She could get lost. *Oh well,* he thought, *it can't be helped.*

"Come on, dear," he said. "Let's get you dressed, and we'll stop off and get some lunch for a picnic. Just like when we first arrived. You remember, don't you?"

Sarah's eyes raced, searching the black screen for information. Owen pulled off her nightgown and dressed her for the day.

Basking sharks circled in Keem Bay as clouds rolled in, covering the sun.

Owen spread a blanket on the sand, easing Sarah down to sit. He slid off her shoes and socks. She closed her eyes as the wind blew in from the ocean and the sun peeked out again.

Couples, families, and friends held the railing on the steep sidewalk. They carried bags of towels and toys and dragged coolers on wheels. Sarah pointed at one couple. Owen watched the waves.

"Cubbies," she said. Owen looked at the man's baseball cap.

Before he could turn Sarah's attention away, the all-too-eager tourists wandered over to say hello, imposing themselves on

Owen's day off.

The man droned on about their driving tour of Ireland, rattling off all the stops in order. Owen nodded along.

"Such a beautiful country. How long are you here for?" the man asked.

"Heading back to Dublin tonight," Owen said.

Sarah shook her head.

"Too bad." The man seemed genuinely upset. "It would have been nice to meet up for a pint."

"Yep, too bad."

The woman chatted with Sarah, whose eyes stayed fixed on the man's Chicago Cubs hat. She seemed to want to say something. The words were forever lost in her head. Much better that way.

Waving goodbye to their new best friends, Owen turned to look at Sarah. "I wish we were heading to Dublin tonight." Helping her up, he folded the blanket and tucked it under one arm while taking her hand in his other. "Then home to Chicago. I want to go home."

His eye caught a woman in a sun hat standing at the top of the walkway, their only exit from the bay. She stood there, staring. Those big eyes fixed on Owen, just like when she'd tried to corner him in the café. This time, he was trapped.

"Let's walk along the beach," he said, turning Sarah around back toward the water.

By the time Big Eyes caught up to them, Owen had left Sarah to sit on a rock as he climbed up another, luring his predator up the algae-covered, jagged edge. *Be careful,* he thought, *even a short fall could crack your skull, and that would be a shame.*

"Excuse me?"

The waves crashed, and Owen stopped. He stared at a dead crab in a tide pool.

"Sir?" Her voice drew nearer.

He waited for the right moment to turn around, pretending to be startled as she came up behind him. He looked around to see if anyone was watching. He had to be careful. Someone might see.

"Owen?"

To hear her say his name gave him pause. He climbed around the corner of a large rock formation. No one would see her fall.

"Yes," he said.

Crossing the bridge back to the mainland, Owen heard the rescue helicopter overhead flying to Keem. He'd hoped for a greater lead time. A hiker on the opposite side of the bay probably noticed her bright yellow coat. They called the Coast Guard before Owen could get Sarah into their car and drive away.

On the television that night, Sarah pointed when the reporter read the news of an unidentified woman who'd slipped while hiking on the rocks. She was alive but in critical condition. Thoughts and prayers for a full recovery. Owen hoped for the worst.

"Ow—Owen," Sarah said, her eyes searching his face.

"Yes, Sarah. We'll go home soon," he said, turning off the TV.

48
Colin

Colin struggled to understand what Detective Green had just told him about Trina.

"What do you mean she's been planning this for years?"

"I can't explain everything right now. Suffice it to say, you spending time with her has only fed into her plan. That's why you need to stay away from her and let me do my job."

"I just want to find my wife."

"Then turn around and let me do my job."

Colin looked at the cars parked up and down the street. A hand waved.

"Like I said, Dr. Clarke." She waved again. "You're giving her exactly what she wants."

"Are you tracking me?" he asked, feeling paranoid.

"Tracking? Go home, Dr. Clarke."

"How'd you know I was driving this way?"

"I didn't. I'm on my way to search Trina's house. We just got the warrant."

She held up a paper, swatting her hand to shoo him away.

"Okay," he said, ending the call.

"What is it?" Anne asked, tapping her knee with her fingertips.

"They've got a warrant. It's too late, Anne." Nodding toward

Green's car—now pulling away from the curb and making a U-turn—he said, "They're on their way to search her house. We should go home and prepare Daniel."

Colin started the car and shifted into drive.

"Wait." Anne reached over and shifted back to park.

"Anne, it's not just Daniel. We should go prepare for the worst." He could hear it in Green's voice.

"No."

"You don't get it. This lunatic has been planning this for years."

Anne looked around. "We're only a few blocks away?"

"Yeah."

"Let's just go and watch. Maybe Liz will come out. Maybe she's in on it with this woman. Maybe she's just hiding out."

"Hiding from what, Anne? From me? From me being such an awful husband for wanting to start a family with her?"

"That's not—it's just a lot of pressure on a young wife when her husband wants nothing more than to have a baby. You don't understand. It's demoralizing."

He didn't know what to say. "Maybe you think so, but Liz was very positive about continuing to try." He wasn't sure what was true anymore. He thought of Trent saying there had been a heartbeat. He tried to remember what Liz had said the last time they discussed the matter. Everything had been corrupted in his memory. Nothing seemed straight. The truth was, they hadn't discussed it. They never discussed it.

He could taste bile and blood rising up his throat. Not now. He focused on Liz.

"I would love nothing more than to go there and see Liz come walking out," he said, thinking of the time he'd spent in Trina's house. He couldn't help imagining Liz tied up in a bedroom upstairs, desperate for his help, while he and Trina sat downstairs, drinking whiskey and watching movies. Or Liz hiding in the basement, waiting for Colin to leave so she could come up and hang out with Trina.

"I have to know what's going on," he said, imagining the

worst once more.

"Then let's go watch," Anne said. "We can park down the block and stay in the car."

His phone rang. Trina again. He sent it to voicemail, then texted Liz's phone. *Enough of your games, Trina. I know it's you. Where's my wife?* He regretted the decision the moment he pressed send and knew he'd have to explain that decision to Green.

Colin didn't know what he really expected to happen when he pulled in front of a minivan just five houses down from Trina's, leaning over to get a better look.

"That's the house?" Anne asked, pointing at the brick two-story with two police cars parked out front. Green knocked at the door while Eddie leaned over the railing to peek in the front window.

Colin nodded to Anne, then looked back at Green. The mood had changed. Eddie said something to Green and jumped toward the door. Green signaled to the squad cars, drawing the gun from her holster.

Anne jumped out of the car and ran. Colin took off after her. Eddie kicked in the door. Officers swarmed inside.

Anne hesitated on Trina's front lawn. Catching up to her, Colin faced her, staring into her eyes. He had seen that look of terror in a patient's eyes once when, just as her baby entered the world, she went out.

Grasping her arm, Colin tried to hold Anne back as she wriggled loose, racing up the stairs into the house. Colin followed, hearing the unholy scream the moment he crossed the threshold. He stopped and watched. Anne pushed past the police officers. Dropping to the ground, she clung to the lifeless body.

"Elizabeth!" Anne screamed, rocking as she cradled her in her arms.

"Ma'am," an officer yelled. "Back up."

"No. No. No. Elizabeth," Anne repeated, flailing her limbs as Eddie lifted her to stand.

"Dr. Clarke," Green said, talking through clenched teeth.

"Take her outside."

"Anne, it's not her. It's not Liz," Colin said, taking in the scene.

"Yes, it is." She sobbed. "It's Elizabeth." Her body went limp as Eddie dragged her across the floor.

"No, Anne." Colin grabbed her from the detective, pinning her against the doorframe. "That's not Liz, it's Trina."

"It's her, it's her, it's her." Her voice rose to a crescendo.

"Take her outside!" Green shouted. "Now!"

Police officers approached. Colin grabbed Anne by the waist and, leaning against the railing, dragged her down to the sidewalk.

"Come on, Anne. Please walk. I have water in my car." He forced her face up to his and met her eyes.

She nodded and took a step.

Staggering to the car, Colin helped his mother-in-law into the passenger seat. Collapsing on the lawn, he caught his breath.

"I can't believe she's dead," Anne said, staring back at Trina's house. "How will I tell her father?" She turned to Colin, searching for answers.

"It's okay. You're just in shock. Here." He got up and walked to the trunk, returning with a bottle. "Take a deep breath. I wish I had something stronger for you." Twisting off the lid, he handed the water to Anne.

"I can't believe Elizabeth's dead," she mumbled.

"Anne, that wasn't her. It wasn't Liz. That was Trina."

Her eyes pleaded with him as the bottle of water dropped, spilling out onto the street. She grabbed his wrist.

"Colin... that was Elizabeth."

49
Colin

"I know you think it was Liz," Colin said, rubbing Anne's shoulder. "It's not. That was Trina. The crazy woman who set this all up. It wasn't Liz."

She closed her eyes as an ambulance passed by. A fire truck blocked them in. Colin looked up at the chaos of lights and people moving around.

"Get in the car, Colin." Her voice was so quiet, he had to ask her to repeat herself.

In the driver's seat, Colin leaned his head back and rubbed his eyes, watching the house for Trina to be wheeled out. And Liz. He watched for his wife, hoping she'd come walking out of the front door and down the steps. Either a prisoner freed from her captor or an accomplice in some crazy scheme. Maybe even Trina's killer. He didn't care—he just wanted to see her alive.

His phone rang. Felix. He sent it to voicemail.

"Anne, we shouldn't have come—"

"Trina?"

"Yes," he said, relieved to hear her sorting it out.

She shook her head. "I don't understand."

"I don't either," Colin said, hoping Trina would somehow pull through and explain herself.

"I didn't know she knew Liz. It all makes sense now."

Colin tilted his head, turning to Anne. "What are you saying?"

"Her name's not Trina. It's Elizabeth. She's my first daughter."

Colin shook his head, biting his tongue for her to continue.

"I was married young, before Daniel. Ben—Benjamin. That was my first husband. We had a daughter. I named her Elizabeth. Things didn't work out. I lost touch."

"I'm sorry."

"Thank you." She squeezed his hand.

"Daniel didn't know about your first marriage?"

"No. He thought he was bringing home such a sweet, innocent girl. I loved him from the moment we met. He's always been good to me. When we had the twins, I named the first one Elizabeth. I knew she would never replace my first little girl. It was just sort of... to honor her, you know?"

"I do." Colin fished around in the glove box for a packet of tissues and handed them to her. "How did you know this was her house?"

"I've been here many times over the past few years."

"You found her?"

"She found me. She needed my help—I owed it to her."

"Money?"

Anne nodded.

He wanted to ask if she was sure Trina was really her first daughter, not just some scam artist. "Was she blackmailing you?"

She wiped her eyes and nodded again. "She knew I hadn't told Daniel."

Colin saw a paramedic emerge from Trina's house pulling a stretcher. Trina's body was covered from head to toe. He felt sick.

"This has been going on for years?" he asked.

"Yes."

"How much money?"

"I don't know. This has to be what it's all about."

Colin was still waiting to see Liz walk out with the police.

"What are you saying, Anne? Did Trina kidnap Liz for some

kind of ransom? Was she threatening to tell Daniel? Did you know?"

"No. Nothing like that."

"Then what? Tell me what you know." Colin tried to restrain the growing anger as his mind searched for answers. He tried to breathe and listen.

"I didn't have a way to pay her without Daniel knowing. I asked Liz to—"

"Liz was paying her for you? Why would she do that?" Colin rubbed his eyes. "Let me guess... two thousand a month."

"She told you?"

"No. It's the reason the police haven't been breaking down doors, looking for her." His breathing quickened, and his heart raced. He tried not to raise his voice. It was too late. "They found her account. She was taking out two grand every month in cash. They assumed she'd been stashing it to make a break from me." He rolled his eyes, shaking his head. "Dammit, Anne."

"I'm sorry, Colin. I didn't realize." She blew her nose.

"Why now?"

"I'm sorry?"

"Liz has been paying her for years. Why now? What changed? Why is all this happening? Help me understand, because you sure as hell seem to know a lot more than you're letting on."

Her sobbing returned, and she held her head in her hands. "I'm sorry. I didn't mean for this to happen."

"The last time you saw Liz, what did you talk about? You said she was worked up about something. You said it was about me. Was it really about Trina?"

"No. No, it wasn't. I didn't know they knew each other."

Colin was losing patience. He could tell she knew more. His fists clenched—he wanted to lean over and strangle the truth out of her.

"Anne," he said, gritting his teeth, breathing hard through his nostrils, "Trina has done something to my wife. That psycho is dead and can't help us now. I need you to tell me what you know.

No matter how insignificant."

They sat in silence, staring at each other. Neither moved an inch. Finally, Anne spoke.

"I think Liz is behind all this."

Colin let out a long exhale and threw his hands in the air. "Why? Why would she do this?"

"My first Elizabeth was a good girl. My second has always been..." She shook her head. "She's never cared about any of us. She's a shell of a human being. Don't look at me like that. It's the truth. She didn't care when Emma almost died in the accident. It never bothered her that she was left a vegetable. She didn't care how it affected us. She's the psycho. Not my first Elizabeth. She was a good girl."

Colin thought he understood his wife. He always knew she wasn't emotional. The words Anne used stung. They stung because they were true. "Why? Why did Liz do this?"

"I don't know," Anne said, blowing her nose. "To get back at me for caring about my first daughter? To punish me for my choices? I don't know. She's always been a mystery to me. Always a liar."

The liar bit caught Colin off guard. *Liz isn't the only liar,* he thought, looking at her. "There's more you aren't telling me. Please, Anne."

50
Colin

"It's no secret to you," Anne said. "You said it yourself—you know how Liz is."

Colin nodded, hating to agree with her. Hating that it was true.

"I always suspected something was off, even as a baby. She never cried. As a little girl, she never showed remorse. Then the accident. That's when I could no longer deny it."

"Tell me about the accident," Colin said. He'd never heard the story from Anne.

"It was horrible. Daniel still blames himself."

"Why?"

"The girls wanted to go see some scary movie. He was planning to bring them, but he had the opportunity to work overtime. He'd been worried about the added expense of them both starting college in the fall. When I think what that overtime check cost us..."

Colin watched the ambulance drive away. Police officers left Trina's house, milling about on the lawn, chatting with each other in between calls.

Anne folded and tugged at the tissue.

"Liz drove to the movie?" Colin already knew the answer.

"Yes. Emma didn't like to drive at night. We'd just had

months of rain. The retention pond next to the theater was full. After the movie, Liz drove into it. Right away, I knew she'd done it on purpose."

"On purpose?" That didn't sound like his wife, the woman who'd bend over backward to save a patient's life.

"Nothing made sense. The story Liz told—she was such a good liar, but even this sounded far-fetched. Daniel wanted to believe her. He was in denial. Still is. The police didn't believe her. Why should we?"

"What'd she say?"

"She claimed that after the movie, some guy ran up to the car, banging on her window and yelling at her. She said she thought he was trying to kill them. Probably just scared from the movie."

Colin had never heard that part of the story. He tried to imagine that night.

Detective Green and her partner walked out of Trina's house. They stopped on the porch, looking around as they spoke. Colin wanted to go to them, to see what they'd found, if anything pointed to where he could find Liz. Firemen returned to their truck beside Colin's car, joking around with one another.

"Is that why she backed into the retention pond? To get away from the man?" Colin asked.

"So she claimed. It never added up. The police said the security cameras didn't catch anything."

"How'd they get out of the water? Liz told me she couldn't remember."

Anne shrugged.

"And no one saw this mystery man?"

"Colin. There wasn't any man."

He watched the firemen climb into the truck and pull away. Starting his own car, unsure of where to go but desperate to get away, Colin looked at Green. She was looking back at him. She motioned for Colin to wait as she ran toward him.

Opening the window, Colin said, "I know. I said I wouldn't come. We just wanted to see if Liz was here. We're leaving now."

"Oh no you aren't, Dr. Clarke. I specifically told you to get out of here, and you came anyway. Now, we'll need to continue this discussion down at the station. If you don't mind?"

Colin pursed his lips. "Okay. Am I free to drive myself?"

Green squinted and raised an eyebrow. "Don't get fresh. Of course, you are free to do as you'd like. Remember, we're trying to find your wife. Unless, of course, you aren't interested. In that case, would you mind letting me know so I can call it a day? I've been working since two o'clock this morning, and my nerves are damn near fried."

Colin rubbed his forehead. "Sorry. I'll drop my mother-in-law off and go straight to the station."

Green laughed. "Like hell. Anne Thompson, I'm going to need you to come with me." Her hand gripped the door handle, and the other held the window. "Unlock the door."

"What's going on?" Colin asked.

Anne froze, her eyes wide with fright.

"Unlock the door," Green repeated.

Colin's hand fumbled for the button. The detective opened the door.

"A witness saw you here earlier today, ma'am." She pulled Anne out of the car.

Colin opened his door as Green slammed the passenger side closed.

"Dr. Clarke, I suggest you get in your car and meet me at the station before I have Eddie come over and give you a lift too."

Colin's foot touched the street, and then he stopped himself. He knew no good could come from ignoring any more of Green's demands.

He watched the detective escort Anne away and picked up his phone. There was a voicemail from Felix. Colin thought of his mother. He couldn't bear to listen to more revelations about his own past. Still, he wondered if his cousin could be of some help. Knowing he'd have to be completely honest with Felix, he took a breath and texted him.

Anne's head was barely visible in the back seat as Colin followed Green's car to the police station.

51
Owen

A fly buzzed in Owen's ear as he listened to the morning news. Every channel reported on the unidentified comatose woman. Then a plea for the public's help in finding the missing woman, Zlata. The image of her pink, fingerless glove flashed across the screen.

Owen exhaled and looked at Sarah. Her eyes raced around the room, seeming to cry out with information to help the police. Owen changed the channel and grabbed his uniform.

Paying close attention to the gossip on the bus and in the café, Owen learned as much as he could about Big Eyes. Rumors and gossip.

Walking along the bus stop queue at Westport, he eyed his latest options. Two young ladies stood arm in arm; one seemed ill. He didn't have the patience for another high-maintenance woman in his life. Two groups up, a young woman with layers padding her slight figure caught his eye. She wore a scarf wrapped around her neck, up to her ears. Checking her watch, she looked around for the bus driver, running late from his break.

"I'm here now," Owen said, tipping his hat to show he'd read her mind.

Looking confused and perhaps not understanding what he'd said, she smiled and nodded.

The passengers filed in, paying their fares and grabbing their tickets. He rushed them along. Then his precious new friend stepped aboard, smiling at him again.

"Good afternoon. Where to?"

"Umm, Dumha Acha."

"Where's that, now?"

"You go to... Dumha Acha? Hotel by the sea?" Pulling out her phone, she swiped around, her porcelain fingers shaking.

He wanted nothing more than to take her for a cup of coffee and show her the sights. Acclimate her to her new surroundings. Lead her.

"Marta." A man, out of breath and red-faced, in ripped jeans and dirty white tennis shoes, jumped up behind her onto the bus.

"Sir, please step back," Owen said, saving her from the pushy, testosterone-fueled slob. Owen's new pet turned around and squealed with delight, throwing her arms around the man.

"Dooagh," he said. "Two for Dooagh." Two fat fingers waved in Owen's face.

Owen would have thrown them both off the bus if he hadn't already marked the girl as his own property.

The drive to Achill was pleasant for the most part as Owen watched Marta between listening to other passengers talk about Big Eyes. One woman said she'd heard the poor woman might never wake up. Owen wanted to be sure of that.

By the Keel stop, his imagination had worked out several ways to finish Big Eyes off. Nothing seemed feasible. He wasn't a huge fan of jeopardizing his freedom with anything too risky.

A buzzer sounded, and he saw the filthy arm of Marta's boyfriend up in the air, pressing the call button like some royalty alerting the servants. Owen pulled off to the side of the road at the hotel. He watched a sheep scratch its backside on the sign. A large cat, black with patches of white, ran off when the couple approached the front steps.

Alone on the bus, Owen turned on the radio and nodded

along to the beat as he drove to the end of the line and went into the pub.

"Hiya, Owen," a regular said. "Did you hear about the mystery woman? Found over at Keem yesterday."

"People on the bus were talking." He nodded his head. "Terrible business."

"Probably trying to take a selfie and slipped," another man said.

The publican set a glass of water on the bar. Owen held it and nodded again, agreeing with the theory.

"Did you see anything?" the first man asked.

"Me?" Owen took a gulp.

"I saw you and Sarah drive past."

Finishing his water, Owen set the glass down on the bar. "Didn't see a thing."

"It's a big place," the second man offered as an excuse.

Owen left.

He always missed that in Chicago, houses were close, but neighbors respected privacy. He missed the city. He'd even started to miss that heart-attack snow.

While switching to the 440 in Westport towards Knock Airport, he hoped to hear news about Big Eyes. He expected maybe a bad update. He paused to pick up some employees and visitors outside the hospital.

No luck, he thought. The day was lovely, and all anyone could think to discuss was the weather as they drove along.

That night, he thought of his new friend Marta and imagined freeing her from that horrible slob of a man. *Perhaps she needs a job*, he thought, drifting off to sleep.

52
Colin

"Felix, I need your help." Colin followed Detective Green's car, his eyes watching his mother-in-law's head sinking farther down as they arrived at the police station.

"Sure thing, cuz, anything."

He took a breath. Now that he was on the call, Colin found it hard to admit he needed the man's help. Ever since meeting his distant cousin, Colin had been irritated by his droning on about one start-up after another. Desperately looking to tap into his newfound relatives' pockets for an influx of Kickstarter cash. Colin would offer a check just to get him to stop. Still, like Felix had said before, they were family, right?

For the first time, Colin had to admit his life was not quite as perfect as he'd always led Felix to believe.

"My wife is missing. It's serious..."

He told the story, trying his best to stick to the basic points: wife missing, the only lead dead, mother-in-law brought in for questioning.

"Dang. You should have told me sooner. How can I help?"

"I'm not sure. The police took forever tracing Liz's phone. When they finally did, it was too late. I thought maybe there's something they missed that can lead to Liz. They don't seem to have the same abilities that someone might..." Never comfortable with outright asking someone to break the law, Colin hesitated to finish his request.

"Ah, I hear ya, I hear ya, cuz. I'll tell you what I'll do. I'll put together a team of hackers on my end and offer a bounty on the dark web."

Colin wasn't sure if Felix was serious or joking. He almost laughed.

Green opened the car door ahead of him and helped Anne to her feet.

"The detective—her tone has changed. I think she's expecting the worst," Colin said. "Felix... whatever it takes to find Liz, okay?"

"Dang, cuz. You don't think... could she be...?"

Dead, Colin thought, not wanting to say the word either. "I don't know what to think. Her mom thinks she's alive and behind all this. What do I know?"

"And this Trina woman? How'd she die?"

"It looked like an overdose. Honestly, she didn't strike me as the type to use drugs." Colin parked his car and walked into the police station. "I have to go. And Felix—whatever it takes."

"Don't worry, cuz. I'm on it."

Colin was brought to an interrogation room to wait. The desk sergeant mentioned it was only because they were having renovations done and there weren't many quiet areas available. The longer he sat staring at his cold cup of coffee, the more he questioned the sergeant's honesty.

"Dr. Clarke," Green said, walking in with the case file and two bottles of water. Kicking out a chair, she sat down. Eddie closed the door behind them and pulled another chair over from the corner.

"Where's Anne?" Colin asked.

"She's fine. Dr. Clarke, why don't we start with you walking me through your movements today?"

"My movements?"

"Yes, we're especially interested in the time leading up to us seeing you driving around Trina's neighborhood."

"I wasn't driving around her neighborhood. I was driving to her house."

"Why is that? After I specifically told you to meet me at the station. Why would you be racing me to her house?"

"I wasn't racing you. She called me saying there was someone in her house. She was scared and wanted me to come over. I told her I'd come. Then you called and told me she was behind the texts coming from Liz's phone."

"Then what'd you do?"

"I went to Anne."

"Why?"

"To prepare her."

"Prepare her for what?"

Colin leaned back in his chair and rubbed his face. "Liz's dad doesn't know any of this is going on. He thinks she's in Phoenix, busy working. He's a good man. I thought he should know before you found anything."

"How were you so certain we'd find something?"

Colin shook his head. He looked down at the file. "I don't know, I just..."

"Okay. Why did you bring Anne with you to Trina's?"

"She insisted on coming. I—"

"Let's talk about our conversation. When I told you Trina had been planning this for years... that made you angry?"

"Angry?" Colin shook his head. He hadn't had time to be angry. He felt confused and wanted answers.

"When you heard she was behind it all, you decided to confront her yourself before I arrived?"

Colin hadn't wanted to confront her. That had been Anne's idea. He wondered how she was holding up after being questioned by the police.

"I thought I could reason with her and find my wife."

"And you dragged Liz's mom along?" She handed Colin a bottle of water and twisted open one for herself, taking a long drink.

"She insisted."

"Right. You do know Trina and Anne knew each other? That's why Anne was seen at Trina's house earlier today, by a witness."

Colin nodded again and opened his water. "She just told me."

"Strange. Here we were thinking this was just some simple, run-of-the-mill love triangle." Green looked at Eddie, who shook his head.

Swiping around on her phone, Green settled on a website.

"Do you recognize this?" she asked. The screen was black, with a lime-green logo in the center.

Colin stared.

Green clicked her pen. "Yes or no."

Colin's eyes traced the lines. *Ask for a lawyer*, he thought.

"Dr. Clarke, do you recognize this website?"

"Yes."

53
Colin

Green set her phone on the table. "I wasn't familiar with the website when I first saw it. Turns out, it's a vigilante group."

Colin didn't flinch.

"The Squatter Squad. TSS. The logo's a monogram. Are you familiar with this group, Dr. Clarke?"

He nodded.

"Why don't you tell me what it is? I'm still a little confused."

"It's a squatter remediation service."

"Meaning what, exactly?"

Colin exhaled hard and rolled his eyes.

"I'm sorry. Am I annoying you?"

"It's stupid—the business... the business is stupid. It's a service to remove squatters from your property without involving the courts."

"Wow." Green turned to her partner. "My friend's mom died a couple of years ago, and before she could get the property fixed up and sold, squatters moved in."

"Is that right?" Eddie asked.

"Tore the place apart, drug paraphernalia everywhere, pawned her mom's stuff, ran up the utility bills... Took almost a year to get them out."

"Terrible," Eddie said.

Green swiped on her phone. The logo glowed. "She could have used one of these—what did you call it—a squatter remediation service? The problem with these vigilante groups is they can be misused. Isn't that right? What do you think, Dr. Clarke? Could people misuse these groups?"

Ask for a lawyer, he thought, but he had nothing to hide. "Can I get a cup of coffee?"

"I suppose," Green said, motioning to Eddie, who stood up and left the room. "So, what do you think?" she asked Colin. "Could people misuse these groups?"

"I couldn't say."

"Couldn't say?"

"I'm not completely familiar with how they operate. So, no. I couldn't say."

Eddie returned with three coffees.

"Hmm." Green blew steam from her cup. "Well, it's my understanding that the homeowner, finding themselves with a squatter problem, would turn to a company like this. They'd remove the problem without the courts—which, like my friend discovered, can be quite difficult."

"And expensive," Eddie said.

"That's right," Green continued. "A company like this offers a quick solution at a reasonable rate. The homeowner pays half up front, and their problem disappears."

"Not completely," Eddie said.

"That's right," Green continued. "It seems some groups forcibly remove the squatter while others just kill them right there on the property. Staging it to look like a suicide or overdose, of course. They leave a calling card to let the owner know they'd been around to exterminate their squatter problem, and the final payment was due."

Colin still thought it sounded stupid.

"Are we going to find a TSS calling card at Trina's, Dr. Clarke?"

"What? Why? No."

"You're sure?"

Colin furrowed his brow and looked at Eddie, then back to Green.

Green set down her coffee. "Dr. Clarke, did you hire The Squatter Squad to kill Trina?"

Colin's mouth opened. No words came out. He cleared his throat. "What?" he asked. "That's ridiculous. Of course not."

Green exhaled. "I have to ask. Did you use The Squatter Squad to have your wife, Elizabeth Clarke, killed or forcibly removed?"

"Removed?" Colin shook his head, his lips quivering. "No."

Opening the case file, Green pulled out a sheet of paper. "Do you recognize this check?"

Standing, he flipped his chair onto the floor. "No, no," Colin said. He held his hands up. "Hold on. Wait—"

"You don't recognize this canceled check from your bank account?"

"No, it's not— Wait. Listen—"

The check he'd signed in haste to get Felix to shut up sat on the table. A glaring incrimination. On the memo line, the letters *TSS*.

"This is your writing?" Green asked.

Colin didn't answer.

"What did you get for ten thousand dollars, Dr. Clarke?"

The amount hadn't seemed like a big deal at the time. Colin didn't want to admit the truth, but he loved to hear Felix grovel for money. Before every ancestry meetup, Colin would be sure to pull out his checkbook just for the occasion. Felix had asked him to simply transfer the funds. Colin refused. He liked the tactile feel of writing out the check. Writing it out slowly, while Felix watched and waited, drooling with greed. Colin had felt superior back then. Now, he felt foolish.

"Pay to the order of... Felix something? I can't make it out," Green said. "Who's he?"

"Felix Everett. Please. Detective Green"—his hands were still up in surrender—"this has nothing to do with Liz. I can explain."

"Sit down, Dr. Clarke." Green walked around the table, picking up the chair.

Colin took a breath and sat.

Green's eyes never left Colin's as he explained his cousin's endless stream of start-ups. "I've given the same amount to a few of them. Check my account. I have an information packet at home. I think it's in the top drawer—"

Green snapped her fingers.

"Hold on," she said, flipping through the case file. Popping her tongue, she tapped her fingertips on her chin, thinking. "Right," she said, opening her notepad. "Here it is. Felix Everett. I thought that sounded familiar." She read her notes and looked up. "What is your wife's relationship with Felix Everett?" Green asked, turning to a clean sheet of paper.

"They've never met."

"Sure they have." She flipped back to her notes. "Right here. She and Aaron Townsend met with Felix for funding. Some apartment building..."

"No, I don't think they—"

There was a knock at the door, and a uniformed officer popped her head in.

"Sit tight," Green said, leaving the room. Eddie followed behind. The door closed.

Dropping his forehead to the table, Colin decided he wouldn't say anything else without a lawyer.

54
Colin

More than an hour passed before Green and Eddie returned to the interview room. The word "lawyer" was on the tip of Colin's tongue.

"Dr. Clarke, sorry to keep you waiting. Let's put a pin in your story." Green opened the case file and flipped through some papers. Skimming a page, she looked up. "It seems Trina has done this before."

Colin furrowed his brow and waited for her to go on.

"Five years ago, she was accused of stalking a man. When he tried to get a restraining order, she allegedly kidnapped his daughter."

"Allegedly?"

"No proof. The girl showed up three weeks later on a playground in Kansas City, unharmed. Then three years ago, she set her sights on a new guy she'd met on some internet dating app. He alleges that after one date, she'd show up everywhere. His home, his work, at his sister's wedding in Vancouver, on a cruise in Alaska. When he finally went to the police, his dog disappeared."

"Did they find the dog?"

Green nodded.

"Let me guess," Colin said. "On a playground in Kansas

City?"

"Yeah."

"So." Colin rubbed his eyes. "You think Liz might turn up there?"

Green spread her hands. "It's worth a look. I contacted KC police. They have a couple of cars out."

Colin realized he'd been holding his breath and let out a long exhale. He was exhausted and hungry. More than anything, he was confused.

"Dr. Clarke, I'd like to start over from the beginning." Green picked up her pen, clicking it three times. "How did you come to meet Trina Scott?"

Back to Trina. Good, he thought, eager to help. "A medical conference in Sarasota. She gave a talk about protecting patients' records. She's in IT, I think."

"And that was last year?"

"Yes." Colin's stomach growled.

Green leaned back in her chair, raising her arms above her head. Stretching, she eyed her partner and said, "We need more people going through all those devices we recovered."

"I'll put in a call," Eddie said, standing up.

"Thanks. Would you mind bringing Anne in here?"

Eddie left, closing the door behind himself as Green continued. "You didn't meet Trina on a dating app?"

Colin shook his head, and she made a face. She seemed to be sympathizing with him.

"You've never met any women on dating apps? Maybe before you met your wife?"

"Well, yeah."

"So, you did have a profile on some app?"

"Yes. I talked to a few women. After meeting one out for a drink, I knew it wasn't for me."

"Picture didn't match reality?"

"Do you think Trina was one of the women I talked to on there? That was years ago." He didn't think it was possible. Still, he couldn't help but feel responsible.

Eddie opened the door, stepping aside for Anne to walk in and take a seat.

"The truth is, we don't know anything about Trina before a few years ago. But I think she does. Have a seat, Anne. We're going to figure this out together."

55
Colin

Colin looked at Detective Green and then back at Anne. He couldn't help but feel like he'd missed some crucial information they both knew. Eddie dragged a chair into the room from the hall and pulled it around for Anne to sit beside Colin.

"We'll check the dating app to see if Trina first saw you there. But," Green glanced at Colin and then Anne, "why not share more about your community?"

Community? Colin stared at Anne. Her eyes stayed fixed on her hands, her fingers tightly interlaced, one thumb rubbing the other.

"What would you like to know?" Anne finally looked up and asked.

"Do a lot of girls leave?" Green asked.

Colin's eyes darted from one person to the next, trying to understand what they were talking about. The detectives remained focused on Anne.

"A few over the years," Anne said.

"And you both left through the same woman." Green checked her notes. "Constance Walters?"

"Yes. I'd been in contact with Connie over the years. She helped me get situated at first. After that, I was pretty much on my own."

Colin cleared his throat to get Anne's attention. She ignored him and kept talking.

"Whenever a girl left, Connie would give her our contact info."

"For support?"

"Yes. Encouragement and financial support."

"And you'd been giving Trina money each month to help her get on her feet?"

Anne nodded. "I know what it's like to struggle on the outside."

Colin couldn't believe how easily the lies rolled off Anne's tongue. *Or did she lie to me before, and this is the truth?* he wondered, waiting for her to mention that Trina was her first daughter.

Green flipped through her notes. "And you're sure you don't know Trina's real name?"

Elizabeth.

"No," Anne said.

Why are you lying? Colin thought as he finished his water, crinkling the bottle to get her attention. Anne wouldn't look.

"Okay," Green continued. "You didn't want your husband to know, so you asked Liz to give her money? Why's that?"

"Yes. He never could understand what it's like."

"Why would Liz give her that much money for years?" Green asked Anne before looking at Colin. "Sorry, Dr. Clarke. It seems all that money your wife was taking from her account each month went to Trina."

"Oh, so not a stockpile of cash to leave me?" Colin asked, not even trying to hide his irritation. His stomach growled again.

"I'm sorry," Green said.

"Fine," Colin said. "I don't understand. How do they know each other?" He pressed the issue, wanting to expose Anne and get to the bottom of her lies.

"Trina's from Anne's community in Indiana."

"Her community?" Colin asked.

"Yes, dear. The Amish community I grew up in," Anne said,

holding Colin's hand.

"Amish?" Colin stifled a laugh.

Anne squeezed. "Yes, Colin. Trina was a girl from our community. When she left, Connie gave her my number. She was struggling to make it on her own. She kept asking more of me. More money. More of my time. She even asked to move in with me. I think she wanted to be my daughter. I had a feeling she was a bit... unbalanced. I thought I could help. I brought her into our lives—it's all my fault."

Anne looked back at the detectives. "I told Lizzie about Trina. That's why she gave her money. She was trying to help me, and she didn't want her dad to be bothered. He's been through so much with Emma and the accident. Thank God for our sweet Lizzie." Dabbing her eyes and shaking her head, she looked down at her lap and sighed.

Colin swallowed hard, but his anger continued to rise. Anne's lies flowed smoothly, as if she had practiced every word. Calling her out would only backfire—she would say to *handle things in the family*. He forced his face to remain neutral, biting back his frustration. *Not here. Not now.*

"Yes, well," Green said. "You couldn't have known she would have done all this. You were just trying to help. Based on everything..." She flipped her notebook pages and set her pen down, folding her hands. "Dr. Clarke, we found detailed records on Trina's computer. They track your every movement from the past few years. Every appointment, every delivery, every shopping trip, everything you've done. It seems the conference in Sarasota presented her with the opportunity to enter your life. Since then, she's been planning."

"What are you saying?" Anne asked.

Green frowned. "It would appear Trina was planning to replace Liz as Colin's wife."

An officer knocked at the door and poked her head in. "Excuse me." She motioned for Green to join her in the hall.

"Replace? What does that mean?" Anne asked, looking at Colin and yanking his hand.

He didn't respond.

Green returned with a laptop and an evidence bag. She pulled out a phone. Colin knew.

"Liz," he whispered.

Green nodded. "We recovered it in a garbage can down Trina's alley. Do you recognize these?" she asked, pouring the rest of the bag's contents onto the table.

Colin looked each item over. There were memories attached to every one of her possessions. The wallet Colin had given her for Christmas. Her mirror compact, its edge chipped on their trip to Vegas. The gross lip balm that had melted on the dashboard of Liz's car.

"Where's her purse?" he asked.

"I don't know. These were found dumped in a box in Trina's basement. Her laptop's been wiped clean."

She exhaled through pursed lips. Her eyes shifted back and forth from Anne to Colin. "I'm sorry to say, but we need to prepare for the very real possibility that Liz has been dead this entire time. Mrs. Thompson, Dr. Clarke... we are now treating Liz's disappearance as a homicide investigation."

Anne sobbed. Colin stared in shock.

He hadn't wanted to go to the police at first. He hadn't wanted to look foolish reporting her missing like he'd done with his first wife, only for Liz to show up the next day. When she started texting, he knew it didn't sound like her. He didn't want to tell the police. Again, foolish. He hadn't known how to explain that it didn't sound like her.

Anne hadn't wanted to go to the police either—Colin was sure of that. He listened to her staccato breaths, sharp and uneven between sobs. She'd said she thought Liz was behind it all, yet Anne was acting as if she had something to hide. Meanwhile, Liz was most likely lying dead somewhere.

Anne *was* hiding something—Colin knew it—and she wasn't planning to tell the police. But if he stayed calm and played it right, she'd tell him.

"Did you find any evidence of my wife being at Trina's

house? You've checked the basement and the garage?"

He knew they had. If only he could think of something to say to spark an idea of where Liz might be. The voice in his head, the one calling him to his apartment to binge, laughed at him now. He thought of all the times he'd run off to be the knight in shining armor for his patients, showing up their husbands. And for what? As soon as the babies were delivered and the euphoria hit, Colin no longer existed to them. He did it all for fleeting moments of pride. All the while ignoring Liz, taking her for granted. Now she was gone.

Green picked up Liz's laptop and phone, piling them with the folder and her notepad. "You should both go home and get some rest. We'll find her."

Not her—her body, Colin thought, but he didn't say it out loud.

He and Anne walked to his car.

"What was that all about?" Colin asked, opening the passenger side door. "Amish?" He shook his head.

"Please, Colin," Anne squeezed his hand. "I have to tell her father."

56
Owen

"Where's your boyfriend today?" Owen asked his newest friend, Marta, as she boarded the bus. He hoped she'd say the boyfriend had run off and abandoned her in Ireland. All alone.

"My husband? He started a job." She counted out her bus fare and handed it to Owen.

Husband. Owen frowned. "Did he? What's he doing then?"

"Construction." She made a face that showed a bit of embarrassment.

Owen winked. "It's a fine job he's doing."

"Thank you," she said, blushing as she found a seat.

The news reports about the mystery woman who'd taken a fall at Keem Bay had quieted down. Owen had hoped that meant she'd died. Unfortunately, it turned out she was still in her coma. The only upside he could find was that she was quiet. Quiet and out of Owen's hair—for the time being, at least.

He thought about her whenever he drove past the hospital and at the end of the line on the island leading up to Keem. Most of the time, though, Owen thought about Marta.

He'd never acquired a pet who had a husband, but it couldn't be helped. Owen had already chosen her that day as she checked her watch, looking for the bus driver. Later, Owen realized Marta had been looking for her slob husband, the one trying to find menial work to make a few bucks.

No, he'd never had a friend with a husband. In some way, the idea sparked a bit of excitement in him. Like the first time he'd approached a nice young lady walking alone in the dark. The way she startled and clutched her purse. So sweet.

The idea of outwitting a husband and taking his wife brought a freshness to Owen's process. Surely, Sarah would die soon enough, and he could go home to Chicago. Until then, he'd have something new to occupy his time.

The next day, when Marta boarded the bus, Owen held his phone to his ear. He held up his other hand for her to wait.

"Yes, that's right. It's not a difficult job. Just looking for someone friendly to sit with my wife while I'm at work..." Owen said into his phone. "Well, sure, let me know if you think of someone for the job." Owen pretended to end the call and set his phone down, mumbling about hoping to find someone soon. When Marta didn't take the hint and offer, he said to her, "You wouldn't happen to know anyone looking for a job, would you?"

Two days later, Marta arrived early, following Owen through the house as he showed her the kettle and how to use the television remote. She wouldn't need to start cooking and cleaning just yet. Owen could tell she'd been a bit spoiled in her earlier years and would need time to learn those things.

"What about that room?" She pointed to the locked door.

"I'm running late." He checked his watch. "I'll show you that room later... I promise."

On the bus into Westport, there was quite a bit of chatter that Owen couldn't quite follow. Either too many passengers were speaking at once, or they were speaking Gaelic. *How irritating*, he thought, trying to eavesdrop. No one mentioned Big Eyes.

"I hope she's dead," he mumbled to himself. Then he worried

she'd recover and return.

Over his break, as he picked at his usual blueberry-lemon crumble, Owen considered going to the hospital to inquire. It was risky. He'd have to think of a convincing lie.

On the 450 to Achill, Owen knew he'd be looking over his shoulder until he knew what happened to her. Amnesia? With his luck? Not likely. No. If she recovered, she'd know exactly what she was doing, who she was, and what she'd come to the West of Ireland for. And poor Owen, tethered to his bus route with nowhere to hide.

57
Colin

Colin tried to come to terms with Liz being dead. He prayed her body would be found soon as he turned out of the police station's parking lot. Still, he clung to the hope that she was alive.

Anne grabbed the steering wheel, yanking it back.

"Are you trying to get us killed?" Colin asked, slamming on the brake.

"I told you. I have to tell her father that she's dead."

"I know. Let go. I'm taking you home."

"No. The police don't know for sure she's dead. Let them investigate. I have to tell Ben."

"Ben?" Colin knew when the name left his lips. Anne meant to tell her first husband that their Trina—Elizabeth—was dead. He couldn't keep her lies straight. "Where does he live?"

"Indiana."

Colin flipped his blinker from right to left and frowned. "Let me guess, near an Amish community. Is that where you came up with that ridiculous story to tell the police? I can't believe they bought it."

"It's the truth."

"Really?" Colin sighed. "Why'd you tell me Trina's your daughter?"

"Because she is."

Colin clenched his teeth and inhaled deeply. "Okay. Why didn't you mention to the police that Trina's your daughter?"

Anne shrugged. "They didn't ask."

"You've got to be kidding..." Colin said under his breath as he checked both ways and pulled onto the road. Everything Detective Green told him replayed in his head. Remembering the part about Liz knowing Felix gave him hope. At the first red light, he swiped on his phone to call.

There was a new text from Liz's phone. A text from earlier, in response to the text he'd sent calling Trina out for her lies. He opened it.

Sorry, Colin. I encouraged Liz to go to him. I thought... I don't know what I thought. Can't blame a girl for trying, right? I really am sorry. Trina.

"What is it?" Anne asked, trying to read over his shoulder. The light changed, and a car beeped.

Him? Colin thought, rereading the text. *I encouraged Liz to go to him?* The car behind him beeped again, swerving around, honking and speeding off. *Him? Felix?* He dialed.

Suicide note. Colin mouthed the words.

"What?" Anne asked as Felix answered the phone.

"Hey, cuz. About time you called me back. I have some news about your mom."

"Where's my wife?" Colin asked, trying not to yell. Another car slammed on the horn.

"Whoa. What?"

"You know her."

"No. Settle down. I've never met her."

"Yes, you have. Years ago. She came to you with Aaron Townsend to fund a building of tiny homes. The Beehive." Colin pulled off to the side of the road, flipping on his hazards.

"Yeah, I remember. Hold up, Elizabeth Thompson? Dang, she's your wife?"

"Don't pretend you don't know. Is she off working somewhere for one of your shady businesses?"

"Shady?"

"What about that surrogacy center? You asked me to head it up. Don't tell me Liz is working at some baby mill."

"Hey, hey. Calm down, cuz. This is all a coincidence. Last time I saw Elizabeth, she was a minimalist influencer..."

Colin listened to Felix plead his case. He hated to admit it, but it was convincing. The adrenaline flooded his body. He needed a release. His thoughts turned to his apartment. He looked at Anne, then got out of the car to pace.

"Look," Felix continued, "whatever it takes—I'll help you find her."

"Thanks." Colin clenched his teeth. "Sorry I called your businesses shady."

"No worries, cuz. We're family. Besides, some are."

He hung up. Slamming his fists on the trunk, Colin took several deep breaths. Turning around to pace, he saw people staring at him. He wanted to run. He wanted to scream.

When he got back in the car, Anne didn't move as Colin sat for several minutes in silence. With a cleansing breath, he clicked his seatbelt and continued on.

As Colin drove, he and Anne compared notes from the police station, starting with Trina.

"The detective said she'd done this before," Anne said.

"Yeah, they told me." It didn't comfort him to know he wasn't the first guy Trina had stalked.

"Said she hacked into security systems to watch people."

"That must have been how she got the pictures of us together," he said, then added, "at the restaurant." Not mentioning the one of himself and Trina kissing or Colin standing in the street with a knife. *She probably hacked the doorbell camera on the house across the street,* he thought.

"That's awful," Anne said, watching the billboards along the interstate to Indiana. "I didn't even know they met each other."

"Trina joined Liz's fertility group. Probably to get close." He thought of Trina lying about adopting a baby. Liz at Trina's house for her baby shower, never knowing she was in danger.

Anne turned to Colin. "I had no idea she was crazy. I thought she was just alone and confused—I felt guilty for abandoning her. I'm sorry."

"Don't apologize." Colin felt guilty too. He thought of Liz saying, *Real friends never need to apologize*. Then he imagined her dead in a ditch. He changed the subject, trying his best to untangle Anne's lies. That proved futile.

They drove the final hour in silence—aside from the random attention-seeking sniffle or sigh from Anne. Colin thought through everything that had happened, desperate to understand the truth.

"Wait a second," he said, picking up his phone.

He dialed Detective Green.

"I think Trina was working with someone."

"What makes you say that?"

Switching the phone to speaker, he flipped to the text and read it to her. "I encouraged Liz to go to him... *Him*. Get it? Trina encouraged her to go to some guy."

"Who?" Anne asked.

Colin swatted the phone at her, swerving into the right-hand lane as he turned the speakerphone off. A truck laid on the horn.

"Sorry, Detective," he continued. "Maybe some guy has Liz."

"Who, Colin?" Anne asked again, snatching at Colin's phone.

"Stop," he said, glaring at her.

"I'll look into it," Green said. "We just started cracking into her cache of phones. There's a lot to weed through."

"Did you see anything about a guy?" Colin asked.

"Pull over, Colin," Anne said.

"Wait," he said to her, turning his attention back to Green. "I'm sorry, a cache of what?"

"Pull over," Anne yelled.

"I'm sorry, Detective. I have to go."

"Forward me that text," Green said.

Ending the call, Colin pulled to the shoulder and stopped.

"What the hell, Anne?"

She didn't answer.

"What?" he asked. "Anne? What is it?"

Silence.

He turned to her. "Look at me."

Her eyes glistened. Her mouth opened. She didn't speak.

"What?" He clenched his fists and teeth, holding back the fury building within.

Anne stared at Colin. She didn't blink. She didn't move. Finally, covering her mouth, she said, "She found him."

"Who?"

"I'm sorry, Colin." She pursed her lips.

"Dammit, Anne!" he yelled, slamming his fists on the steering wheel.

Anne flinched. "I'm sorry," she said again.

"Stop saying you're sorry. Just tell me the truth. Are you even capable of telling the truth?" He tried to control his rage. He knew then that she hadn't left her Amish community willingly. She'd been shunned. He'd like to shun her himself. He'd like to do more than shun her.

"You're right. There's more," she said, crying and wringing a tissue in her hands. "You have to understand, when you said Liz was missing and they said you were having an affair... I didn't put two and two together."

"What do you mean?"

"They're wrong about everything," she said, shaking her head. "The day she went missing—" She bit her lip.

Colin rubbed his face and let out a growl of frustration. He shifted the car into drive. "Maybe the police can get it out of you."

"Fine, take me to the police."

That wasn't the response he wanted. He wanted Anne to shift the car into park and talk.

"On second thought, Daniel can get it out of you."

That did the trick.

With a deep inhale, Anne said, "I know where she is."

58
Colin

"I hoped this wasn't part of it. It probably isn't," Anne said. "You do realize this will kill Daniel?"

"Enough. Tell me what you know."

"Fine," she said, clearing her throat. A truck raced past on the interstate, shaking the car. "Daniel didn't know I was married before him or that I had a daughter. He also didn't know..." She looked down at her hands, then closed her eyes.

Pulling the key from the ignition, Colin dropped it into the cupholder. Waiting.

Anne looked up. "When Daniel and I had been married two years without any babies, I knew getting pregnant wasn't *my* problem. Daniel wanted kids so badly, and I knew he'd make a great father. I would've done anything to give him a family." She shrugged and wiped her eyes.

"Liz and Emma aren't his," Colin said, understanding the words she'd left unsaid.

She nodded. "I probably should regret it, but I don't. I did what I had to do to give him the family of his dreams."

"That's why you told Liz not to be desperate to have kids—to give me kids."

Anne nodded again and picked pieces of tissue lint from her pants.

"I never regretted cheating. I regretted not planning better. It was a spur-of-the-moment thing. I could have picked a better..."

Sperm donor, Colin thought. "What does this have to do with Liz missing?"

"At lunch, the last time I saw her, she mentioned she was going to send her DNA to that website."

"What?"

"That horrible DNA business you're always trying to get her to join."

"No. She never signed up," Colin said, ignoring her accusation.

"Yes, she did."

Colin wasn't about to argue the point. Liz joked about his monthly meetups. She wondered why anyone would want to find more relatives, especially if they didn't like the ones they had. He couldn't imagine her sending in her DNA. It didn't add up. He didn't know what to believe.

"Maybe that's what she was trying to tell me about before she went missing," Colin said. Then he refocused on the point. "What did she say at lunch?"

"She was planning to send in her DNA, and she wondered what I thought about the idea. I tried to discourage it by reminding her how silly she'd always thought it was when you'd meet crazy, long-lost relatives."

"Do you think she sent in her DNA and already knew the truth?" Colin asked.

"I didn't at the time. When she went missing, and the police asked about you having an affair, I didn't think it was pertinent to mention."

"Why wouldn't that be pert—" He stopped himself. There was no use asking when he knew what she'd say. *It would kill Daniel.* As if that was enough of an excuse anymore. He thought of all that had happened. Just moments ago, he was imagining Liz lying dead somewhere. Now, she was simply off meeting her biological father—probably on the sly to save face after all her jokes about Colin's ancestry quest.

"Okay," he said. "It's fine. Just tell me where she is."

"Okay," Anne said, nodding. "Turn around."

"Where are we going?"

"My house first."

Traffic sped past. Colin started the car, shifting into drive. A small part of him regretted not confirming Anne's Amish story as he took the first exit and turned around. His phone rang.

"Hey, Felix. Did you find anything?"

"Sorry, cuz. No, I haven't. It's just... the reason I'm calling... we lost our biggest investor."

Colin drove as he listened to Felix pitch several pointless tech companies, all in desperate need of more money. He looked over at Anne as she dozed, wishing he could read her mind.

"I'll look through the press kit you gave me," Colin said.

"As soon as you can. Thanks, cuz. This is really important."

Life or death, right, he thought. "Yeah. Oh, and Felix, you'll see if there's anything you can find on my wife, right?"

"For sure."

Colin hung up just as he pulled to a stop in front of Anne's house.

The curtain moved in the front window. Anne waved to her husband as she opened the car door.

"Wait here. I'll grab my passport."

"Wait? What?"

"Liz went to Spain to find him."

"No," Colin said, shaking his head. "Her passport's at home."

"It's the only way to find him."

Colin leaned his head back. "We should call Detective Green." Pulling out his phone, he swiped to her number.

"That'll take too long. We can call the police in Spain." She grabbed the phone. "Trust me."

Colin couldn't hold back a sudden laugh. "The nerve—"

"Colin, if she went to him, she's not safe."

"What do you mean?" He furrowed his brow. The scared look in her eye seemed honest, for once. "You know he's in Spain?

For sure?"

Anne nodded.

He rubbed his eyes, trying to think. His brain felt completely broken. "This better not be some wild goose chase," he said, dropping his phone.

59
Colin

"How did you know where to find Liz's biological father?" Colin asked Anne as they stood in line for a taxi in Spain's Costa del Sol.

"Not father. Brother," she corrected, frowning. "Half-brother. He already had two kids when..."

"Hold on." Colin grabbed her elbow, pulling her out of line. "I thought we were coming to see her father."

"He left Chicago years ago. His son's here. He'll know where to find him."

"I told you no wild goose—" Colin stopped when a few people in line shot him irritated glances. He exhaled and held up his hands. "Fine. How do you know his son's here?"

"He was in the news a couple of years ago."

"The news? For what?"

"He was on trial."

That was when Colin learned they wouldn't just be meeting Liz's half-brother — they'd be visiting him in prison. As the taxi cut through Málaga's narrow streets, Colin sat in silence, turning it all over in his mind. Asking Anne questions had proven a waste of time, but that didn't mean he didn't *have* questions — plenty of them.

He couldn't believe he was halfway across the world,

following Anne with only half-truths and lies. Why hadn't he pressed harder to involve the police? Why would Anne spend a day dragging him to Spain instead? And why had he followed?

The truth was, he knew why — because he'd hoped, despite everything, that whatever Anne was chasing might lead them to Liz. Part of him still believed Anne knew more than she was letting on — something she hadn't told the police or him.

By the time they reached the hotel, Colin's patience was wearing thin. Jet lag, frustration, and doubts about Anne made him feel he'd made a mistake.

Hours later, they were in the visitor line at Albolote Penitentiary. The heavy door creaked open, and a scrawny man with thick glasses shuffled in. Anne stood up and left without saying a word.

"Scared her off," the prisoner said with a crooked smirk. "I seem to have that effect on the ladies. Who are you?"

Colin hesitated. The sterile room and stale air felt all too familiar. Years ago, he had volunteered at a prison program, working with mothers who wanted to keep their newborns with them for the first year. He'd walked away jaded, manipulated more than once by women who twisted his kindness to gain more time with their kids. Prison was a world of half-truths and careful lies, and Colin wanted no part of it now. Probably why Anne had waited until they'd arrived in Spain to tell him that Liz's brother, Joey, was still inside.

He resisted the urge to go after Anne. Whatever she knew, whatever she was hiding, it was time to stop chasing her for answers. Joey was right in front of him. Colin looked the man in the eye.

"Do you know Liz Clarke?" Colin asked.

"Who wants to know?" He crossed his arms and smirked.

Colin wanted to say never mind and leave. He'd call Detective Green and tell her what he knew. She'd have the Spanish police look into things. He rubbed his eyes.

Joey tapped on the glass.

"Hey, I'm just giving you a hard time. Yeah, I know her.

She's my sister," he said, looking proud.

"She's my wife."

"I know," Joey said, laughing. "The guard told me when you checked in. Colin, right? It's nice to meet you. Is she here?"

"No."

"She said she'd come back to visit." He looked past Colin, to the door.

"She's been here before?"

Joey looked confused by the question, as if of course she'd been there every day for years. "Yeah."

"She was looking for your dad?"

He leaned back, taking Colin in. His eyes filled with suspicion.

"What do you want?" he asked.

"Liz is missing."

"Really?"

"Yeah." Colin cleared his throat. "We think she came here to find her dad—your dad. Did you tell her where he is?"

His body stiffened. "No."

Colin could tell he'd hit a nerve. "You met Liz through the ancestry site?"

"In a way. They used my DNA from the system. Sleazebags."

"What do you mean?"

Joey crossed his arms. "Some investigator matched my DNA to hers from one of those sites. Tried to use it to get me for some crime. I don't get how it's legal."

"What kind of crime?"

He cracked his neck. "Same thing they got me in here for."

Colin wanted to ask what that was, but he didn't have to. Joey seemed happy to talk.

"She didn't tell you?" he asked, smiling. "Yeah, I don't blame her. I came out here ten years ago to DJ. It was amazing. Best time of my life. Fueled by drugs and alcohol. I got into transporting cocaine from South America. Always doing my part for the party scene."

"And you got caught smuggling drugs?"

"Nah. I had girls do the work. Sent them out two by two like Jesus sending out his apostles." He laughed.

"I'm sorry, you sent girls to South America for cocaine?"

"Yeah." The look of pride grew as Joey sat taller in his chair.

"You got caught sending girls—"

"Nah. Couldn't link me to that. No, I got caught when one of the girls got nosy. Called her dad, who sent an investigator to sniff around. Find where the bodies were buried."

"Bodies." Colin laughed with Joey, then felt like an idiot. He'd thought Joey had meant cocaine, saying "bodies" instead to sound cool. He rubbed his forehead, in desperate need of sleep, irritated he hadn't slept on the plane. Looking up into Joey's eyes, he understood. Real bodies. "You'd kill the girls after they brought the drugs back to Spain?"

"Not always—that was my fault. My mistake. Got greedy."

"Isn't that always the way..." Colin rolled his eyes, trying to think of something to say to get back on track.

Joey nodded and laughed again. "Who was that?" He tilted his chin to the door.

"Liz's mom."

His smirk faded. "She has a lot of nerve coming here after what she did."

"What'd she do?"

A guard knocked at Joey's door and motioned that his time was almost up.

"Tried to break up my parents. She's not trying to rekindle something with my dad, is she? Is that why Liz came looking for him?"

"No. I swear to you, she has no interest in rekindling anything."

Colin knew the guard would be opening the door soon and leading Joey away. He didn't have time to beat around the bush anymore, and he certainly wouldn't return for another visit.

"Where's your dad, Joey?"

"That's not a good idea. They disowned me when all this—"

The guard opened the door.

"I have to go."

"I won't mention you." Colin stood up. "I just want to find my wife. Where's your dad? Please."

Joey shook his head and walked out of the room.

Colin slammed his hands on the wall, angry with himself for wasting the visit, listening to a murderer gloat about killing women.

"You're sure you don't have any idea where her dad moved to?" Colin asked Anne as the cab stopped in front of their hotel. He pulled out his phone.

"No."

A message popped up, and Colin called his voicemail to listen.

"Dr. Clarke. I wanted to give you an update, and I had some questions about your dealings with Felix Everett. Since it seems you've fled the country, I have a whole lot more..." Detective Green did not seem pleased.

"Anne..." His voice trailed off as she passed through the lobby to the front desk to check in to her room.

Colin followed and inquired about a nearby Chinese restaurant, needing a release. Then he thought twice. "Never mind." He sighed and asked to be pointed to the bar instead.

"I don't know about you," Anne said, looking worn out, "but I'm heading up to get some sleep."

"I will too. Let's meet at seven for dinner."

Sitting at the bar with a bottle of beer, Colin considered calling Detective Green back. He pulled her number up on his phone. No. Meeting Joey—knowing Liz had been there to see him—she felt so close. Colin was certain Joey gave her their father's address. Putting his phone down, Colin decided he'd return to the prison in the morning and try again.

As he finished his bottle and signaled to the bartender for another, his phone rang.

"Ah, Dr. Clarke. So nice of you to pick up this time."

"For the record, I didn't flee the country, Detective."

Green laughed. "Don't worry yourself. Spain will extradite if needed."

"Extradite?" He wondered how she knew where he was. The bartender popped open another bottle, swapping it with the empty one as a couple sat down next to Colin.

"When are you coming home, Dr. Clarke?"

"You said in your message you had an update?" he asked, ignoring the part about her also having questions.

"I'd rather talk in person. What brought you to Spain?"

He considered telling her and asking for help, then changed his mind. He knew he'd have a better chance of getting Joey to talk.

"I'll be back soon," he said, ending the call.

60
Owen

Having had no news regarding Big Eyes' fate, Owen's nerves were on edge as he watched over his shoulder. Every stop on his route was a potential risk of interaction. He knew who she was and what she was after. She wouldn't just give up. He needed a vacation.

"I just have a few questions," she had said that day at Keem, introducing herself as an investigator. The liar.

Investigator or not, that wasn't his problem. His pride was the problem. After Owen took her around the rocky corner, waves crashed nearby. Basking sharks circled in the bay. He mistakenly thought her fall would kill her. It had worked before. He was sloppy and proud as he confessed everything he'd done. It felt invigorating to admit the truth to someone.

Now she knew the truth and would return with the police. He didn't know for sure. She could be dead. The news was no help. Twice he attempted to go to the hospital and chickened out. *Coward*, he thought, pulling the bus to the curb and opening the door.

A swarm of unnaturally chirpy Americans boarded his bus. He tried to turn them on to a tour company. They weren't having it. "Keen to travel like a local," the most irritating of the lot said, then asked Owen where he was from.

He tapped his fingers on the ticket machine and mumbled the name of a town he'd just made up. The man counted out his euros, commenting on the different sizes of their money.

"Yes, yes, fascinating," Owen said. He turned on the radio to a Gaelic talk station. It helped drown out the constant chatter of those damn Americans.

His desperation to return home to Chicago grew as he listened to the women coo at the lambs and comment on the beauty of the purple flowers.

"What kind are those?" one lady asked another.

"Oh, I don't know. The purple ones?" another asked.

"Very exotic, don't you think?"

"I've never seen such flowers..."

Owen screamed in his head at those mindless tarts. *Rhododendron, you twits!* That felt better.

After his shift, he stopped at the grocery store for a box of Barry's tea to spite his wife, who only drank Lyons brand. She had told him that they'd go to Ireland and drink Lyons, then travel around Europe. It would be fun and exciting, a whole new chapter in their lives. They'd be new people. New people. She was right about that. She went and lost her mind and left him to entertain overly friendly, idiot Americans. The same people who, if he saw them in America, would know how to keep their eyes forward and their mouths shut.

At home, with his cup of Barry's—which tasted exactly like Lyons—he could sense Big Eyes was getting close. He had no other choice but to be done with their time in Ireland. He frowned, not wanting to end things with Marta so soon. He had such fun plans for her. *Oh, well, it can't be helped,* he thought. Their time together was up.

A knock came at the front door. Finishing his cup of tea, he wondered if Big Eyes had brought the police. If she hadn't, he'd invite her in. *There might still be a chance out of this entire mess.*

"Oh, hello," Owen said, stepping outside the house and

pulling the door shut behind him. "My wife's just gone down for a nap, or I'd invite you in."

"Is my wife here?" Marta's slob husband said, trying to see inside the stained-glass window.

"I'm sorry, she's taken today off. I believe she's in town shopping."

"Shopping?"

"Well, yes, I paid her today, and you know how wives are..." Owen regretted stepping out onto the porch with such a large man. He looked around and started to walk to the sidewalk out front. "I'm just heading out to get a curry. Care to join me?"

Slob Husband frowned. "Do you know which shops? I leave tonight for a job in Dublin."

"I wish I could help," Owen said as he waved him off.

A minute later, from around the corner, he watched as the brute drove away, remembering why he avoided girls with husbands.

In the rabbit room, Owen pulled back the plaid blanket from the extra-large dog cage. The pet store clerk had corrected him, calling it a crate. Owen had laughed at the attempt to make it sound more humane.

Standing there now, watching Marta's pleading eyes, he knew the reporters wouldn't call it a crate. No, they would call it a cage to make Owen sound less human.

"Your husband's run off to Dublin to give us a little more time."

A scream pierced the silence, and he jumped. Throwing the blanket down, he ran into the kitchen to find Sarah rolling on the ground, cupping her hands to her chest. Barry's teabags had been thrown around the room, several in flames on the stovetop.

He tried to force her hands apart to check the damage. Skin stuck to her nightgown, peeling off as he tugged. Seeing her bones exposed shocked Owen. He tried to quiet her and think.

"Just hold them still," he said as he led her to the hall to slip on her shoes. Then he escorted her to the passenger seat, strapping her in. The seatbelt pressed against her clenched hands. She screamed.

"I'll be just a minute," he said as he closed the door. He hurried back inside to lock the rabbit cage and the room. Then, he checked the front door, making sure it was secure. After that, he drove to the hospital.

61
Colin

Light peeked in from the edge of the curtains. Colin looked around the room, expecting to be in the staff lounge on the Labor and Delivery floor. Instead, he rolled over in his hotel room in Spain. Turning off the alarm, he took a quick shower and dressed for dinner.

Anne had already ordered when Colin arrived at the hotel's restaurant. He motioned for the waiter.

"Did you sleep?" she asked.

"Yeah." He felt hungover, with a headache, and wished he hadn't. "I take it you knew all about Liz's brother's crimes."

Anne rubbed the edge of her plate. "I didn't want to mention—"

"It doesn't matter." Colin checked his phone.

"What is it?"

"Nothing. I'm just used to being tied to my phone. I keep thinking my phone's broken." He set it down as the waiter approached to take his order.

"Was he like Liz?" Anne asked.

"Joey? In what way?"

"I don't know. What did he say?"

"Oh, I don't know. That he had a bunch of women run drugs for him and then murdered them."

Anne leaned over to the chair next to hers and unzipped her purse. “Here.” She handed Colin a folded-up newspaper article. The headline: *The Reaper of Ibiza.*

The details were far more horrifying than Joey had led him to believe. Colin was relieved that Anne had kept this information to herself before having him sit across from that disgusting monster. Now, he dreaded his plan to return to the prison.

As he folded the paper and handed it back, his phone vibrated.

“It works,” Anne said, looking at his phone.

He answered.

“Hey Colin,” Felix said, his voice cracking. “I have to ask you something.”

“Okay?”

“Remember when you asked me about The Squatter Squad? You wanted to know what was to keep someone from having anyone taken care of. You didn’t...”

Colin leaned back as the waiter brought his food. He nodded a thank-you.

“I take it you talked to Detective Green?” Colin asked.

“You know I’m just a middleman. I don’t have anything to do with these companies. Just raise money and take my cut. You know that, right? If you used—”

“I didn’t.”

“Didn’t what?” Anne asked. Colin waved her off and walked to the lobby.

“Right, right,” Felix said. “You need to know... If you did, I can’t just undo it.”

“What’d you tell the police?”

“The truth. That you asked about using the service for people other than squatters.”

Colin clenched his fist, then closed his eyes. He felt sick. He wanted to scream. Finally, someone had told the truth, and it pointed directly at Colin. He wanted to laugh at the absurdity of it all. Still, he knew it didn’t look good.

“It’s fine,” Colin said. “I swear I didn’t use the service.”

"Cool. Hey, the cop said you're in Spain? Do you want me to come out there and help?"

Hating the excitement he heard in Felix's voice, Colin declined the offer and ended the call.

Having made the mistake of sleeping a few hours during the day, Colin spent the night staring at the ceiling, waiting for morning. At 2 a.m., his phone rang. A blocked number.

"Colin?" a man's voice whispered.

"Joey? How are you calling—"

"Is she really missing?"

Colin sat up, switching on the lamp. "Yes." He wanted to thank him for calling. As he started to speak, he stopped himself and listened.

"You asked me if she had come looking for my dad. Yeah, well, I told her it was a bad idea. She insisted."

"It's okay. Please, just tell me where he is."

"Okay."

Colin jumped from the bed, fumbling around the desk for a pen and paper. He heard another voice through the phone telling Joey to hurry up. Colin scribbled the address as the call ended. Swiping around his phone, he booked tickets on the first possible flight.

Anne looked like she'd been up all night when Colin found her at breakfast, calling the waiter over for more coffee.

"You look like you slept," she said, sounding jealous.

"Not really."

"What happened?" she asked, folding her napkin.

"I found Liz's dad."

Anne frowned. "He's not her *dad*. Daniel raised her, he's—"

"Sorry," Colin said, as the waiter returned to take his order. "Just a croissant and a coffee, please." He looked at Anne. "We have to get to the airport."

"I don't know if I can face him."

"You won't have to," Colin said, looking at his watch. "You can come and wait somewhere while I go." The waiter brought Colin's order and checked on Anne. "Or you could return home and I'll call you as soon—"

"No," Anne said, grabbing her purse. "I'm coming with you."

62
Colin

On the flight, Colin tried to think of the best way to approach Liz's father. He decided to keep it simple and just show up.

When they arrived, Anne stayed in the car.

Colin knocked and waited. Then he knocked again. He hadn't planned on no one being home. For a moment, he worried Joey had called, scaring him off.

"We'll come back later," he told Anne, getting into the car. "Let's find a hotel."

"There's a neighbor," Anne said, pointing.

He saw a woman wrangling her kids into the car for school and walked over.

"Drives the bus," she said, handing a doll through to the toddler in the backseat. "Passes through town at Mill Street. Goes out to Achill. It's a nice scenic loop, if you're interested."

He thanked her, and they left.

"Might as well have a look," Anne said when they pulled into town and found themselves approaching the bus stop. Colin parked.

"Hiya. Where to?" the bus driver asked as the door opened.

"Can I loop around the island?" Colin asked. "A woman

mentioned—"

"Sure. It's a fine way to see Achill."

The bus driver took Colin's money and pointed to the ticket printing out of the machine.

"You be sure and keep that with you in case the inspector comes along."

As the door closed, Colin called Anne's phone. He saw her settling down in the café window.

"Is it him?" he asked, looking at her as the bus turned off Mill Street heading out of Westport.

"Yes. Yes, that's Owen."

Colin looked at the mirror in the front of the bus and saw Owen's eyes firmly fixed on the road ahead as he chatted with another passenger. He overheard the woman saying she had come from Wexford. She thought Achill was much prettier than Hawaii, claiming to know as she'd worked in Hawaii for nearly thirty years before returning home.

"Hiya, Owen. How's Sarah?" an older man asked as he boarded, chatting and holding up the bus.

"Just home from the hospital," Owen said.

The Hawaii woman looked at her watch.

Colin planned to wait for all the other passengers to get off, then he'd move up to the spot just behind the driver and casually start chatting. Perhaps mentioning he was from Chicago. That'd be common ground.

As they drove along, with people boarding and leaving the bus, he worried the Hawaii woman had had the same idea to make the entire loop. Just when he thought it was all for nothing, she pressed the red call button above her head. The bus slowed to the side of the road. She lingered to chat a few more moments as she stood outside. Owen's eyes looked into the mirror to the back of the bus, fixing on Colin as he closed the door.

"You're from America, then?" Owen asked.

"I am." Colin looked around to see they were now alone. "Chicago. What about you?"

Owen's eyes darted back and forth from the road to Colin. "You're not a tourist."

Colin stared at the man's face in the mirror.

"I don't mean anything bad by it," Owen said, smiling. "Driving a bus, you see all kinds of people every day. Most American tourists have an excited, nervous way about them. You don't."

Colin laughed.

"Besides. You don't have a camera. Not even your phone's camera out to take pictures of this haunted landscape. No, sir, you're here for something else..."

Colin looked out the window to the harsh, rugged islands rising out of the ocean. Green fields dotted with white sheep, their black heads rooting around the ground.

They passed the Keel stop and snaked up through town. The coffee shop, restaurant, and pub on the hill. Up, up, around by the church. Back down the hill through the last town on the island. He didn't know how much more time he'd have alone with Owen. As he began to say something, he noticed the final bus stop sign at Dooagh come and go. Colin looked up at the mirror, but Owen's eyes remained fixed on the road ahead.

Colin looked back at the final stop receding into the distance. "Wasn't that the—"

"I always thought it such a shame the bus line ends three miles shy of the most beautiful beach in Ireland."

"It's all right. I wouldn't want you to get into any trouble."

Owen laughed. "Don't worry about me. They can't fire a man who'll be quitting soon."

The road rose quickly up the mountainside, where sheep clung to the edge. Colin looked down at the steep fall to the ocean waves below.

"Really. I don't need to see it."

"It'd be a shame." Owen turned on the radio, country music flowing through the bus as he swerved. Slamming the brakes, he allowed an oncoming camper to pass.

"That out there is called Bills Rocks," Owen pointed and told stories of the British using the cluster of jagged points for target practice. "And this here was an Amethyst mine. Local kids from Dooagh used to sell pieces they'd dug up to tourists. Long time ago."

They came around the steepest curve, perched high above the ground. Colin found himself looking straight down.

"These guard rails were only recently put in. You can imagine how terrifying this drive used to be."

Relieved to be starting the descent into the bay, Colin then noticed two cars in the parking lot and took a deep breath. Owen hit the gas, the bus barreling down the winding road.

"I know who you are," Owen said, bringing the bus to a stop in the middle of the parking lot.

Colin froze, his heart racing. "How do you—"

"Come along. I'd like to show you something." Owen opened the door and hopped down. "I don't bite."

Colin gave a nervous laugh and followed.

Together, they strolled past the two cars as one backed up to leave. The parked car was empty. Colin looked up the hiking path and down to the beach. No one in sight. Then, as he followed Owen past the picnic benches, a car approached over the ridge on its way into the bay.

"How do you know who I am?" Colin asked. They walked down the concrete ramp to the beach. Colin grabbed for the railing, his foot slipping. A trickle of water seeping down from the mountain.

"Liz showed me a picture—from your wedding."

"She was here?"

"She was."

Owen's tone was flat. Colin couldn't decide what to make of it. There was something cold and distant about the man. *Melancholy*. He felt sad for him and hesitated to deliver bad news.

"She's missing," Colin said.

"Oh, I'm sure she'll turn up." He winked.

Colin stopped and stared as Owen strolled along the shore.

"Wait," Colin called out, catching up. "Is she still here?"

63
Colin

"Owen, is Liz still here?" Colin asked again.

Slowing his stride, Owen looked out to the horizon. A huge cruise liner passed by, lost from time to time in the fog blowing in over the island. He shook his head.

"She looked just like my older sister, Rose," he finally said, picking up a frond of seaweed. "Eyes like the sea. The shade of blue changing with the tide. That's how I knew who she was." He tore a bit of seaweed, dropping it on the sand. "She looked terrified when she saw me. Almost didn't get on the bus."

"She came looking for you. Why would she be terrified?"

Owen walked along the shore, picking at the seaweed. "The last time she saw me, I must have scared her. I just wanted to tell them the truth."

"What do you mean?"

"That I'm their father." Owen shrugged. "That their mother is a pathological liar."

Colin almost smiled at that. "What do you mean, tell *them*? You saw Liz and Emma?"

Owen nodded.

"Oh, the accident?" Colin asked. "You were there? The man Liz said—"

"Don't look at me like that." Owen waved his hands. "I

jumped in and saved those girls. Thank God I did, or they wouldn't be alive."

"I get it," Colin said, trying to understand. "You found out you had twins and went to tell them the truth."

"I didn't just find out. I knew about them the whole time."

"Really?"

"I saw Anne pregnant. I watched her and her husband bring them home from the hospital. My girls playing in their yard. The metal swing set. The swing on the right squeaking. I can still hear it. When my daughter, Sheena... When she died, it was time. I showed up at their door. Anne wouldn't let me in." Owen's voice rose as he spoke. He took a breath, releasing it slowly. "I just wanted to be part of their lives. She refused. What could I do? I waited until they were eighteen. I just wanted to hold my daughters." Dropping the last bit of seaweed, he hid his face in his hands.

"I'm sorry for your loss," Colin said, resting his hand on Owen's shoulder.

Owen tensed, then relaxed. He nodded, patting Colin's back. "I brought her here," he said, continuing to stroll toward the rocks.

"Liz?" Colin looked around, imagining Liz walking beside them. "Do you know where she is? Is she still here? In Ireland?"

"No. Why?"

"When she left, did she say where she was going?"

Owen turned, looking toward the parking lot. "How'd you find me?"

"Liz told me."

Owen closed his eyes and shook his head. "That's a lie."

"Your son," Colin said, feeling stupid for being caught.

He watched the subtle shift in Owen's posture, from vulnerable to defensive. Holding back.

The rocks towered out of the sand behind Owen. Waves slapped and churned, foam rising into the air. A cave of black lay farther on.

"What was it you wanted to show me?" Colin asked, trying to sound casual.

Owen pointed. "Just up ahead."

Colin noticed his tone had changed too. "Do you know where she is?" he asked again.

"I told you. No."

"You're sure?"

Owen let out a laugh, squaring his shoulders. "What are you asking me, exactly?"

"I'm just trying to find my wife."

The man looked around. "I don't know what my son told you. That degenerate. You know what he's in there for? Disgraceful. If your wife really is missing, you should talk to him."

"Sorry. It's just—" Colin raised his hands. "I think you're the last one to see her."

Owen shook his head, looking down at the sand.

"She was here, yes," he said. "I told her the truth, and she thanked me. Then she left. Oh, I see..."

"What?"

Owen took a step toward Colin.

"It is my fault."

"What is?"

"The truth. The truth scared her off."

"What do you mean?" Colin felt Owen moving toward him. He wanted to step back. To breathe.

Owen stepped closer, reaching out for Colin's arm. "Sorry, kid. I should have told you."

"Told me what?"

"You didn't know she was coming to meet me. You didn't know about her brother? That bad seed." Both hands were now stroking Colin's arms.

Colin stared, smelling Owen's warm breath between them.

"I'm so sorry," the man said. "She told me she's always felt different. She asked me for the truth."

Colin shook his head. Owen grasped his arms tighter.

"I saw it in her too. Just like my son," Owen said, his eyes sympathetic to Colin's pain. "When I saw her, there it was. My bad seed."

Taking a step back, pulling out of Owen's grip, Colin tried to think. Joey in prison talking so matter-of-factly about the women he'd murdered. The psychopath. Colin had always known there was something different about Liz. Not this. No. He shook his head.

"You've seen it too," Owen said. "Something different."

Colin nodded. "I was on call the night I met Liz. It was busy. Crazy. Full moon. A woman came in, high as a kite, in labor. All she wanted was to get out and get another fix before she started to come down. We had to restrain her. The police were called. The baby's head started to crown, and I focused on my part of the job. The woman broke loose..."

Owen stepped closer again, his hand on Colin's shoulder. Grains of sand whirled up in the wind, racing along the surface of the beach.

Colin continued, "As soon as the baby's head came out, the patient reached down, ripped the baby out of herself... twisting her baby's head almost clean off."

Owen tsked. "Drugs are a powerful thing."

"They are," Colin nodded. "We've all seen a lot, but that—it just happened so fast. It was shocking. My best nurse, Selena, lost her lunch in the corner and still has PTSD. Another one spent months in therapy and transferred to a different unit."

"Not Liz."

"No. She stayed calm and acted as if this sort of thing happened every day. Just looking at her, I knew she was different."

"You saw the same thing in her that I saw," Owen said, staring, searching Colin's eyes. Colin averted his gaze, embarrassed that he'd wanted Liz because he knew she was different. She wouldn't be emotional and dramatic like his first wife. He wouldn't have to bother fixing what had broken in him when he was thrown in that dumpster as a baby. His mouth watered, craving a binge. He thought of the hours after that delivery.

Colin had managed to hold it together in the moment of the horrific scene. Afterward, someone ordered Chinese. Beef and mushrooms, shrimp pad Thai, egg rolls, one order of egg foo young for Selena. No one could eat. When the nurses clocked out, Colin ate it all, trying desperately to keep it together. Only when he began to choke and ran to the bathroom did he feel right again.

Owen gripped the back of Colin's neck. "If I were you, I'd stop looking for her."

"Why would you say that?" Colin pulled away.

"The night of the accident. Do you know what she did when she reversed into the pond?"

"No... what?"

"She smiled."

Massaging his forehead, Colin tried to think straight. He imagined the scene, Liz smiling as she plunged herself and Emma into the water. He shook his head. It couldn't be true. No.

Owen turned, looking up at the rocks, and hesitated. Hikers stopped to take pictures of the landscape.

"This has been a shock," Owen said, patting Colin on the back. "Why don't we head to my house for a cup of tea?"

"Thanks," Colin said. He needed time to think. "I should get back."

Owen shrugged. "You're welcome anytime."

Anne was still sitting in the café window when the bus returned to Westport. Owen switched buses with another driver and drove away as Colin stepped onto the sidewalk in a daze.

"What'd he say?" Anne stood as he walked in, passing a group of teens leaving.

"She was here, but she left. Let's go."

"No, sit down. I've been a nervous wreck the entire time. When the bus was late... I got worried. Just tell me what he said."

Colin picked up her purse and jacket. "Come on, she's not here. Maybe the police can make something of this." The thought of her passport at home popped into his head.

"How?" Anne asked, following Colin out onto the sidewalk.

He turned to the right, but remembering the hotel was across and to the left, circled around instead, confused. Anne nipped at his heels.

"I don't know." He had to call Detective Green, even if she suspected him of being involved somehow.

"Colin, wait, you're walking too fast."

He heard Anne fall and turned to help her. An older couple had stopped to assist, and they moved on as he came back.

"I'm sorry, Anne. Are you okay?"

"I'm fine." She sat dazed, tugging at her shirt.

"I'm sorry. I'm out of ideas. By the way, you were right about Owen." He helped her to her feet. Another woman stopped to pick up her purse and dust off her coat. Colin smiled his thanks and took the purse.

"What do you mean?" Anne asked.

"What?"

"How was I right about Owen?"

"You should have done a bit more research before having his kids. Something about him... something off." *The strain of his son's crimes?*

Anne clung to Colin's arm as they walked, her ankle causing her to limp.

"He was charming when I met him. Why would you say that?"

"Nothing."

At the hotel, Colin helped Anne to her room to rest and ice her ankle while he went to order a sandwich from the hotel's restaurant. A sandwich and a pint of Guinness.

"Do you mind if I sit?" a woman said. He thought of Trina sidling up to him in Sarasota. *What's the harm in a drink?* he'd said to himself back then. He wouldn't repeat that mistake.

"Actually, I'm just leaving." Picking up half of the ham and cheese panini from his plate, he turned to leave.

In the stairwell, his phone rang. Detective Green. Colin sent the call to voicemail and waited for the ping. Sitting on a dusty step and taking a bite of his sandwich, he listened to her message.

"Dr. Clarke, we found something on one of Trina's phones. Call me back. Now."

64
Colin

Colin dropped his sandwich and returned Detective Green's call. No answer. Hanging up, he waited.

As soon as the phone rang, he answered. "What did you find?"

"Trina had so many devices. We've been working around the clock. It'll take weeks to get through. I think we found something. I can't be certain it was Liz she was talking to. Not yet. However, you being in Spain made me think it might be useful."

"What is it?" he asked, not mentioning that they were now in Ireland.

"Trina had contacted someone about getting a fake passport for a friend. I'm assuming you think she's there in Spain, right? That's why you went?"

"Trina got Liz a fake passport? Why? Why not just use her real one?"

"I don't know. Why are you in Spain? What do you know that I don't?"

"Liz's mom lied ... to everyone," he said, standing to pace as he told Green about meeting Liz's brother in prison. "He gave me her father's address—in Ireland."

"You're not in Ireland, are you? I'll have—"

Three girls in matching tracksuits and braids skipped into the stairwell, squealing. They looked at Colin. His sandwich lay on the dirty black and white tiles. Laughing, they raced upstairs. A door slammed.

"Dr. Clarke?"

"Sorry, I couldn't hear you."

"Does your wife have another phone?"

"No, why?"

"There are texts from one of Trina's phones to a number. It's not your wife's number, but I think it's her. You'll see. I'll email you the preliminary transcript. Read it, and call me back right away."

In the hotel's restaurant, Colin found an empty table and refreshed his email, waiting. He looked around the room. The woman who'd tried sitting next to him at the bar was chatting up two other men, their backpacks stashed by their feet.

Colin's phone pinged. He opened the email.

Unknown: *Hot on the trail! Send the first text. Thx!*

Trina: *On it! This is so exciting!*

Trina: *Text sent!*

Trina: *Update, please???*

Trina: *Hello??? I'm dying...*

Trina: *I hope everything's okay??*

Unknown: *Hey, don't send the second text. I'm coming home.*

Trina: *Oh no! What happened???*

Unknown: *I can't do this.*

Trina: *Okay.*

Trina: *You know, you could always turn this into a nice little vacay!*

Unknown: *LOL! Not gonna lie, I could use it!*

Trina: *Spa????*

Unknown: *LOL*

Trina: *It can't be that bad.*

Trina: *I'm sure you can do it.*

Unknown: *I know him.*

Trina: *NO! HOW??? What'd he say!!!???? What'd you*

say???!!!
Unknown: *Nothing.*
Unknown: *I froze when I saw him.*
Unknown: *Don't send the text.*
Unknown: *I'm heading to the airport tonight.*
Trina: *No! You've come so far.*
Trina: *Go to him!!!!!*
Unknown: *I can't.*
Trina: *You owe it to yourself!!!*
Trina: *Please answer my call.*
Trina: *You'll regret leaving without talking to him first.*
Trina: *Call me back.*
Trina: *Think of everything we talked about.*
Trina: *Remember how important this is to you.*
Eighteen-minute call: *Unknown to Trina.*
Trina: *I meant what I said. I think of you as my little sister!*
Trina: *I'm proud of you.*
Trina: *And super impressed!!*
Trina: *You're the strongest woman I've ever met!!! SERIOUSLY!!!!*
Unknown: *Haha! Thanks! Big sis! LOL!*
Trina: *You got this.*
Trina: *Call me as soon as you talk to him!!!! Or else!!*
Unknown: *Oh no! I'm sooooo scared! LOL!*
Trina: *Well?? How'd it go???*
Trina: *I'll assume you're still with him and everything is magical! Call me!!*
Trina: *Hello?*
Trina: *How'd it go??? Where are you??*
Trina: *Talk to me.*
Five missed calls: *Trina to Unknown.*
Trina: *I'm getting worried. Please call me.*
Twelve missed calls: *Trina to Unknown.*
Trina: *If I don't hear from you by tomorrow, I'm going to the police.*
Three missed calls: *Trina to Unknown.*

Trina: *Please call me.*
Trina: *Okay. I'm calling the police.*
One-minute call: *Unknown to Trina.*

Colin placed his phone on the table, watching the screen turn black as he processed Liz's conversation with Trina. He dialed Green.

"It's your wife, right?"

"Yes."

"Her brother's in prison. I've already been in contact with the Spanish police." Green took a breath. "You said he told you where their dad is? I need you to tell me his address."

Colin listened to Green's tone as she tried to sound calm and confident. In control. He'd done the same countless times as he delivered bad news to his patients. Standing up, he pulled the keys from his pocket.

"She never left," Colin said.

"What?"

"There's no time."

"What happened?"

Colin knew there was something off about Owen. "I just met him. If she's with him... there's no time."

Once more, Colin imagined the worst as he ran through the hotel lobby to his car.

65
Colin

Owen's house was quiet and dark when Colin arrived. He started for the front door, then hesitated. Walking the perimeter, he tried peeking in windows, looking for any movement. By a side window, a pungent smell caught his attention. The curtains were drawn to the edges, overlapping in the center. He heard a sound.

"Colin," Owen said, smiling as he stepped around the corner. "So glad you changed your mind. Come in. I'll put the kettle on."

Colin's heart raced as he watched the man walk to the trash to toss something in, then return to his house.

Unlocking the front door, Owen whispered, "My wife just got home from the hospital, if you'll please be quiet. She needs her rest."

Colin followed him into the entryway. Owen locked the door, tucking the key in his pocket.

"Don't mind the smell. I'm a bit behind on cleaning up after the pets," Owen said, turning out of sight. "How do you take your tea?"

Colin winced at the stench. He looked to the right. A dim hall of closed doors. He turned left, making his way to the kitchen, pausing to peek into rooms along the way. First, the living room, then a bedroom—a woman asleep in bed. Not Liz. *Owen's wife,* Colin assumed.

The television flickered in the dark. Passing through the dining room, he glanced at the table stacked with newspapers and magazines. The clinking sounds of teacups and saucers led him to the kitchen.

"Your wife was in the hospital?" Colin asked.

"She had an accident. Dementia."

"Her hands," Colin said, having seen the bandages in the light of the TV.

Back through to the living room, where Owen prepared two cups of tea with sugar and milk as Colin studied family photos on the fireplace mantle. A blurry shot of himself and Liz leaving their church caught his eye.

"You were at our wedding?"

"I thought you'd get a kick out of that one." Owen laughed, relaxing back in his chair. "Have a seat."

Colin sat across from Owen, picking up the cup and warming his hands.

"The truth is..." Colin said, watching the ripples in his tea pulsing in time with his heartbeat. He looked at Owen. "Liz isn't missing. She left me."

Owen leaned forward.

"She must have been planning it for a while. Saved up some cash. Got a fake passport. A new phone."

"You think so?"

Colin sighed. "She's done it before. Years ago."

"I'm sorry to hear that," Owen said, setting his cup on the table. He looked at the photo of Colin and Liz. "I wish I could do something to help."

"You can."

"Oh?"

"When she saw you, she recognized you. She was scared and reconsidered." Colin shook his head, thinking of Trina encouraging Liz to return. "She came back here. Then disappeared for good."

Owen nodded. "Me confirming the truth must have done it."

"That's not the whole truth, though, is it?" Colin asked,

setting his cup down.

Owen smiled. “What more is there?”

“Is she here?” Colin looked toward the hall.

“What on earth? Who put you up to this?” Owen asked, standing. Crossing the room to the window, he slid the curtain open. “Her mother...” Owen added. “I saw her in town. Thought I wouldn’t notice. She put you up to this, didn’t she? Is she here?” He yanked the curtains shut.

“No,” Colin said, watching the man pace.

“That one’s a real piece of work.” He sat back in his chair. “You know what I mean. The night I met her, she was all over me. Told me she was single. Liar from the word go. Yes...” He winked. “You know exactly what I mean.”

Colin realized he’d been nodding along with Owen’s description of Anne.

“I’m sorry,” Colin said. “All I meant was... maybe Liz came here and knew she could hide out.”

Finishing his drink, Owen let out a yawn. “I wish that was the case. Sorry.” Standing, he offered his hand to Colin. “If she does turn up, I’d be happy to ring you.”

Colin stood. Taking Owen’s hand in his, he thanked him. The plan had worked out differently in his head on the drive to Owen’s house.

Following him to the front door, he watched Owen fish out the key and turn the lock.

Resting his hand on the man’s shoulder—feeling him flinch, just like at the beach—Colin backed up, returning to the main hallway.

“For my own peace of mind... can I just check those rooms?”

Owen lowered his head, the door handle still in his grip. He sighed.

“By all means.”

Colin followed Owen as he led the way, opening and closing doors. He peeked into two bathrooms, a den, and a linen closet.

The pet smell grew with each step forward. Owen's hand rested on a doorknob.

"The rabbit room," he said, leaning his forehead against the door. "I'll have to get the key from the kitchen."

Colin looked at the last door. "That one?"

"Spare bedroom." Opening the door to it, Owen moved aside for Colin. "It's not what you think," he said, taking a step back.

Colin's eyes focused on the bed. The blankets were rumpled. Women's clothes lay draped over a chair, plus a purse on the nightstand. Colin entered, looking at a bookshelf. A pink glove was arranged as if on display. Sunglasses. Hats. Other belongings. Odds and ends. On the desk, a tangled mess of blond hair.

"It's not what you think," Owen repeated.

Taking the hair in his hand, Colin gave it a shake. The thick bangs fell into place. A blond bob with bangs. He remembered Emma pointing it out in the catalog. Number 294037.

"Where is she?"

"She's not here."

Colin pushed past Owen to the locked room. It reeked of urine and sweat. He rattled the handle.

"It's not what you think. Get out of my house." Owen grabbed Colin's arm. "Go. Leave now."

Colin pulled away and rammed his shoulder against the door.

"She dropped that at the beach. She's not here!" Owen yelled. "Leave!"

"I know what death smells like," Colin said as he kicked the door. Owen grabbed him, trying to drag him away. Colin pushed him off. The man staggered backward and fell, landing hard on the floor, his head bouncing against the wall.

"All right, all right," he said, smoothing his hair. Lifting himself off the ground, he pulled a chain from around his neck. "You'll see it's not her. Then leave. Got it?"

Colin controlled his breathing as he watched Owen slowly unlock the door.

66
Colin

Colin burst past Owen into the room. The room was black, the air thick with stench. Colin felt for the light switch on the wall and flipped it on. Nothing happened. Shuffling his feet to the window, he tugged at the curtains. Dust motes shimmered in the light. His eyes adjusted to the sudden change as he scanned the cages lining the walls, the largest one peeking out from under a plaid blanket. Forgetting Owen, Colin raced toward it and pulled off the cover.

Dropping to his knees, he searched the heap of bare flesh and hair. The limbs were curled into a ball for warmth. The lock dangled open. His hand grabbed the latch.

"Don't," Owen said, stepping closer.

Colin turned to see a knife in his hand. He took a breath. "You said I could be sure it wasn't Liz."

Owen hesitated. "Fine."

Colin opened the cage. Brushing the hair from the woman's battered face, he searched for a pulse. Her skin was already cold to the touch. He took his time, checking her over, thinking, planning. He thought of Liz with the Minimalist Mentor cornering her at knifepoint. Her quick thinking, her ability to remain calm. He closed the cage and stood up with a smile.

"You've got a really nice setup here," Colin said, looking at the smaller cages crowded with rabbits. Some alive. Some dead.

"Smelly little buggers. I assume they're to mask the smell of your other... *pet*?"

Owen's eyes were wide, searching Colin's face. He nodded.

"Look," Colin said. "I don't care what you have going on here. All I want is to find my wife. I think you know where she is."

Owen inched over to the doorway, still holding his knife toward Colin. "I can't let you go after—" He pointed the knife at the cage.

"That? You don't need to worry about that. Don't you see?"

"See what?"

"The same bad seed in me that you see in Joey and Liz. You've got it too. I see it." Colin let out a shriek of laughter. "I almost forgot Anne. Now there's a true psychopath to the core. I don't blame you for hating her. I hate her too."

Owen leaned against the doorframe, the knife dangling at his side.

"She was going to be my first."

Colin smiled. "Your first?"

"When I met Anne, I thought she was a lovely young lady. Beautiful, naïve, a little timid. Still full of passion for life, hopeful for the future. You can imagine my disappointment when I found out how boring she was."

"Boring?"

"Throwing herself at me... I prefer a little fight in 'em."

Colin looked at the woman's body. "I know what you mean."

"Marta," Owen said with pity in his eyes. "She looked like my daughter, Sheena. I keep thinking, if I could go back—I could get it right this time."

"How'd Sheena die?"

"Joey."

"Your son killed her?"

"Police never proved it, but I knew." Owen shrugged. "When she died, I had an idea. It was perfect. Liz may have looked like my sister, but Emma looked like Sheena. That's why I went to Anne."

Colin tried to maintain a neutral face as he processed Owen's plan. "You'd replace Sheena with Emma." He nodded in agreement. "Anne wouldn't go for it?"

"No. She was bent out of shape when I showed up unannounced. Threatened to call the police. I didn't need them sniffing around any more than they were."

Colin understood. "Like father, like son?" He tried to laugh.

Owen smirked. Colin watched one bunny stand on another, sniffing the empty food dish while several chewed hay. He thought of the blond wig on the desk, then looked back at Marta and imagined Liz having been in that very cage. No. Something didn't feel right.

Colin's apartment flashed into his mind. The ritual had to be followed just right to get the release. The look on his face in the bathroom mirror when it was over. He looked at Owen.

"Marta looked like Sheena," Colin said. "She started in that other room, but she wasn't just right. That's why she's in here." He tapped his foot on the cage.

Owen raised his eyebrows. "You do get it."

"Do they always end up in here?"

Owen shrugged.

Colin understood. He had other rituals. Not just the cage.

"Tell me about your sister," he said.

"Rose? Why?"

"What happened to her?"

"No." His posture shifted. His tone changed. Colin realized he'd overstepped.

The smell of the room was suffocating. He could feel the sweat prickling on his skin. He wanted desperately to leave and get some air. Thinking again of Liz keeping calm under pressure, he took a breath.

"Did you hurt Liz?"

Owen sighed. "I would never hurt my daughters."

"Then where is she?" Colin regretted not telling Detective Green the address. "Why don't we have another cup of tea?"

Owen didn't budge. He shook his head, then met Colin's

eyes. “Tea’s gone cold by now.”

Colin looked at the knife clenched in the man’s hand. “You said I could leave.”

Owen just stared.

“I’ve seen too much. It’s okay. I get it.” Colin’s shoulders slumped. He took one last shot. “If you’re going to kill me anyway, what will it matter to tell me the truth?”

Colin had treated knife wounds before. It wouldn’t be pretty. Still, he braced himself to charge past Owen and run for help.

“I would never hurt my daughters,” Owen said.

“I know you wouldn’t.”

“It was an accident.”

Colin’s eyes searched Owen’s face for answers. “What happened?”

“I never meant—”

A banging thundered from the entryway. Heavy boots stomped inside the house. All color drained from Owen’s face as he leaned into the hall to see who was there.

Owen opened his mouth to speak as a man came barreling down the hall, tackling him to the floor.

“Where’s my wife?” the man screamed, yanking Owen’s body up from the ground. Owen’s Bus Éireann sweater twisted in the man’s fists.

Watching from the doorway, Colin made his move. Slipping out of the room, he ran down the hall to the front door.

“Hey you!” the new man yelled from behind.

Colin didn’t turn back. He imagined the man chasing him outside, dragging Owen along in his strong grasp. Colin fumbled for the keys in his pocket as he raced out the front door. A work van was blocking his car against the curb. Colin braced himself and turned back to face the irate man, but no one was in the doorway.

He took a breath, opened the car door, and slammed his fists on the roof. Looking back at the house, he knew if he wanted to find Liz, he’d have to save Owen.

67
Owen

"Marta," Slob Husband screamed, opening the cage.

Owen rolled onto his side in the hallway and pushed himself up on his elbow. *If you'd been a better husband to her, you wouldn't be in this situation.*

His chest ached. *Broken rib*, he thought, as he tucked his arm to his side. Grabbing his knife from the floor, he pushed himself up to stand, leaning against the wall.

"Marta." The man sobbed and groaned.

Owen saw the key on the floor, just inside the rabbit room. Dropping his knife in his pocket, he braced himself to make a dive for it. He had to be quiet, or the brute would overtake him again. His little knife was no match for such a monster. He thought of Sarah in their bedroom. He had to protect her.

Owen inched closer to the door as the sobs of grief began to subside. He knew what would come next. The rage would overtake him. He tried to move quicker.

There was a sudden movement in the room. Owen looked at the key and pounced.

Holding it in his hand, he turned to see that the man's grief had not yet turned to anger. Owen watched, transfixed, as he laid out his wife's lifeless body, straightened her limbs from the disfigured knots Owen had tied. He smoothed her hair, tucking it behind her ears. Grabbing the plaid blanket, Marta's husband covered her naked body down to her toes, made the sign of the cross, and bowed his head.

Slowly closing the door, Owen tried to turn the key. It jammed. The handle turned. The door swung open. Owen was thrown down the hall. He looked up at the man—a raging bull ready to end it all. Then a movement from behind.

"He did it!" Owen yelled, pointing down the hall.

Slob Husband turned. The terror in Colin's eyes was delicious. Owen smiled to see Colin backing away into the dining room, trying to explain. Marta's husband, deaf to reason, pursued Colin into the kitchen. Glass shattered. Owen hurried.

"Sarah, dear," he said, grabbing her robe, dragging her out of bed to the front door. "It's time to go."

Sarah struggled, her bandaged hands slamming the doorframe as Owen yanked her outside, into the car.

"What a lovely evening," he said as he drove away. He watched through the rearview mirror as Slob Husband and Colin's fight erupted onto the lawn.

With only one road in and out of Achill, it was a risk. Sarah had always loved the island, ever since her summer holidays as a child. He knew this was what she wanted. It was time.

"Isn't that right, dear?" he asked as he drove.

Sarah's eyes were confused and questioning. Owen wished he'd brought one of her pills to take the edge off.

Keem would be nice, but it could be busy at that time of day. Minaun Heights would not. Besides, he wouldn't mind saying hello to his pet Lika. *That was her name, wasn't it?* he wondered as he drove over the bridge, waiting for a car trying to park at the grocery store.

The steep road up to Minaun Heights was quiet except for a herd of sheep idling precariously on the edge. At the top, a woman started her car and passed by to leave. The parking area was empty.

"If you prefer Keem..." he said.

"Owen," Sarah whispered, her eyes pleading.

He no longer tried to hide the thirsty look he'd get each time. He smiled to think of the stories she would tell the police, if only she could.

Pulling her from the car, he walked, arm around her waist, up the gravel path to the rocky, sopping bog.

She tried to say something and tugged at the bandages on her burned hands.

Owen nodded. "You're right, it must have rained recently." It made it harder to drag her along in the muck. "This would be such a lovely place if they'd put in a paved path," he said, trying to carry her on his side. Pressing her into his broken rib, he thought of Marta's husband attacking him like a wild animal. For no good reason, at that.

The statue of Mary beckoned them forward as clouds rolled in over Keem.

At the top, settling Sarah on the bench, he looked out at the silhouettes of islands in the distance. Clare, Inishturk, Inishbofin, and his favorite, Inishshark. Then over to Keem, Keel, Dugort—gorgeous beaches he'd recommend time and time again to those irritating tourists. He tried to see the bridge in the distance, the only connection to the mainland. Then the derelict castle of Grace O'Malley, the Pirate Queen.

"This was your dream," he said, sitting on the bench next to his wife. "All of this." He waved his arms. "And people are right. It is lovely." He took her face in his hands and looked into her eyes. Locked deep inside her mind, she knew all his secrets. "I have a dream too. This isn't it." He shook his head and kissed her cheek. "It's time you fulfill your dream so I can return home to mine."

Owen lifted her up to stand. Sarah resisted.

"I should have brought wine," he said, looking back at the parking lot. Seeing another car approach, he sighed. "It can't be helped. Come on, let's go."

Dragging Sarah to the edge of the cliff, he listened to the

crashing waves. A storm cloud broke open overhead, pouring down on them.

"Be careful—I wouldn't want you to slip," he said, pulling her closer. He looked into her eyes one last time, then pushed.

Sarah moaned as she reached out to him, the gauze on her hands unfurling in the wind. She caught his arm and yanked.

Owen wrenched himself free. A sharp pain stabbed his ribs. He winced as he doubled over. Sliding in the muck, he teetered forward. Catching his balance for just a split second, he lunged at Sarah, pushing her again. The hair blowing in her face couldn't cover the joy in her eyes as she fell over the edge.

Owen's hand gripped his side. He thought of Marta's husband and the weight of that brute. He felt something else. Not just a broken rib. His side was now warm and wet. He tried to make sense of what had happened. His fingertips felt the handle of a knife. His knife. As the rain washed the blood from his hands, he smiled for his wife—one final lucid moment before she died.

"Good girl," he whispered.

With every inhale, Owen heard a wheeze in his chest. He tried not to panic. He had to get away. To get off the island and back onto the mainland. Then leave Europe altogether. He had to get home. Back to his life in Chicago. That nice little hobby. *I have to get back there,* he thought as he steadied his breath and looked at the knife.

Gripping the handle, Owen clenched his jaw and pulled. In pain, he dropped to his knees. The wheezing sound rang in his ears as he panted for breath. The knife remained lodged in his side.

"Owen, stop!" Colin yelled, tripping as he ran.

"Sheep slowed you down?"

Slowing his stride as he approached, Colin raised his hands. "Let me help you."

Owen winced, struggling to breathe. "The trick is to keep moving. Sheep aren't afraid of cars. People stop. The sheep lie down."

With both hands gripping the knife, Owen pulled again.

"Don't," Colin yelled.

Blood gushed from the wound. The wheezing noise from each inhale was replaced by a gentle gurgle in his throat. Owen stood up and walked to the edge of the cliff, fighting the wind as it blew in from the Atlantic. Rain pelted his face. Dropping the knife into the water, he fell again to his knees. His mouth filled with blood. He knew he'd never return to that nice little life in Chicago.

"I believe you. It was an accident," Colin pleaded. "Please, just tell me where she is."

Spitting out blood, Owen leaned back and fell over the edge.

68
Colin

Police lights illuminated the sky as Colin arrived back at Owen's house. A crowd of neighbors chatted and watched, straining to get close.

"That guy must have broken in..." one man said of Marta's husband, pointing to an ambulance.

A paramedic was treating wounds on the husband's face. Wounds from a crystal fruit bowl. It had been the first thing Colin could grab as the man cornered him in the kitchen. Stopping beside a police car, he noticed his own face and wiped dried blood from his brow. His body ached from the man's pummeling.

The crowd stirred as a body bag was carried out. Marta. Her husband sobbed, running to her side.

People speculated that the couple had been renting one of Owen and Sarah's rooms. They wondered where Owen and Sarah were. One neighbor tried to call. No answer.

Colin rubbed his forehead, wishing he had asked Detective Green for help. She could have notified the police, and Owen would be alive. Maybe he wouldn't talk to the police. Maybe he'd never admit what happened to Liz. At least there'd be hope.

Time slowed as Colin watched more vehicles arrive. Boxes were brought in to gather evidence. An officer spoke to Marta's husband. Then Colin. She took Liz's details: name, description.

No, Colin didn't know what she'd been wearing when she went missing. Known aliases? Anyone's guess. Yes, there was more he'd like to tell them.

"She has a fake passport."

The officer stared. Her lip turned up to a slight smile, waiting for Colin to say he was joking. He wasn't.

He thought of Felix and his businesses. The facial-recognition software he'd been developing. Colin had invested—CIA-level tech, he'd called it. Colin offered to reach out.

"Thanks. We'll take it from here," the officer said. "You'll need to make a formal statement." She pointed to a woman in a dark blazer.

Slipping away into the crowd, as floodlights were set up, he listened to the chatter. Confusion about the events turned to prayers for Owen and Sarah to be found safe. Then, with one comment, the mood changed.

"Looks like a fresh grave in the back garden."

"Sarah? Owen? Both?"

The news spread. The mob gathered, closing ranks, demanding answers.

Colin felt sick. He swayed, bumping into a kid on a scooter.

"Sorry," he said, leaning on a car.

He tried to breathe. He thought of Liz. All hope was gone.

A laugh. A joke about having their very own serial killer. Fear turned to excitement. Cell phones were held up, recording the scene. Other crimes were remembered. Tales retold. It was too much.

Anne pounced on Colin as he walked into the hotel lobby, demanding answers. She'd seen the news.

"You're hurt," she said, touching his face. "Tell me everything."

People stared. Some whispered.

Colin couldn't speak. He had to get away.

Taking to the stairs, he climbed them two by two. Anne

chased, falling behind quickly.

"Colin," she yelled. "How dare you?"

Colin stopped. His mouth dropped open.

Anne caught up, clinging to the railing, panting for breath.

"How dare I?" Colin asked, shocked by her nerve. Continuing to his room, he slammed the door and ordered Chinese.

That precious instant upon rising. That sweet moment on the edge of dreamland where nothing was real. Trying desperately to cling on, he lost it nonetheless.

Opening the curtains, Colin took in the soft pink clouds forming in the sky, then turned to the bags of Chinese takeout—all left uneaten.

He flipped on the news. The digging had begun. One body had already been recovered. *Liz*, he thought, sitting down and taking several deep breaths.

He thought of Anne. No matter how mad he was at her for withholding information, he felt petty for not filling her in. Finding his shoes, he opened the door.

Two officers approached. *The body... Liz*, he thought. They were there to notify him. He looked down at one's hands.

"Sir—"

"Her purse..." Colin said, reaching out.

"May we come in?"

Colin led the men inside.

"We found this in Owen's house. Is this your wife?" The officer held open a passport to the photo page.

"Liz," Colin said, nodding as he took the passport in his hand.

"We have in our notes, from your description, brown hair."

Colin looked at the picture. Blond bob with bangs. "Number 294037."

"Pardon?"

"It's a wig," Colin said, looking at the name. "It's a fake

name—fake last name, at least. Elizabeth Miller." *Trina's real name*, he thought, rubbing his neck. He ran his fingers over the gold crown on the cover of the fake passport. The fake Canadian passport. Opening her purse, he pulled out a cheap black cell phone. The battery was dead.

"Sir, do you have a recent photo of your wife?"

Grabbing his phone, he swiped through albums, one officer watching over his shoulder.

"One with her hair down?" the officer asked.

Colin found one he loved. Her brown curls filled the frame.

Realizing it would be the photo plastered over the news alongside some tragic headline, he swiped more.

The officer looked at his partner, then back at Colin.

"Sir, we need you to come with us—"

The officer explained as they walked. "Identify her..." were the only words Colin could understand. Shocked and confused, he followed the policemen out of the hotel.

At the hospital, a staging area had been set up for families with missing loved ones. People discussed the latest updates. Under a fuchsia bush, another body had been found in a mass grave of bunnies.

Colin went to the elevator. There, a hospital administrator introduced herself and repeated what had happened.

"I don't understand," Colin said, stepping into the elevator. He was still expecting to arrive in the morgue to identify Liz's body. "She's alive?"

"Yes. Please, follow me."

The woman stopped outside a hospital room, gesturing for Colin to enter. He hesitated. Taking a breath, he opened the door.

"Her face is badly bruised. It might be difficult to..." she said, following Colin inside. "There's no hiding those curls."

Colin stepped closer. Hair burst in every direction around the bandages. He froze.

"Sir? Is this your wife?"

Colin exhaled, then nodded, taking Liz's hand. As he pressed it to his lips, his knees buckled.

Coma. When he'd first heard the word, Colin couldn't understand. He'd thought Liz was the body recovered from Owen's yard. When he heard she was in a coma, he imagined she'd been buried alive.

"A woman fell in Keem Bay. Some hikers saw her and called for help. The poor thing must have seen your wife and slipped when she was trying to help."

"The woman didn't make it?"

The administrator shook her head, then filled him in on Liz's condition. "The doctor will be around soon."

Liz's nurse entered and introduced himself, offering Colin some coffee or tea and something to eat. He pulled over a chair, guiding Colin to sit.

"We'll give you some time," the administrator said.

Colin stared at Liz, transfixed, then turned.

"Wait. She was... is she?" He looked back at Liz. "Is she still pregnant?"

The administrator looked to the nurse.

"Yes," he said. "The baby's just fine."

69
Colin

Hours turned into days, and days blurred into weeks, interrupted every so often by the breaking news of another body found. Owen's crime scenes stretched out far beyond his bus route, to the bogland and mountains of Achill.

Anne had returned home to tell Daniel the truth. *Or not,* Colin thought, wondering if she'd ever admit to it all. He checked Chicago's news. Reports were breaking as police cordoned off Owen's old house in the city. They prepared to dig. More bodies would be added to the tally.

At the hospital, Colin had his own tally to maintain. He'd made a chart of Liz's vitals and the baby's growth. Snagging a Doppler monitor from the hospital's labor unit, Colin turned the volume up to listen to their baby's heartbeat. "Our baby's right on track," he told her, hoping for a response.

Over the years, he'd experienced a variety of births, but never a coma delivery. Still, he was thankful. He thought of Tess Apel, the woman who'd slipped and died trying to save Liz. When the helicopter arrived for Tess, they'd found Liz clinging to life. He felt guilty for feeling thankful.

"You can wake up now, Liz," Colin said. "You're safe." Every day the same words, trying to sound confident. Every night, the same despair as he imagined the return to Chicago. Their baby in his arms, Liz's casket in the cargo hold.

Colin rested his head on her stomach, listening as the baby's heartbeat ticked away the time.

He felt something move and looked at Liz. Just his phone. It vibrated again. Turning off the fetal monitor, he wiped the gel off her belly and answered.

"How is she?" Detective Green asked.

"No change. I saw the news. They're digging up Owen's old yard there, too?"

"We just started. Did you see the report about Tess?"

"Nothing new. Why?" Colin thought of the picture of Tess on the news, the reports hailing her a hero for saving Liz. Her big blue eyes haunted him. He stepped out into the hall, closing the door.

"We've been working with Irish police. They've recovered CCTV footage of Liz in Owen's bus the day before she was found at Keem, and..."

"What?"

"It seems Keem was one of Owen's... locations of choice."

Colin remembered the man leading him out onto the jagged rocks, farther and farther.

Green continued. "Tess didn't slip trying to save Liz. She was pushed by Owen, too."

Colin rubbed the back of his neck, pacing the hall. "Why would he—"

"Tess tracked Owen down. She thought he killed her little sister, Nora."

"Did he?"

"We haven't confirmed, but..."

Colin couldn't help but imagine Liz struggling to stay alive as her father returned with another victim. He wondered if Owen had seen Liz's body—if he knew she was still alive.

"Listen," Green sighed. "We finally got into the last of Trina's devices. The best we can tell, she was going to contact customs with a tip that Liz was traveling on a fake passport, causing her to be detained in Dublin. From there, I have no idea what she planned. I know it doesn't matter now—"

"Thanks for the update," Colin said. Wanting to lighten the mood, he considered a joke about Green having thought it was just a simple love triangle. Yet walking back into Liz's room and looking at her battered face, he couldn't make light of this. Her eyelids fluttered. Her fingers moved.

"Liz?" Colin said, dropping his phone. "You can wake up, Liz. It's okay."

Her head tilted toward him. He repeated the same line over and over.

"That's it," he said. "Open your eyes."

Drawing the curtains to dim the glare on her face, he repeated, "There you go, Liz. Open your eyes."

Her eyelids flickered, and she opened them.

Colin squeezed her hand and waited.

"Colin?" Liz asked, looking around the room. She searched his face, looking for understanding.

"You're in the hospital."

"Hospital?" she asked, still unsure.

"In Ireland."

Her eyes changed. Colin could tell she was piecing things together. She pulled her hand away from him. Feeling her belly, she looked into Colin's eyes.

"The baby's fine," he said, smiling.

"I meant to tell you..."

"There's a lot you didn't tell me." He winked. Pulling up her shirt a bit, he applied a glob of clear gel again and switched on the Doppler.

Liz smiled, listening. "You know everything?"

"There better not be anything else."

Liz squeezed his hand. "You know how I say real friends never need to apologize?"

He nodded.

"I'm so, so sorry, Colin." Her lips quivered as tears filled her eyes.

Colin broke down, unable to hold back his own. "What I

don't understand is why you had to go to such lengths to hide this from me. A fake passport? Why?"

"I know it seems like overkill. I thought so too. My friend from the fertility group helped me plan everything—she has a similar family history. Never mind. It doesn't matter—I wasn't hiding it from *you*. I was hiding from my mom."

"Why?"

"It's hard to explain. I was worried she'd find out and interfere. Then I'd never know the truth. She lies... a lot."

Colin laughed for the first time in weeks. It felt good.

"I'm serious," Liz said. "You have no idea."

"I believe you." He wiped her cheek with a tissue. "You still should have told me."

"I planned to, but when I went to lunch with my mom, I slipped up. I could tell she was suspicious. We had everything set. When I stopped by the hospital to tell you, you were busy with a bunch of deliveries. I figured I'd be back before you even noticed I was gone. Sorry." She gave a sheepish smile. "I left all my things with my friend so my mom wouldn't try and track me down. And I just went for it."

"Your friend from the fertility group?"

"Yeah, Trina. She was supposed to text you for me so you wouldn't worry. She did, didn't she?"

"Oh, yeah. She texted me."

"Good."

Colin took a long inhale, unsure how to broach the topic of Owen. He dreaded the thought of her turning on the news.

"What happened out here? With your father?" he asked.

Liz waited a few seconds before responding. "I knew him. He was the guy from my accident. My mom..." She looked away, closing her eyes.

"What about your mom?"

She took a breath. "After the accident, a sketch artist drew him. It looked just like him. My mom said she'd never seen him before. She told the police I admitted to making him up." Liz shook her head. "When I saw him, I couldn't bring myself to say anything. Then I decided I owed it to myself to know the truth."

Colin rubbed her arm. "He took you to Keem?"

Liz nodded. "I was still unsure. I wore the disguise from my fake passport photo. It felt silly. He called me Blondie. It wasn't until the end of the line that I built up the courage to face him. At the beach, we climbed up to his favorite spot to talk. There were dolphins swimming and jumping around. It was incredible."

Colin nodded, remembering.

"He explained everything. Their affair. Him trying to be in our lives. My mom lying, saying we weren't his. He told me I look just like his sister. Emma looks like his daughter. He was sorry for scaring us that night at the movie. I didn't realize I was in reverse. I just slammed on the gas to get away. When we went in the water, he jumped in to save us."

She looked around as if to think.

"I told him the good news," she said, her hand on the baby. "Then, I don't know... The tide was coming in. We got up to leave... he said something about the baby. Something about a seed? I don't remember. Then, I must have slipped." She looked toward the door. "Has he been here? What'd he say happened?"

"No. No, he hasn't," Colin said. "I should let the staff know you woke up."

"Colin?"

"Yeah?"

"I just realized—this is the second time he saved my life." She smiled, rubbing her belly. "Our baby, too. You were right about that DNA site. I should have joined a long time ago."

"Yeah."

"Maybe I can get some T-shirts made like you guys. I wonder if we have anyone as famous as your snake-oil salesman gramps." She laughed, turning her eyes to Colin. "What's with that look? I said you were right."

"Yeah, no... I don't..." Colin said, fumbling for the truth as he called Liz's nurse.

70
Colin

"Just one more tiny push, Liz," Trent said.

Colin tried to steady his breathing and stop the trembling in his hands. Selena turned to him. He knew that look. He shook his head and smiled—he didn't need a chair.

Then it happened.

Better than he'd imagined. Better than any pills or purge. True euphoria.

After cutting the cord, Colin placed their daughter on his wife's chest. Tears blurred his vision as he stared at her—tiny, perfect, his.

"Where did she come from?" he whispered in awe.

Liz smiled, her eyes never leaving their little girl, her fingertips stroking the peach fuzz on the baby's ears and back.

Colin felt he'd entered an alternate state of perfection as he watched every movement of their precious miracle. Everything that had happened over the previous months no longer mattered. Nothing else mattered. Nothing bad could touch them in their surreal world of three.

"Congratulations," Trent said, shaking Colin's hand and kissing Liz on the cheek. "We'll get out of your way."

Selena gave them both a hug, then left as well.

Alone in their room, Colin cradled his baby in his arms. Her pink fingers curled into a fist, tucking under her chin as she slept. The thought of his own mother tossing him in the dumpster filled his mind. For so long, he had wanted to prove himself to her. Now, looking at his daughter and his wife, that no longer mattered.

"But it does," he whispered.

"What does?" Liz asked.

"Nothing. I just... looking at her, so helpless. I need to know why she did it. I think... I think I need to meet her."

"Who? What?"

"My biological mother. I need to know why she threw me away."

Liz rubbed his arm. "I understand."

Colin kissed Emma again, watching her sleep. *No more secrets.*

"Colin?"

"Yeah?"

"Do you think I'm like them?"

Colin saw the concern in her eyes. He'd seen it too often since he told her the truth. He knew she was thinking of it now—all of it. The crimes committed by her brother and father, Trina's plans, her mother's secrets. Countless lies. Trying to piece them together, accepting they'd never know the full story.

"No," Colin said. "You're nothing like them."

Their baby's lips began rooting around, looking for food.

"I had an idea." Liz smiled, then pursed her lips.

"Oh no. No way," Colin said. "Your last idea almost got us killed."

"Stop," she said, sitting up. "I was just thinking... maybe... we could name her Emma."

"Really?" Colin handed her their daughter.

"Yeah. My sister always talked about getting married and having lots of babies. After the accident, I just think... she deserves this."

Colin smiled. *You're nothing like them.*

Leaning over, he kissed his precious little girl. Emma.

Epilogue

Sitting in the nursery, watching Emma sleep, Liz thought about everything that had happened.

The scars of the past months lingered, yet there she was—a mother. Her resentment toward her own mother had softened. Forgiveness. Or at least understanding. She saw it clearly now—how desire had led to desperation, and desperation had led to choices best kept secret.

She brushed Emma's hand, smiling as tiny fingers curled around her own.

"All worth it," she whispered.

Her phone pinged, startling her. Reaching for it, she hesitated. Trent.

They hadn't spoken in weeks.

Liz stepped out of the room, closing the door behind her before answering.

"Hey," she whispered.

"Hey," Trent said. "I know we agreed, but there's something I need to say. I won't..." His voice wavered. Silence.

Liz closed her eyes, leaning against the wall. "Don't, please."

"I just..." Trent cleared his throat. "I want you to know... I won't tell Colin."

"You can't," Liz said. "Not now. Not after everything he's been through."

"I know. But I think... you should."

Liz took a breath, shaking her head. "It would kill him."

"It's up to you, but if something happens... if she ever needs me—"

"She won't. We're fine. Everything's fine now."

"Is it?"

"Yes," Liz said, standing tall. "I have to go."

"Liz?"

"Yes?"

"Don't forget... I was there."

She inhaled, closing her eyes. "I know."

"And if this comes out..." Trent hesitated. "It's not just you he'll hate."

The front door opened. Colin's keys clattered in the ceramic bowl.

"Goodnight, Trent," Liz said, hanging up.

Back in the nursery, she smoothed Emma's fine hair with her fingertips and listened to Colin's footsteps on the stairs.

In the quiet moment just before he walked in, she felt it—unstoppable, inevitable. The truth seeping through the cracks. She knew the life she had built was too perfect, too fragile. And some cracks could never be sealed.

Coming Soon

Trapped by lies—one in a stranger's home, the other in a toxic marriage—two women spiral toward a truth more dangerous than they imagined. When their realities collide in a twist no one sees coming, the fallout is deadly.

Out of the Fog is a taut, addictive psychological thriller about control, survival, and the women who refuse to stay lost.

Read more at: **alisonlyle.com**

About the Author

Alison Lyle writes fast, twisty psychological thrillers that explore the secrets we keep, the lies we tell, and the breaking points of ordinary people. Her debut novel, *Her Family Secrets*, is a dark, gripping suspense about obsession, betrayal, and the women written out of their own stories.

Originally from Chicago, Alison now lives on Achill Island, Ireland, with her husband, seven kids, too many pets, and the occasional trespassing sheep.

Learn more and sign up for her monthly newsletter at:

alisonlyle.com

Share Your Thoughts

Your support means the world to me. Thanks for reading!

– Alison

Scan below to share your thoughts with other readers:

Made in the USA
Coppell, TX
10 August 2025

52955056R00187